Healing Hearts

Book Two (The O'Connors)

Jax Burrows

Jax Burrows / Manchester UK

Jax Burrows
P O Box 599
Manchester
M12 0DY
United Kingdom
https://www.jburrowsauthor.com

Publisher's Note: This is a work of fiction. Names, characters, places, and incidents are a product of the author's imagination. Locales and public names are sometimes used for atmospheric purposes. Any resemblance to actual people, living or dead, or to businesses, companies, events, institutions, or locales is completely coincidental.

Book Layout © 2020 Polgarus Studios
Cover Design by James T Egan https://www.bookflydesign.com/

Healing Hearts/Jax Burrows. — 1st ed.
Print Edition ISBN:

Contents

Chapter One

'Hi, Riordan, sorry to bother you at work. Thing is … I need a favour.'

Riordan smiled. His younger brother was always asking him for favours, usually advice about something or other. 'No problem, the clinic's running smoothly this afternoon, so it looks as if we might all be able to go home on time for a change.' He moved his mobile to his left ear and studied the next patient's details on his computer screen as he listened to Casey.

'Well, that's great to hear. You'll have plenty of time to get ready then.'

'Get ready for what?'

'That's the favour I want to ask. You know that Lexi has joined the WI?'

Riordan chuckled. 'Yes, Dad told me. She's really embracing the role of doctor's wife, isn't she?'

'She's made quite a few friends there. I was a bit worried about her, to be honest, when Jess and Craig moved up to Scotland to live with Billy. I thought she'd be lonely, but she's full of community spirit, and they're raising money for the women's half-way house. Shelley's going as well.'

'Going where?' Riordan pressed down his sudden impatience. 'Sorry, Casey, I really need to get back to work, could we talk about this another time?'

'I'll be quick. There's a fund-raising event in the community centre tonight and I promised I'd help out, but we're two consultants down with the 'flu and I'm going to have to work a double shift. Which means I need someone to step up and, obviously, I thought of my big brother.' Casey sounded remarkably cheerful considering he was volunteering to work in A&E all night, having already worked a day shift.

'Look, I'd love to help, but I was planning on spending the evening with Tom—'

'Ah, except … I've already told them you'll do it. All they need you to do is serve tea and scones, and it's only for a few hours.'

'Well …' Riordan expected that the Women's Institute had changed a lot since his mother's time. Then most of the members were retired, widowed, or single with plenty of time on their hands. He had no idea what it was like nowadays. It was for one of his father's favourite causes, however, and his brother needed his help. 'Okay then, I'll do it. What time do I have to be there?'

'Great! I knew I could rely on you, Bro. Just turn up whenever you can, there'll be people there most of the afternoon making the tea and setting stuff out. All you need to do is serve it.'

'Okay, but—'

'I've left your costume hanging up in the little room off the kitchen, you can't miss it.'

'Hang on—costume? You never mentioned a costume. What costume? Casey—'

'Sorry, Riordan, got to go, duty calls. I hope it fits. Good luck and keep your back to the wall.' Casey was laughing and Riordan had a sinking feeling in the pit of his stomach.

'Casey, what are you talking about? What is the costume? Casey?'

But his brother had already ended the call. The four siblings were always pranking each other. If this was one of his jokes …

Riordan told himself that maybe he was panicking for nothing. Perhaps they wanted him dressed up as a waiter? That wouldn't be too bad. So long as he didn't have to wear a pinny.

The nurse in charge of the outpatient clinic stuck her head around the door. 'Are you ready for the next patient, Dr O'Connor? She's had her ECG and is getting a bit twitchy.'

Riordan sighed and returned his attention to the patient's notes on the screen. Mrs Fitzpatrick. She'd first attended with a rapid pulse and a sensation of being able to feel her heart beating. She also suffered from confusion, dizziness and shortness of breath, and was found to have atrial fibrillation, a dangerous condition that threatened heart failure and stroke. A risk that would increase with her obesity, smoking history, high blood pressure and high cholesterol.

'Yes, bring her in please.'

The nurse nodded and disappeared.

He'd have to impress on Mrs Fitzpatrick again the importance of a healthy diet and exercise. Many of his patients had good intentions, smiled and nodded, agreeing with everything he said. Then, as soon as they were out of the hospital, they forgot all the advice he'd given them and went back to their old ways. All Riordan could do was to keep trying.

*

The community hall was noisy with the sound of a dozen conversations from the women who sat in groups around tables covered with pristine white tablecloths.

'Shall I pour?' Lexi asked, and Zoe smiled and nodded. At least she didn't say, *shall I be mother?* which always made Zoe cringe.

'Milk, no sugar thanks.'

'What made you choose Leytonsfield?' Shelley asked Zoe.

An interesting woman, Zoe thought, with her pink and orange highlights and eyes that looked as if they had seen the darker side of life. Lexi had filled Zoe in on Shelley's history;

parents that turned away from their daughter when she got pregnant, a miscarriage, trying to take her own life, and ending up as a punching bag for some lowlife who, thankfully, was now serving time.

'I wanted a change and had grown tired of inner-city Manchester, so I thought I'd try the peace and quiet of a Cheshire town.'

'And what do you think of it?' asked Shelley.

'Well, I've only been here a day, but I like what I've seen so far.'

Zoe was looking for somewhere to put down roots. A place she could feel a part of and be happy to call home. Manchester used to be that, but now there were too many sad memories. When she'd answered the advert for a locum GP in a quiet Cheshire practice, she never expected to even get an interview, never mind a second one with an invitation to visit and look the place over. Now, if everyone liked each other, the job was hers.

'Do you have family?' asked Lexi, handing out the cups and saucers. Not the regulation white mugs that most community centres and church groups used, but a pretty bone china tea-service and teapots to match.

Zoe was looking forward to the sandwiches and scones, her stomach complaining at the absence of food. It seemed hours since breakfast.

'Yes, my mum and dad, and three older brothers. Two of them are married and have children.'

'That's lovely,' said Lexi. 'I used to be alone, but now I have Casey, Jade our daughter, and the rest of the O'Connor family.'

'Good for you,' said Zoe gently. She liked Lexi, she was a sweet girl and, judging by the way Lexi's hands hovered over her midriff in a protective fashion, Jade would be joined by a brother or sister in time.

Lexi noticed Zoe watching and blushed. Zoe leaned in and whispered, 'How far gone are you?'

She whispered back, 'Nearly three months, but we're not telling anyone yet. How did you know?'

Zoe laughed. 'I'm a doctor, remember.'

The murmur of conversation from the other women in the room swelled, and the laughter rose. Zoe looked around and put a hand over her mouth.

'Who on earth is that?' she asked through her fingers.

'Wow ...' said Shelley her eyes nearly popping out of her head.

Lexi said, 'It's Riordan, Casey's brother. Oh dear, I think Casey's in big trouble. He was supposed to be wearing that, not Riordan. There's going to be fireworks.'

*

'I'll kill him,' muttered Riordan as he wriggled inside the gladiator costume. It consisted of a skimpy leather skirt that just about covered him at the front and sides but was open at the back, so his buttocks were exposed for all to see. Another piece of leather with silver studs sat on his shoulders, a band went over each wrist, and gladiator sandals that itched like crazy adorned his feet. Casey had left two thongs with the costume and pinned a note to them saying that he didn't know what size Riordan was, so he'd played safe and left small and ultra-small. Ha bloody ha, very funny. When Riordan examined them however, they were medium and large, which healed his damaged ego slightly.

But he wasn't amused. Not one bit.

'He won't be laughing when I catch up with him,' he growled again.

'Did you say something, Dr O'Connor?' asked Millie. Red in the face and puffing slightly, she was pouring hot water into the china teapots from a large heater. There were a lot to fill, and normally Riordan would have offered to help. In this costume he intended to stay away from anything as dangerous as hot tea. He had too much exposed flesh at risk.

'Nothing I can repeat in front of a lady, Millie.'

'How about you open that wine then? They'll be wanting their alcohol, if I know that lot.'

'Wine … right.' Riordan carefully opened the Prosecco and poured it into the wine glasses. 'I imagine we're only giving them a glass each, are we?'

'Oh no, they can have as much as they want. There's crates of the stuff back here. Your father has been more than generous. He's a lovely man is Dr O'Connor Senior.'

Plenty of wine—that was unfortunate. The more they drank, the quicker they lost their inhibitions. And in this costume, the last thing he wanted was to be at the beck and call of a room filled with rampant women.

He said, 'I'll pour it and you can take it to them.'

Millie shook her head. 'It's you they want to see, Dr O'Connor. I'll stay here and cut the sandwiches and then you can take them round too.'

Riordan peered fearfully through the doorway at the women chattering away like magpies. He spotted Lexi and Shelley sitting with a dark-haired woman. They were laughing and looking over at him. He ducked back inside the kitchen.

The crowd were getting restless. He couldn't hide forever. Riordan had Googled the Women's Institute before he left the hospital. As he'd suspected, it had undergone some major changes in the last few decades, by all accounts. No longer content with making the perfect Victoria sponge, it had raced joyfully into the twenty-first century with nude calendars and strippers. Riordan had a horrible feeling he was supposed to be the WI's answer to a stripper. Casey's comment about keeping his back to the wall made sense now.

The other thing that had changed was the average age of the members. They were young, professional, and ready for anything, eager for the entertainment to begin.

And he was it. Like a lamb to the slaughter.

'Right then, Dr O'Connor, there's no time like the present. Get those drinks out and then when you've finished, I'll help you serve the sandwiches.'

'Ah … Millie, may I make a suggestion? Why not get the food out first so they'll have something to soak up the alcohol?'

Millie laughed. 'Oh, you don't need to worry about that, Doctor, there's not a woman out there who couldn't drink you under the table.'

'Right.' Not reassuring. There was nothing else for it. He'd have to get himself and his bare arse out there. He'd bluff, and pretend he did this kind of thing all the time. If he could get through an outpatient clinic in the Cardiology Department relatively unscathed, then he could survive the comments and giggles of a group of drunken women.

Here goes.

Chapter Two

Zoe couldn't take her eyes off him. So that was Dr Riordan O'Connor; tall, slim, but with muscles in all the right places, a tidy six-pack and long—amazingly beautiful—legs. Strong thighs too. That outfit left absolutely nothing to the imagination. Zoe couldn't wait for him to turn around. Lexi had just whispered the best bit about the costume, which caused a strange heat to warm Zoe's face. A feeling she'd not enjoyed for a long time.

'What's he supposed to be?' asked Shelley, craning her neck to follow Riordan's progress as he made his way slowly to each table and gave out glasses of wine.

Zoe already hoped there'd be seconds. Dan O'Connor had told her it would be a nice drop of Prosecco, her favourite wine. One glass wasn't going to go far.

'A gladiator, I imagine,' said Zoe.

'Like in the movies?' Shelley asked.

'Yes. They date back to Ancient Rome when slaves and the like were made to fight each other to the death in an arena.'

'Why?' Shelley looked horrified.

'For entertainment. Blood excites people. Even today, people go to boxing matches to see someone being knocked unconscious.'

'Well, it don't excite me,' said Shelley, 'I've been on the receiving end. It's not funny. Trust me.'

'I agree wholeheartedly,' said Zoe.

'Me too,' said Lexi. 'You've escaped that life, Shell, I'm really proud of you.'

'Thanks, Lexi.'

Zoe had heard the story of how Casey and Lexi helped Shelley. They were good people, the O'Connor family, and she was going to enjoy working with Dan and the other doctors. Yes, she decided, she was going to like Leytonsfield. It was exactly what she needed at this point in her life. A more pressing need was for Riordan to turn around so she could catch a sight of his naked bottom. She liked men's bums and not just the ones that were buns of steel. Although they were worth looking at too. The softer ones could be just as sexy, but in a different way. Zoe wondered what the other women thought.

She had an idea.

'Do we have any paper and pens, or pencils?'

Lexi said, 'I could find some notebooks from when they have the AGM. They'll probably be in a cupboard somewhere. What do you need them for?'

'I think we should give Riordan O'Connor marks out of ten. For service, smiles, and appearance. I'd give him a good score.'

'So you think Riordan is hunky then?' Lexi was grinning in an evil fashion, so Zoe returned the look.

'I've seen a lot worse.'

'Riordan's very sweet. I thought he disapproved of me once, before Casey and I got together properly, but he was just being cautious.'

'Is he a cautious person by nature?'

Zoe thought that there must be another side to him. The side that lets the world ogle his bare bum.

Lexi nodded. 'Oh yes, he has to consider a question from all angles before he commits himself to an answer. At least, that's what Casey says. But then, my husband is impetuous and rushes in where angels fear to tread.'

'Casey sounds like a fun guy.'

'He is. But so is Riordan, just in a different way.'

'Good afternoon, ladies.' Riordan had returned to the kitchen for more glasses twice and theirs was the last table he served.

'Hi, Riordan. Loving the costume,' said Lexi.

'Well, I'm glad I'm bringing some happiness into your life on this dull January afternoon.'

'Oh, you're doing that alright,' said Shelley, leaning backwards in her chair so she could get a better view.

'Aren't you cold in that costume?' asked Zoe. Although, on studying him closely, she couldn't see any goose pimples. Just lovely smooth skin with a light smattering of light brown hair on his chest.

'This is Zoe,' said Lexi quickly.

'Pleased to meet you, Zoe. Sorry I can't shake hands at the moment.'

Riordan put a glass of wine in front of each of them and started to back away from the table. He obviously had no time to answer silly questions, thought Zoe, willing him to turn around. When he did, walking back to the kitchen quickly, they all stood up as one to get a better view.

'Whoar …!' said Zoe. 'I think I might have to give him the full ten points for that one. Not seen a bum as nice as that for a long time. And I'm a doctor and see bums on a daily basis.'

They all laughed and clinked their wine glasses together.

'I'll get those notebooks. This could become a regular event on our group's schedule. I must have a word with the president. Pity she couldn't come today.' Lexi got up and scurried away.

Zoe sat back and concentrated on the Prosecco. Dan was right. A lovely drop of wine.

*

All the wine was served. Riordan had distributed the bottles that were left so that the ladies had plenty of alcohol to fuel their merriment for the rest of the afternoon. And, boy, did they know how to enjoy the moment. He'd been photographed from all angles, had selfies taken with the younger ones, and even been smacked on his butt cheeks several times to the point where he didn't know which one was pinker.

'Right ladies, shall I take the sandwiches around?'

Millie had been joined by her sister, Mavis, and the two little ladies, who must have been hitting their eighties, were heads down buttering bread and making sandwiches like a small, well-oiled machine.

'Yes, Dr O'Connor, thank you,' said Millie. Or was it Mavis? They looked almost identical.

He picked up a cake tier in each hand. There were tiny, neat sandwiches in white and brown bread on the top layer, small dainty cakes and éclairs on the middle, and scones fresh from the oven and served with tiny ramekins of strawberry jam and clotted cream on the bottom. He rehearsed the sandwich fillings in his head as he left the kitchen.

This time, he went to Lexi's table first.

'Right ladies, we have chicken, cheese and pickle, egg mayo, and cucumber and tomato.'

'Is there anything suitable for people who are dairy and gluten free?' asked the dark-haired woman.

Riordan had forgotten her name already—and damn, he hadn't thought of dietary requirements. It wasn't his responsibility was it? He was merely serving and making a spectacle of himself.

'Umm … do you want me to ask?' He must have looked completely flummoxed as the three women started laughing. The dark-haired one had a very sexy laugh and her eye contact was direct and teasing.

She said, 'Sorry, just kidding. We can eat anything, can't we girls?' Zoe appealed to Lexi and Shelley, who nodded enthusiastically.

'Oh, I see,' Riordan said tightly. This woman was starting to get on his nerves. Almost as if she sensed Riordan was out of his depths. 'Good, then I'll leave you to it.' He placed one of the tiers on the table and moved away. This time he didn't bother to try to hide his naked bottom, what was the point by now?

Then Riordan wished he had as Lexi, Shelley, and the other one started clapping and cheering. Bloody women. He could feel himself shrinking inside. He hated being teased. He'd been bullied in high school because he was a nerd who wore glasses and always had his nose in a book. Not one of the cool kids. It was only Casey, and his threats to beat anyone up who touched his big brother, who saved him from physical harm.

Riordan went through his routine again with the sandwich fillings at the next table, and the next, until the novelty really started to wear off. He hurried back to the kitchen.

'Right, I have to leave, I'm afraid.'

'Oh, but Dr O'Connor, we were hoping you'd stay for the raffle and pick the winning ticket.'

'Much as I'd love to, I'm afraid I can't. I'm wanted back at the hospital. Patients need me. Sorry.'

'Oh well, we're sorry to see you go, aren't we, Millie?'

'We are, but if it's the patients, then … well, duty calls.'

'Dr O'Connor Senior was always dashing off to see patients as well. Like father, like son.'

The ladies beamed at him. They looked like two rosy, cuddly grannies and Riordan hated himself for lying to them. But he'd done what he'd promised Casey and now Riordan needed to get away. Too many women gathered in one place could only spell trouble. Especially when you threw alcohol into the mix.

Riordan ducked into another room and pulled off the ridiculous costume. He was still going to kill Casey when he saw him. Was this some kind of a joke or bet? Riordan felt more relaxed once he was wearing his own clothes. After bundling everything into a carrier bag, he left by the back door.

Chapter Three

Riordan was exhausted. He'd started work early to get some paperwork done before a ward round but was bleeped as soon as he arrived in his office. A new patient had been admitted overnight, an elderly gentleman named Jack Dempsey, who had suffered a myocardial infarction and was in the coronary care unit. The patient wanted to speak to "the man in charge".

Mr Dempsey was refusing to do anything the nurses told him, afraid that he'd be put in a care home, and he was saying, 'I won't be left to rot in one of those places. I'd rather be dead.'

Riordan had done his best to reassure the old man they would do everything possible to allow him to go back home. Unfortunately, Jack Dempsey lived alone in a house with stairs, and the chances of him being able to manage unaided were slim.

By the time Riordan had finished the ward round, he was late for a meeting of the multi-disciplinary team to discuss another of his patients, one who was badly in need of a heart transplant. The odds of that happening were almost zero as things stood. The patient, Mrs Murgatroyd, was a heavy drinker and smoker, and was clinically obese. The decision was made, though, to refer her to the transplant team for an assessment. Meanwhile, Riordan would do all he could to encourage the woman to lose weight.

Then there was a clinic to run and more paperwork, before yet another meeting. By the time Riordan got home, he was wrung dry.

'Hi Tom,' he called as he walked through the door.

'Hey Dad, wanna play a video game with me?'

Riordan was aware of how little time he'd spent with his son recently. Tom was nearly nine and, at the moment, they had a close relationship. Riordan was conscious of time passing and hated to think of a future when Tom, as a teenager, would be scornful of spending precious evenings with his old man.

All Riordan really wanted, however, was a hot shower, a drink, and to collapse in front of the news.

'Okay. Just a quick one though, before dinner.'

'Okay.'

They played for about half an hour while Riordan's mother, Eloise, made the evening meal. Then his father, Dan

O'Connor, returned from the surgery. He wasn't alone. Riordan stood up abruptly when he saw who was with Dan.

'Ah, Riordan, glad you're home. May I introduce who I hope will be my new locum? This is Dr Zoe Angelos. Zoe, this is my eldest son, Riordan.'

Zoe stepped forward with her hand out. 'So, now we get the chance to shake hands.' She was smiling, her eyes bright.

'Pleased to meet you—again. So you're not a member of the Women's Institute after all?'

'No, but I am thinking of joining. I had fun yesterday, and I think it's important for a GP to be part of the community, don't you, Dan?'

'Of course. After all, they are the people you're going to be looking after. Should you decide to join us, that is.'

'So it's not definite then?' asked Riordan hopefully.

He wasn't sure if Zoe was the right kind of person to take the weight off his father. Since Dan's heart attack the year before, he had gradually eased himself back into work. But Riordan wasn't happy. He would have preferred his father to retire and leave the practice altogether, perhaps work a few days a week at most.

'No, I'm here to have a look at the place, and for Dan and the others to have a look at me,' said Zoe.

Dan said, 'Well, I'm happy if you are. I'd love it if you joined us. You're exactly the cheerful, enthusiastic person the practice needs. And I'm sure the rest of the staff will agree.'

Eloise stuck her head around the door. 'Casey, Lexi and Jade have just arrived so I'm going to serve out. Would you like to sit down?'

'Tom, go and wash your hands please,' said Riordan.

Dinner time. Good, Riordan needed a word with his younger brother.

*

Now that Zoe saw the two brothers together, she could see the family resemblance, although they didn't really look alike. Casey was slightly shorter and obviously worked out. He had broad shoulders and a strong chest. She seemed to remember something about him being a swimmer. He was cheeky with a twinkle in his eye and a mouth that was full and smiled easily. Riordan was serious and, Zoe suspected, shy despite evidence to the contrary the day before. A shyness he covered up with a sparkling intellect. A memory of his body in the gladiator costume flashed across her mind and Zoe felt that warmth again.

Eloise had made a chicken casserole with onions and plenty of peppers. There was a buttery mashed potato and lightly cooked cabbage. It was absolutely delicious, and Zoe was so intent on eating it was a while before she noticed the tension around the dining table.

Riordan said to Casey, 'You told me you were doing a double shift.'

'I was, but then I found someone to cover. It was too late to tell you.'

'You set me up.'

'You agreed to do it. Oh, come on, Bro, it was just a bit of fun. Lighten up,' said Casey.

Zoe glanced at Lexi, but she had her head down, eating. Jade was staring at Zoe as young children do, with an open and frank interest. Zoe winked and Jade grinned. Zoe looked at Tom and he was grinning but had his head turned away from his father. Dan was eating and frowning. Eloise was expressionless and also seemed to be avoiding eye contact with anyone.

Riordan said, 'Dressing up and making a complete fool of yourself in public may be your idea of fun. After all, your humour has always been infantile, but it certainly isn't mine. You should have warned me, Casey.'

'What, and spoil the surprise?'

Dan guffawed, which turned into a cough, and Lexi chuckled.

'Now boys, let's not get into a fight, especially as we have a guest,' Eloise said.

Zoe said, 'Oh, don't worry about me, I have three older brothers, this is making me feel right at home.'

'How lovely,' said Eloise. 'Do you have nieces and nephews?'

'Yes, Markos and Jacinda have three boys, Caleb and Jo have two girls. Caleb's twin, Damon, isn't married yet, but he has a steady girlfriend.'

'That sounds wonderful, doesn't it, Dan? And what lovely names.'

'Our grandparents were Greek.'

Eloise smiled and Zoe sensed that this sweet, gentle lady was the centre of the O'Connor family, like the sun with the planets orbiting around, receiving her light and warmth. Eloise reminded Zoe of her beloved grandmother, her *ya ya,* the person she had always turned to for support and love. When her grandmother died, a bit of Zoe died with her.

'Anyway,' Casey continued, 'you were a roaring success by all accounts. The Women's Institute collectively awarded you an average of nine out of ten. They would have given you a ten if you'd smiled more.'

'What are you talking about?' Riordan's face was like thunder and Zoe realised she needed to 'fess up.

'That was my fault, I'm afraid. I had the idea of all the ladies awarding you marks out of ten. We were thinking of more fundraisers, you see, like a slave auction—'

Casey erupted into hysterical laughter and could hardly speak. 'Can you imagine … Riordan …'

'Not just Riordan, Casey, we were thinking of you as well,' said Lexi.

'What …? Me? A slave?'

'Oh yes,' said Lexi sweetly. 'I think you'd be perfect.'

Zoe said, 'It was just an idea. Please don't think we were laughing at you, Riordan, because we weren't. If it's any consolation, I awarded you full marks.'

Riordan was glaring at her and she wilted a little under his intense grey-eyed stare. His glasses made him look more serious and his eyes bigger.

'I'm sorry to disappoint you, but no, it's absolutely no consolation whatsoever.'

'Oh come on, son. Casey's right, you need to lighten up a little. It was for a good cause.'

'Would you have worn that costume, Dad?'

'Me, no. Nobody wants to see my flabby old bottom.'

Tom and Jade gasped and started giggling together.

'Granddad, did you show your bum?' asked Jade, giggling loudly.

'No, darling, I didn't,' said Dan.

'It was your Uncle Riordan,' said Casey, dissolving into laughter again.

'Did you, Dad—really?' asked Tom with what, to Zoe, sounded like respect.

Riordan sighed. 'Yes, I did.'

'Why?' Tom stared at his father in awe.

Riordan leaned towards his young son and said quietly, 'Because sometimes, Tom, a man has to do what a man has to do.'

Tom laughed and put his hand up for a high five, and Riordan solemnly obliged.

Then everyone was laughing, even Riordan. A sound that started quietly, then built up in an upsurge. A family united in love and having fun.

Chapter Four

'First of all, let's welcome our new locum, Dr Zoe Angelos.' There was a smattering of applause as Zoe nodded, smiling at each of the people around the table.

'We've already met, but welcome again,' said Louis, a GP, grinning.

'Yes, it's lovely to have you here,' said Imelda, the Office Manager. Zoe noticed Imelda was wearing slippers, although the rest of her attire was pure professional. She had a smart black skirt and jacket with a pristine white blouse. Imelda must have been in her forties and looked well-groomed—and slightly harassed.

Zoe always felt uncomfortable being the centre of attention and today was no different. As the new girl, it was unavoidable. Zoe couldn't wait to feel that she belonged.

'Are you liking Leytonsfield so far?' asked Bilal, the other GP partner.

'Very much, thank you. Everybody's been very welcoming and friendly. I'm looking forward to starting work and meeting the patients.'

Dan said, 'Well said, and with that in mind, let's get on with this agenda. I think we should keep it as short as we can, okay?' He glanced at them over his glasses and they all nodded.

He went on, 'So, first item; phone consultations. Now, you all know how I feel about them. Face-to-face is the only way to treat patients. There is so much you can pick up with body language and the person's general appearance. And I think we need to go on good old-fashioned instinct as well. We all know patients who come to the surgery and spend almost the whole time talking about something trivial and then, at the last minute they come out and say what is really on their minds.'

A discussion ensued which Zoe listened to with interest. Everyone had a valid opinion and eventually they decided to give it a go for six months and evaluate the effect it had on the practice before making a final decision.

'Right. Imelda, could you liaise with these three and get this in motion please?'

'Of course.' Imelda didn't look pleased, probably because it involved much more work for the receptionists.

'Right, next item on the agenda is the redistribution of tasks. Zoe, I wanted to ask you if you'd like to take on the mother and baby group. Do you have any interest in that area of medicine?'

Zoe felt cold in the pit of her stomach. She took a few deep breaths as if she was in her yoga class. 'Actually Dan, I wonder if someone else could run it? I'm not terribly good with babies, to be honest. I'm more interested in the elderly and keeping people living in their own homes for as long as possible. In fact, I would like to run some exercise classes, mainly aimed at patients with diabetes and obesity. Would that be alright with you?'

Dan was frowning, and Zoe worried this had earned her first black mark.

Louis said, 'Do you know, Dan, this is something I've wanted to bring up for a while. We really need to move away from this gender stereotyping. Just because Zoe is the only female GP doesn't mean she should have to do all the baby stuff. Not when you've got a willing volunteer right here?' He grinned and Zoe could have kissed him for rescuing a sticky situation.

Bilal chimed in, 'I agree. Louis is obsessed with babies, everyone knows that. We all need to play to our strengths for the good of the patients. I'd like to work closely with you, Zoe. I have an interest in diabetes and curing type two with diet and exercise. I think we need to push that aspect of health care.'

Dan shrugged. 'Fine, you all seem to have everything sorted. Maybe I'll leave you to it and go and play golf.'

'That would make Riordan happy anyway,' said Imelda, who had pushed off her slippers revealing huge bunions on both her feet. Zoe tried not to look. Imelda caught her gaze and grimaced. 'My bunions are killing me at the moment—I hope you don't mind …'

'Of course not. You poor thing.'

'I'm a martyr to my feet. Always have been.'

'Right,' said Dan. 'Let's get back to the patients.' They all stood up and Dan gestured for Zoe to remain behind.

He said quietly, 'I hope I didn't upset you just then, asking if you could do the mother and babies? It's just that … well, you looked a bit emotional. If there's something you need to talk about, my door's always open.'

'That's very kind of you, Dan, and I will remember that, but I'm fine, honestly. Anyway, are you going to join the exercise class? It would be great for the patients to see us taking part. I'm thinking of line dancing to start off with. It's not too strenuous and really fun.'

'So all the old codgers could see another old codger like me strutting his stuff?' Dan's eyes were twinkling, and Zoe laughed.

'Something like that, yes.'

'Go on then. I need to get more exercise. Just let me have the details.'

Going back to their own offices, Zoe knew she'd dodged a bullet. She would tell Dan and the others eventually. But not yet. It was still too painful.

*

Zoe was in the middle of afternoon surgery and things had been going well, until a young mother came in with her newborn baby.

'He's not thriving, Doctor. He should be putting on weight.'

'How old is he?'

'Two weeks old tomorrow.'

'Okay, well in the first few days of life your baby will probably have lost a little bit of weight. You'll have noticed the thick, tarry poo?'

The mother nodded. 'Ugh, yes, that was horrible.'

Zoe forced a smile, but her heart was racing. Zoe tried not to stare at the baby lying peacefully asleep in his mother's arms.

She said, 'That's the stuff that's built up in the baby's bowels when he was in your womb. Nothing to worry about, it's perfectly normal. When he gets rid of that he'll lose weight, but put it back on by his third week. How are you feeding him?'

'Oh, breastfeeding,' said the girl proudly.

'Well, I think you're doing everything right and I'm sure he'll be fine.'

'Aren't you going to examine him?'

Zoe had been dreading this moment. She *should* look at the child, weigh him and more, but sat frozen. Eventually Zoe grabbed the phone and asked Shona Sutcliffe, the advanced nurse practitioner, to check over the infant. The patient was looking at Zoe with an expression bordering on disgust. Zoe didn't blame her.

Shona bustled in without knocking and swept the child into her arms. 'Come on now with me, lassie, let's take the little fella into the next room and I'll have a good look at him.'

'Thanks Shona,' said Zoe weakly, well aware that what she'd just done was unacceptable. Patients could start complaining.

Her next patient was easier, a middle-aged woman newly diagnosed with stage two diabetes. Zoe inwardly sighed with relief. Back in her comfort zone, Zoe explained that weight loss and exercise would help and could even get rid of the diabetes altogether. The woman was happy and left the surgery, promising to attend the exercise classes.

Next was a man with terminal cancer who wanted to change his pain relief. Zoe put him on a regime of regular Codeine and paracetamol, with breakthrough Oramorph when the pain was worse.

Her next patient was a sixty-five-year-old woman, who hardly ever came to the surgery because she didn't believe in "running to the doctor for every little ailment." She had been told that, now she was sixty-five, she should have a 'flu jab in winter. Well, she didn't want one, that was for sure, and she was there to tell the doctors not to bother sending her an appointment for one either.

Zoe patiently detailed the need for the jab.

'Will it make me sick, Doctor? Because I won't have it, if it does. I look after my husband, see, and he's got dementia. If I'm sick, there's no-one to look after him.'

'Don't you have carers?'

'Oh no, we don't need anyone interfering in our lives. We can manage, we always have.'

*

Zoe was shattered by the time the clinic ended.

On the way to reception, she bumped into Shona.

'How was the baby, Shona?'

'Oh, the wee lamb was fine. Just a nervous young mother, that's all. She went off happy.'

'Thanks for your help, I really appreciate it.'

'Aye, well, I did hear you're not one for babies. Shame, they're such adorable little things when they're newborn. Still, we can't all have the maternal instinct, I suppose.' Shona moved on before Zoe could answer.

Zoe stood rooted to the spot, fighting back tears. This couldn't go on. People would think she was hard and uncaring. Zoe needed to tell Dan—and soon—before her reputation was in tatters.

Chapter Five

The sun was just beginning to set below the pale wintery sky when Riordan left the hospital. He was bone-weary and would have loved to have gone straight home, but it was Sally's birthday and Riordan had given her flowers for the last fifteen years and wasn't about to stop now.

He parked the car on a side road and slipped through the gates which would be locked soon. This wouldn't take long.

Riordan walked briskly down the grassy aisles, looking neither right nor left, until he came to his wife's grave. He stood for a few minutes, examining the headstone for damage by either the weather or vandalism, and then knelt and replaced the dead flowers with the fresh blooms. A mixed bouquet; Sally's favourite.

'Happy birthday, sweetheart,' he murmured then sighed deeply. Each year he came to the cemetery on the seventh of

January—and on other days as well, of course, and sometimes brought Tom, even though the boy didn't remember his mother very well. Tom was two years old when Sally died.

The first few years after Sally's death, Riordan had cried, wringing himself inside out emotionally, not caring about making a spectacle of himself in public. Gradually, as the years went on, his grief became more contained, quieter, more like a heavy weight that he learned how to carry by holding it in a certain way. Not that there weren't times when Riordan didn't still feel a deep, uncontrollable rage that the only woman he had ever loved, and ever would, had been taken from him and Tom so cruelly. Those times, however, were less often. Riordan had been taught how to deal with the pain and, most of the time, unless under a tremendous amount of stress, it worked.

He walked slowly back towards the gates, deep in thought. Riordan didn't see the short, female figure, standing quietly watching, until she spoke.

'Hi, Riordan.'

He stared through the gloom. 'Martha?'

'Yes, I knew I'd find you here at this time. I rang Casey who told me you'd been on duty today, so you would pay your respects on the way home.'

Riordan ran towards Martha and lifted her in the air. 'Martha! How wonderful ... I didn't even know you were back.'

'Oh no,' she said, laughing. 'Put me down, you'll give yourself a hernia.'

'You are a sight for sore eyes.' He set her down gently.

'And you. You're looking well. Cold, but well.'

'It's freezing. Come on, let's get into the warm. Have you got time for a drink? Where are you staying?'

'Yes, it's freezing, especially after the Yemen. I'm only here for a short while, and then I go back until Easter. Then home again. I'm going down to London tomorrow, but in April I'll be able to stay for longer.'

He said firmly, 'Then at Easter, you'll stay with us.'

When they were both in the car Riordan headed in the direction of Leytonsfield Town Centre.

'How about the Leytonsfield Hotel? I know you like it there,' Riordan said, his mood improving with every minute he was in Martha's company. She was the first person he had approached in medical school and they became best friends almost instantly.

Riordan bought two halves of bitter and two packets of crisps and searched around until he found Martha. She was sitting in a corner people-watching. He felt his spirits lift at the thought of being in her company again. She was the bravest, kindest, most down-to-earth person Riordan had ever met. He owed her so much. When Sally died, it was Martha who held Riordan for hours as he wept. She was his rock and best friend, and even though he only saw Martha once in a while, Riordan couldn't imagine life without her.

'There we go.'

'Oh, lovely, cheese and onion.' She opened the packet so they could share. Another typical Martha trait.

'So ... how's *Médecin Sans Frontières*?'

Martha gave him a sideways look. 'Busy. Stressful. And still the best thing I've ever done. I couldn't imagine doing anything else, Riordan.'

'I admire you, I really do,' he said, feeling a rush of affection. 'You're doing something I wouldn't have the courage to do.'

'You say that every time you see me.' Martha smiled at him gently. She was one of the few people Riordan would let tease him.

'That's because every time I see you, which, by the way, is never often enough, I'm bowled over by the life you lead. The dedication in the face of such overwhelming danger.'

Martha laughed. 'You sound like an advert for MSF. If you ever get sick of the NHS you can be our copywriter.'

'I get sick of the NHS nearly every day. But never the people.'

'Things no better then?'

'No, not really.' He thought of Jack Dempsey's desperate need to stay in his own home.

'Penny for them? You're wandering, Riordan.'

'Sorry, I was just thinking about a patient of mine. Wants to stay home, lives alone, needs care ... the usual story. But compared to the people you help—limbs blown off by landmines for instance—we don't really have the right to complain, do we?'

She said, 'The thing I've discovered about the patients is that every single person we treat has problems and it's not for us to judge how big or small that problem is. If it's affecting their lives, then it's our job to help, nothing else.'

Riordan was silent, watching her. Martha never looked any older, despite the horrors she must have to deal with on a daily basis. She'd never married, and never—to his knowledge— fallen in love. She was totally dedicated to her work.

'What are you looking at?' she asked suspiciously.

'I'm looking at the most remarkable woman I've ever known.'

'There's nothing remarkable about me, Riordan, trust me. I'm the same as any woman.'

'No, my dear friend, you're not.' Embarrassingly, Riordan felt tears coming. But, as always, Martha understood.

'This is a difficult day for you. Is it getting any easier?'

He thought before answering. 'Yes, it is. Very slowly, but surely, I'm finding a way of living without her. I have Tom, my family, work and I have you—periodically.'

She smiled again. 'You'll always have me.'

'Likewise. You know I'd be there for you, if you ever needed me.'

'I know.' Martha took a long draught of her beer. 'But you should think about dating again. You must get lonely some-times.'

'I don't have time. Anyway, what about you? Have you met anyone?'

'Me? No, I'm married to the job.'

Riordan drained his pint and sat back. 'And I imagine you don't get the time to dwell on your own needs. Too busy looking after everybody else.'

Martha narrowed her eyes in a challenging look. 'That's right.'

He stifled a grin. She hadn't changed one bit. Work came first, and always would. Sometimes Riordan envied her. Martha didn't seem beset by doubts, never bothered by other's opinion of her. She was completely content in her own skin. But, as Martha said, she was a woman like any other, with needs, hormones and moods.

'Well, Martha, when you come to stay at the O'Connor's for Easter, you'll be spoilt rotten. You'll not lift a finger the whole time.'

'That sounds good, and I gratefully accept your kind offer. But now, I need to go. So if you could drop me off at the station, I'll catch the train to Manchester.'

'Are you getting the early London train tomorrow?'

'If I can get up in time.'

Riordan said, 'It's great to see you again.'

She had restored his equilibrium, as always. And Martha knew it. It was why she had gone all the way to the cemetery to see him. Because better than anyone else Martha remembered the hell Riordan had gone through when he lost Sally.

Chapter Six

The cottage was warm and cosy with a roaring log fire and thick curtains at the windows to shut out the chill of the January night. There was little sound outside. Zoe had chosen this tenancy out of about half a dozen because it was the last cottage in the row and promised the seclusion and quiet that she needed.

She could have chosen the centre of town in a more modern area. Smart, but cramped townhouses that were near shops, bus routes and schools. Also, on the estate agent's books were cottages in the older district of Leytonsfield. Beautiful old stone houses with large fireplaces and tiny gardens at the back. And then, of course, there were flats, which Zoe didn't even bother to look at. She'd spent enough time in digs and hospital accommodation, and never wanted to go back to that style of living.

Rosemary Cottage, as it was grandly called, had everything she wanted. Privacy, a lovely large garden at the back that wasn't overlooked—except by cows in an adjoining field—and easy access to the canal and woodlands for long walks in summer. The front garden was small with a hawthorn hedge protecting the property from prying eyes. It was perfect.

Well, almost perfect. Some of the rooms were damp, with peeling paint that made the walls look as if they had a terrible skin disease. The windows were tiny—and some didn't open, and the bare floorboards were uneven and creaked terribly like in an old Hitchcock horror film.

Nonetheless, Zoe knew she had struck gold and signed the agreement for a six-month let.

After a long soak in the bath with the water as hot as she could stand it, and bubble bath filling the air with fragrance, Zoe sat on the sofa with a hot chocolate, staring into the flames and trying to fight the depression threatening to overwhelm her.

She had been so looking forward to moving to Leytonsfield. Starting afresh with people who didn't know her history and would accept Zoe with no preconceived ideas. No pitying looks or walking on the other side of the street to avoid her. After today, Zoe realised how unrealistic that was—to think she could pretend it hadn't happened, when every waking, and sometimes sleeping, minute was filled with it. The hollowness inside echoed with pain and loss to the point where Zoe sometimes felt she was going mad.

She owed it to herself and the people she worked with, especially Dan, to be open about it. Then, at least they would realise she had good reason for any peculiar behaviour.

Tomorrow. She'd channel her inner Scarlet O'Hara and think about it tomorrow.

Despite the relaxing bath and hot chocolate, Zoe couldn't sleep. She tossed and turned for two frustrating hours, then admitting defeat got up again and put some more wood on the burning embers. Soon, the fire was blazing merrily, and Zoe sat on the sofa and shut her eyes, trying some meditation. Emptying her mind was hard as the same thoughts drifted back in time and again. She was supposed to let them drift without acknowledging them, not making any judgements, just accepting them and gently turning back to the flames. Zoe had discovered that a candle worked well for meditation, but she didn't have any candles and stared at the fire instead.

Zoe was just starting to relax and feel peaceful when the headlights of a car lit up the room like searchlights, followed by the sound of the car door opening. It was late for visitors. Zoe was up and at the window in seconds, her heart racing, mouth dry. It was so isolated here, which is what she'd wanted, but now Zoe wished differently. Adrenalin, the fight or flight hormone, was surging around her veins.

The road was dark and with few streetlamps. A copse of trees on the other side was solid and black. The full moon, shining through a gap in the clouds, gave just enough light to see the car, the headlights now turned off. A man leapt out of the car, pulled open the back door and grabbed something from the back seat. He threw it into the ditch on the far side of the road, jumped back into the car and left in a tearing hurry, without turning the headlights back on first.

The following silence was eerie. Zoe stood at the window for ages, wondering what to do. What was it? And why had he come all the way out here to get rid of it? Zoe peered intently towards the other side of the road but could see nothing in the blackness. The moonlight didn't penetrate the thick shadows at the bottom of the trees and the camber of the road made it impossible to see into the ditch.

There was only one thing to be done. She'd have to go outside and look. Zoe ran up the stairs and pulled on jeans and a sweatshirt, then ran back down again and shoved her feet into wellington boots that were permanently near the door. Outside, Zoe shivered in the chill air, and wished she'd worn a coat— and had the foresight to buy a torch.

The road was empty of traffic. A tawny owl hooted in the distance. A break in the clouds revealed a night sky dotted with stars and the moon seemed to be directly over the cottage. Maybe it was shining just for her, knowing she needed help to find … whatever it was. Zoe could see something in the ditch and moved cautiously towards the dark shadow.

She thought it moved.

Zoe hurried over and pulled it out of the ditch. It was in a bin liner and the plastic had torn. Then the bundle whimpered.

Frantically, Zoe tore the plastic off and unravelled a bundle of rags. A small terrified dog was curled up, cowering and crying.

'Oh, you poor little thing!'

The dog was obviously hurt, but Zoe couldn't see how badly. She scooped it up in her arms and, leaving the plastic and the rags to retrieve later, hurried back into the cottage and over to the fireplace. She placed it down gently, near enough to the fire so it could get warm, then ran her hands over its legs and back. Zoe couldn't feel any breaks, but she wasn't a vet and couldn't be sure.

The dog was a lovely sandy colour with a white patch on its chest. She stroked it gently, talking soothingly, and the little thing made no attempt to get up or move. It just lay on its side shaking and whimpering.

The dog needed help, so there was only one thing for it. Zoe grabbed her phone and searched for vets in the local area. There was a practice in the middle of the town, and the website claimed that there was a vet on duty around the clock for emergencies.

No need to ring first, just come in, we're never closed.

'Right, sweetheart,' she said to the dog. 'I'm just going to put my trainers on and then we'll go.' The dog hadn't moved, but its ears twitched slightly, which Zoe took as a good sign.

She dashed up the stairs, grabbed her winter coat and struggled into her trainers, all the time wondering what to put the dog in for the car. All the cardboard boxes for moving to the cottage had been dismantled and put into the recycling bin.

Zoe solved the problem by putting the dog, wrapped in a soft towel, on her lap while she drove. It was the early hours of the morning and there was little traffic on the road, so she drove slowly, never reaching thirty miles per hour. Apart from quiet whimpering when Zoe slid carefully into the car and started the engine, the dog hardly reacted.

Zoe parked in the almost deserted car park at the side of the vets and slid out from behind the wheel, talking gently to the dog and trying not to make any sudden moves. She carried her precious bundle into the building and stood in the reception area with the dog in her arms, wondering what to do next. The place was spotlessly clean and looked deserted.

She walked over to the desk to see if there was a bell or something. The dog had hardly moved.

'Hello.'

Zoe turned at the sound of a man's voice. 'Oh … hello.'

Wearing pale blue scrubs, he was over six feet tall with curly brown hair and the most intense blue eyes. It was his smile that floored Zoe. Perfectly white teeth as if he had come straight from a toothpaste commercial, and the sexiest mouth with a wide grin that showed a dimple in his cheek.

'What have we got? Bring the dog in here quickly.'

He turned and went into a room, holding the door open. Zoe followed, realising how she must look. No make-up, hair dishevelled after the bath, and wearing jeans and sweatshirt over pyjamas. Zoe wasn't even wearing a bra.

Typical. When a Greek God turned up in her life, she was looking as bad as it was possible to look.

'What's the story?' asked the vet.

Zoe told him. The muscles in his jaw clenched and the smile disappeared. He shook his head, and then listened to the dog's heart. After performing a thorough examination, he stood with his head bowed, absentmindedly stroking the animal. It lay on the examining table, unmoving and unresponsive.

'Is it alright?' Zoe's heart was in her mouth. She desperately wanted this small scrap of life that had been thrown away like a bag of rubbish to survive. 'I can't believe how vile some people are,' she said, before bursting into tears.

Zoe stood there sobbing and wiping her nose on one sleeve. She rifled through her pockets and couldn't find a tissue.

Without a word the vet handed her one.

'Thank you,' she said. 'I'm so sorry, I'm not usually like this, it's just that … I couldn't bear it if the dog died after being so cruelly treated, never knowing what human kindness is.' The tears wouldn't stop flowing. 'I'm sorry.'

'Stop apologising,' he said.

She looked up expecting to see an exasperated look on his face. It wasn't even her dog and here Zoe was blubbing like an idiot. But he was smiling, and his blue eyes were kind.

'She's not going to die. She's had a nasty shock but is in surprisingly good physical condition. There's nothing broken and her gums are a good colour. If you saw some of the sights we see … well, that's our job, not yours.' He deftly inserted a needle and took some blood from her leg. The dog didn't even flinch.

'I can imagine,' she said. 'So, why did they treat her so badly, if they were looking after her so well?'

'Only *they* can answer that. Although I suspect it has a lot to do with not wanting the hassle and expense of a litter of puppies. Maybe they just couldn't be bothered. I see that a lot, especially with dogs. People don't realise that they're not toys, but living, breathing creatures that have needs only their owners can meet.'

'Puppies? What, you mean she's...?'

'Pregnant. Yes. And not too far away from her due date.'

'How far?'

'I'd need to do a more thorough examination, but I'd guess about a week.'

'Oh my goodness.' Zoe stared at him.

What was it with the world and babies? It was almost as if the universe was conspiring against Zoe. Okay, a gross exaggeration, but Zoe's head was spinning from lack of sleep and trying to keep it together. The bout of crying didn't help.

He said, 'Don't worry, there's a woman who sometimes takes in strays for us, especially in cases like this. I'll give her a ring and see if she can take this little lady in. The puppies won't be a problem I shouldn't think. People always want them. It was good of you to bring her to us.'

'Oh no, I ... it's okay, I want her. I'll look after her.'

He straightened. 'Are you sure? You did a good deed by bringing her in, but you really don't need to take her on, especially with puppies on board. Maybe you need to think about it?'

'No, I don't. I'm sure.'

He looked doubtful and studied Zoe for a moment or two. She felt uncomfortable under his gaze, but stared back with raised eyebrows.

'I haven't seen you around town. Are you from Leytonsfield?'

'Manchester, but I live here now.'

He smiled and put out his hand. 'Toby Dean, pleased to meet you.'

His hand was warm and the grip firm but gentle. She couldn't help smiling back. 'Zoe Angelos, and likewise.'

'What brings you to this neck of the woods?' he asked.

'I'm a GP. I've just started at South Leytonsfield Medical Centre.'

'A doctor? At Dan O'Connor's place?'

'Yes, do you know Dan?'

'Everyone knows Dan.' Zoe waited for him to elaborate, but he didn't.

'Can I take her home?' she asked. Zoe moved nearer to the examining table as Toby gently stroked the dog's side. Zoe wanted to get the dog back into the warmth and peace of the cottage. Toby frowned and shook his head.

'To be honest, I'm still a bit worried about her. I want to do a thorough examination and some blood tests to make sure the puppies are healthy before letting her go. She is a bit too unresponsive for my liking. We'll keep her here overnight and you can pick her up tomorrow. How's that?'

'She will be alright, won't she?' Zoe didn't like the worried tone that belied his matter-of-fact words.

'Oh, I'm sure she will. And she's in the right place. Just fill in one of the forms in reception and leave your details including mobile number, and I'll give you a ring, okay?'

Zoe watched anxiously as Toby carried the dog effortlessly through a swing door at the back of the room. Zoe followed.

The room was full of cages of all sizes. There were only two occupants; an old Labrador with a muzzle streaked with grey who gazed mournfully at them but didn't even lift his head, and a Corgi who was fast asleep, his paws working. Maybe he was dreaming of running away.

Toby placed the dog in one of the cages with a beanbag inside. Zoe marvelled at how gentle Toby was for such a big man. Even his hands were large, but he had the deftest of touches.

'Right,' he said, closing the cage door. 'I'll let her get used to things, then see if she is more responsive in a short while.'

'Is she in shock?'

'No, her gums are a good colour and there's none of the physical signs of shock. I need those blood test results to see if I'm right, but I suspect she's been sedated somehow. I can't see how else someone could wrap a dog in rags and a plastic bag without the animal going ballistic and barking, not to mention biting and snarling. It would be natural for any animal to fight back. I know I would.'

'Me too,' Zoe said, close to tears again. 'Poor little girl.'

'Yes.' The smile was back, and Zoe knew she was leaving her new pet in safe hands.

'I better go then. I may be in surgery when you ring, but if you leave a message I'll ring back.'

'Okay. What are you going to call her, by the way? I suppose you haven't got that far—choosing a name.'

'I have, as a matter of fact. I'm going to call her Luna, in honour of the moon that helped me find her.'

'Good name.' Toby grinned and Zoe thought she could get to like this guy—too much, if she wasn't careful.

'Til tomorrow then. 'Night.'

'Goodnight Zoe, and don't worry, I'll take good care of Luna.'

Chapter Seven

When Zoe collected Luna the following afternoon before surgery, she arrived at the vets carrying a lead and a small dog carrier. She'd left the rest of the things in the boot of her car. These included a beanbag, a dog bed in case Luna didn't like the beanbag, bowls, food, biscuits, brushes, combs and toys. She'd bought a collar with tiny gems that sparkled and would ask Toby to microchip Luna. Not that she had any intention of letting the dog out of her sight.

Zoe also made sure to look her best. A smart skirt and blouse, immaculate make-up, a squirt of her favourite perfume, and hair brushed and shiny. She didn't examine her motives too closely, having no intention of getting involved with a man again at this stage. Recent relationships could be summed up in one word—disaster. After the way Zoe had looked the night before, she just wanted Toby to realise that scruffy bag-lady wasn't a normal look.

The noise hit Zoe as she walked through the automatic doors. There were dogs barking, cats meowing, a parrot squawking and various small mammals in cages.

There was no sign of Toby.

Behind the reception desk was a woman who smiled calmly at Zoe as she approached, apparently oblivious to the cacophony filling the room.

'I've come to collect Luna,' Zoe said.

'Oh good, come this way.' The woman led Zoe to where the cages were kept. 'She's a lovely little thing, isn't she?'

'Yes. Quiet, but lovely.'

The receptionist said, 'There, Luna, didn't I tell you your mummy was coming to fetch you?'

The sinking feeling Zoe normally got when anyone mentioned the word "mummy" was swallowed up by the joy of seeing her dog. Luna was sitting up and wagging her tail as hard as she could. Seeing Zoe, she started barking and jumped up, placing her paws on the bars of the cage and trying to stick her nose through.

Zoe bent down. 'Oh, look at you! She's like a different animal.'

'She is indeed,' said a deep, male voice. Zoe turned around to look into the blue eyes of Toby Dean. He added, 'And so are you, if it's not impertinent to say so.'

Zoe straightened and looked around. The receptionist had gone. 'No, it's understandable after the way I must have looked last night.'

'You looked like a woman on a mercy mission.' He grinned. 'Actually, you looked fine.'

'Well, thank you for that, but ... anyway ... Luna. You've performed miracles.'

'It was as I suspected. They'd used a sedative called Benadryl which is safe if administered properly but Luna had far too much of the stuff in her system. If you hadn't brought her in, she would have died. You saved her life, Zoe.' His words warmed Zoe.

'I rather think you were the one who did that'. They smiled at each other and Zoe heard a small, warning voice inside telling her to be careful. Toby was charming, intelligent, gorgeous—and exactly the kind of man she needed to avoid.

She said, 'Okay, let's call it a team effort.'

He nodded. 'I've taken the liberty of micro-chipping Luna with the details from the form you filled in. Hope that's okay?'

'Yes, of course, I was going to ask you to do that anyway.'

He unlocked the cage and let Luna, frantic for freedom, swarm all over Zoe.

'Hello, gorgeous girl,' Zoe said, as Luna licked her face, hands and ears. The smart skirt was already covered in dog hair and the make-up mostly licked off. So much for trying to look her best.

'Okay,' said Toby decisively. 'Shall I help you get her in the carrier?'

'Yes, thank you.' He was plainly keen to get back to work. Anxious patients and their even more anxious humans waited for him.

'Do you want to pay now, or we can send the invoice to your home address, if you'd prefer?'

'I'll pay now.'

'Okay, give me your car keys and I'll put her in the back, shall I?'

'Thanks. It's the silver Ford Mondeo.'

Zoe handed the keys over and went to pay the bill. She tried not to react when she saw it; the total was more than Zoe had been anticipating, but she'd never owned a pet before and had no idea what to expect really.

Zoe returned to the car just as Toby was placing the dog carrier on the back seat.

'Thanks for everything, Toby.' She didn't know what to say. Zoe felt the occasion merited something profound, and all she could think about was being late for surgery if she didn't leave now.

He said, 'I've been thinking. As you were so kind as to take Luna and she's had such a rough time at the hands of humans, she deserves special treatment. Just ring me when you think she's about to pup and I'll come over and supervise. Here's my card.'

Toby handed his card over and Zoe blushed. He was a nice man, and a good vet. 'Thanks, I will.'

'Right, better go.'

'Yes, me too. 'Bye, Toby and thanks.'

'So long.' He walked off and Zoe jumped in the car.

'Right Luna, it's just me and you now girl.'

*

The traffic was heavy on the way back to the medical centre, with mums on the school run, people shopping, and delivery vans at every turn. A normal working afternoon in Leytonsfield town centre, Zoe imagined.

Zoe didn't have the time to go back to Rosemary Cottage, so she took Luna into the medical centre. Fortunately, the dog had calmed down and seemed happy to settle on the beanbag next to Zoe's desk. Zoe would have loved to skip surgery and take Luna home so they could get to know each other. There was a waiting-room full of patients to think about first.

Surgery consisted mainly of people presenting with 'flu-like symptoms, coughs, sore throats and the like. Typical January ailments. Most of them smiled when they saw Luna, and luckily no one complained, which was Zoe's biggest fear.

A small boy, who had looked terrified when he crept into the room, broke into a wide grin when he saw Luna and spent the whole time talking to the dog. His mother told Zoe her son's symptoms and Zoe managed to examine the boy easily with his attention focused on Luna. A simple case of glue ear. Zoe told the mother it would probably clear up in three months but to bring him back if she was worried.

The mother said, 'He's always wanted a dog, Doctor. Do you think they're safe? You must know.'

'Yes, if you get the right kind, they're perfectly safe.' Zoe hoped the woman wouldn't ask *what* the right kind was—Zoe had no idea.

'Do you always bring her to the surgery?'

'No, but she's pregnant and I need to keep an eye on her.'

'Puppies!' The little boy was suddenly animated. 'Mum, can I have one—please?'

'Oh, I don't know, we'll have to ask your father. But the doctor may already have homes for them. Have you?'

'No, actually, I haven't. I can put your name down provisionally, if you like.'

'Yes, please!' said the boy, and his mother shrugged.

There was one patient who took little notice of Luna. She was too upset, a young black girl called Mary, living in the battered women's shelter and heavily pregnant, and near due. Mary was scared for the baby. Her boyfriend had kicked Mary in the stomach, saying he didn't want the brat. Mary only wanted to see a female doctor.

Zoe rang the antenatal clinic at the hospital and booked an appointment, before examining the girl closely. This time, Zoe wasn't calling in Shona.

'I can't find anything, but I want you to be checked over just to make sure. They will see you as an emergency this afternoon and do an ultrasound. Are you able to get there?'

'Yeah, Hannah'll take me. She's taken me to all the appointments so far. She's in the waiting room.'

'Good. Here's my card. Ring me if there are any problems, and don't hesitate to come back and see me any time, okay?'

'Okay.'

A young man called Andrew, who lived on his own, also made a fuss of Luna. Zoe slipped into the conversation that there would be puppies.

'I'll have one,' he said.

At the end of surgery, Dan came in and glanced at Luna before looking at Zoe with raised eyebrows. 'I didn't know you had a dog.'

'Neither did I until yesterday.'

Over coffee, Zoe told him the story.

'I hope it's okay to bring her into surgery. It's only until the puppies are born, in about a week.'

'It's fine by me. Unless one of the patients complains, it'll be okay with everyone else, I should imagine.'

'Thanks, Dan. I need to talk to you about something else too. It's a bit delicate.'

'Do you want to tell me now?'

'No, not right now. When there's more time.' Zoe wasn't ready despite her earlier resolve. Now definitely wasn't the time.

'Then just let me know when.'

'I will, Dan. Thanks.'

He smiled, petted Luna and left.

As Zoe typed up the patients' records, she wondered if offering the puppies to patients was ethical. How could it not be? The puppies needed homes, and Zoe knew as much as was needed about the people who wanted them. It was a win-win.

Chapter Eight

'So, how is the new GP shaping up?' Riordan passed the potatoes down the table and waited for his father to answer.

Like Riordan, Dan O'Connor never answered a question without giving it careful consideration. This made some people think he hadn't heard or was ignoring them. Riordan had picked the habit up and found it useful.

'She's shaping up very well, thanks.'

'Right,' Riordan nodded.

Dan didn't want to talk about Dr Zoe Angelos, but Riordan did. Zoe had been employed to take the heat off his father and Riordan intended to make sure she did.

'She's a lovely-looking girl, all that dark hair and the deep brown eyes. She's a looker,' said his mother.

'Dad, can I leave the vegetables?' asked Tom.

'Eat some of them.'

'I don't like them,' he whispered in a loud voice.

'Your gran has spent all day cooking you a lovely meal and you're not eating it.'

'I am, Dad … I've eaten the meat and the spuds.'

Riordan reached over and took Tom's knife and fork off him. He moved a small portion of the peas and cauliflower to the side of the plate. 'Just eat that tiny amount, okay?'

Tom slumped in his chair and said, 'Okay,' in a resigned voice.

'Has Zoe taken on any of the extras that you wanted to offload?' Riordan asked.

'Yes, she's organising a keep-fit class and plans to introduce walks in spring and summer. She's working with Bilal on trying to get the Type Two patients off medication and encouraging the obese patients to lose weight. Zoe is an asset and we're lucky to have her.'

'Why don't you like her, Riordan?' His mother always knew what Riordan was thinking.

'I hope it's not because of that stupid costume joke,' said his father.

'No, of course not, I'm not that petty—that's long forgotten. It's you I'm concerned about. You need to take it easy, Dad.'

Ignoring this, Dan said, 'Oh, and she's got a dog. She rescued it, apparently. Someone … well, let's just say they didn't want it. It was in the surgery with Zoe, lying on a beanbag. Sweet little thing.'

'She brought a dog into the surgery with her? Is that hygienic?'

'A dog!' said Tom, 'Dad, can we go and see it?'

'No, Tom, not today anyway.'

'It's having puppies,' added his father, putting the lid on any hope Riordan had of distracting his son.

'Puppies! Dad, can I have a puppy? Please?'

Riordan shot his father a *thank you very much for that* look. Dan smiled back innocently.

Eloise said, 'Riordan, if you do go around tonight, will you take some food with you? I've made some buns and an apple pie. At least Zoe can have some home cooking in case she gets homesick, living on her own in that isolated cottage.'

Now Riordan had no choice.

'Yes, of course.'

'Can we go after tea, to see the dog, and tell her we want a puppy?' Tom was beside himself with excitement and Riordan knew he wasn't going to win this one. And would it be so bad? Tom was a good kid, he hardly ever asked for anything and was grateful for any present he got. At Tom's age, Riordan and his siblings had owned enough pets between them to start a small animal farm. And boys loved dogs.

'Yes, if it's convenient. I'll have to ring Zoe first to check. We can't just turn up unannounced.'

'Well, you do that now,' said his mother. 'Tom can help me load the dishwasher and then you can go.'

*

'Hello?'

'Hi Zoe, it's Riordan. Riordan O'Connor.'

'Ah … the gladiator.' Zoe heard him laughing and couldn't help smiling. 'Does this mean I'm forgiven?'

'Forgiven for what?'

'Whatever I did to upset you.'

'Of course, and it was Casey I was mad at, not you—or anybody else for that matter. I'm still going to get my revenge, I just haven't decided how yet.'

'Poor Casey.'

'My son is desperate to see your dog, and my mother has been cooking for you. She's convinced you're not eating. I just wondered if it's okay to pop round? We won't stay long, I promise. It's a school night and I like Tom to be in bed early.'

'Of course. It's Rosemary Cottage, but I expect you already know that.'

'I did. See you soon.'

'Yes.' She ended the call.

Zoe gazed around at the cottage and wondered if it was worth trying to tidy up. Since coming home with Luna, the living-room had undergone a major reconstruction. It looked as if a bomb had hit it—a small, furry bomb. Luna had made herself at home very quickly, sniffing everything and piddling in the corner when she got too excited. Zoe hadn't stopped to consider if her new pet was house-trained. Newspaper was put down in strategic places and Zoe took Luna into the garden regularly in the hope the dog would get the message that certain things were meant to be done outside.

One of Zoe's slippers had found its way into Luna's bed and the dog was now curled up with her head on the slipper. She looked so sweet, as if butter wouldn't melt. Zoe snapped a photo.

The doorbell chimed and Luna, barking madly, shot out of the bed. Zoe knew better than to try to discipline Luna; she was only defending her new home. Perhaps it was a good sign.

'Come on, Luna, come with me and we'll see who it is.' Luna wagged her tail and obeyed, walking at Zoe's side.

She opened the front door and Tom made a beeline for Luna.

'Hi, Tom.'

'Oh look, Dad, isn't she beautiful? Hi, Zoe.'

'She's tiny,' said Riordan. 'Not sure why, but I was expecting a bigger dog.'

'She's a Sheltie-Jack Russell cross, according to Toby,' Zoe said.

'Toby Dean?' Riordan frowned and turned away.

'Yes, do you know him?'

Riordan's expression was blank, but the muscles in his jaw were clenched tight. 'Our paths have crossed.'

'Right. He was very good with Luna.'

'I'm sure.' Riordan's words were clipped.

'Come in, come in,' said Zoe, disappointed by Riordan's manner. He obviously didn't like Toby for some reason.

'Thanks. We won't stay long. Here—Mum's offering.' Riordan handed Zoe a basket.

Zoe peeked inside. 'Thank your mum for me, will you? Actually, I haven't eaten yet, so I might have some of this delicious apple pie. Would you two like to join me?'

'No thanks, we've just had dinner.'

'Coffee? Tea?'

'Coffee, please. Tom can have juice or milk.'

Zoe went into the kitchen, leaving the two of them to fuss the dog. As she cut a slice of apple pie and made the coffee, she wondered what to talk to Riordan about. He was reserved, but not unfriendly. Perhaps she'd keep quiet and let them do the talking.

She returned to the living room with the drinks and food to find both of them sitting on the floor play-fighting with Luna. Zoe sat quietly on the sofa, eating the apple pie, and watching them.

'Is it okay to play with her like this?' asked Riordan. 'It can't damage the puppies, can it?'

'I wouldn't think so, she's been like this ever since I got her home. I meant to ask Toby how old he thought Luna is, but I forgot. I imagine she's quite young.'

Riordan stood up and brushed his trousers with his hand. Then he sat next to Zoe on the sofa and picked up his coffee. Tom stayed on the floor playing with Luna.

'So, how are things at the surgery? Dad says you're settling in well.'

Zoe nodded, swallowing some pie. 'I'm enjoying myself. It's early days yet, of course, and I'm still on trial, but I think I'm going to like it here. I'd really like to stay.'

'Good. You do know my father had a heart attack last year, don't you?' Riordan spoke quietly, so Tom wouldn't listen.

Zoe did the same. 'Yes, I did. Dan told me he was taking on another doctor so he could do a bit less. But he's not the kind of person to just sit around and do nothing.'

'It's a balance, Zoe. As a cardiologist I see the results of not getting that balance right. I don't want that to happen to my father.'

Was Riordan warning Zoe that she wasn't doing enough?

'Well, I will do all I can to help Dan. He's been very good to me and I know how lucky I am to be able to work with such an experienced doctor. We all have our own ideas of how to treat the patients and my belief is that keeping active is the best way forward.'

'Could you elaborate on that?'

Riordan still spoke quietly, but Zoe detected the edge behind his words. He also had a pleasant voice and Zoe imagined the junior doctors would find his teaching fascinating. In Zoe's family everyone talked loudly and all at once, as they wouldn't be heard otherwise. It was a free-for-all in the Angelos household.

She said, 'Some patients have a heart attack and think their life is over. I don't mean Dan, of course, but I've seen it happen. They give up so many of their interests because they are frightened of doing some kind of physical damage. I try to encourage my patients to live their lives as normally as possible, and that includes exercise and having fun. Yes, and sometimes taking risks.'

'So, in your opinion, my father should continue as if nothing had happened?'

'No, Riordan, I'm not saying that. The MI he had was real, but the days of telling patients to take it easy are long gone. Regular exercise is essential for good health, and work is essential for a man like your father to maintain quality of life.'

Zoe stopped and took a deep breath, in danger of getting on her soapbox and spouting more favourite theories about patients and exercise. But Dan was Riordan's father and quite rightly, his son worried. Zoe would be exactly the same if it was her father. The fact that Riordan was a consultant cardiologist was irrelevant. When it's your own family, logic can fly out the window.

'Dad, can you ask Zoe about the puppies?'

'What about the puppies, Tom?' asked Zoe, happy for a change of subject.

Riordan sighed deeply. 'Tom wants one of Luna's puppies, if that's alright with you, of course.'

'Fine by me. If Toby is right, she's having four, and there's only one more to rehome.'

'How did you find homes for them so quickly? Dad said you only rescued her yesterday,' said Riordan.

'I didn't have time to bring Luna home before surgery and had to take her with me. Two of my patients expressed an interest. Of course, they could change their minds.'

'We won't, will we, Dad?' said Tom, still on the floor with his arms around Luna.

'No, once I make a decision, I usually stick to it.'

'Good for you,' said Zoe, and smiled to show she wasn't making fun of him.

'Okay, Tom, I think it's time to leave Zoe and Luna in peace.'

'Ah, Dad ... can't I have five minutes more?'

'I tell you what—if we leave now, you can have an extra ten minutes when I read to you.'

'What if I'd rather stay here for an extra five minutes?'

'Then you go straight to bed when we get home.'

Zoe laughed and watched the discussion between father and son with interest. They had such a good relationship and Riordan treated Tom with respect, not something all parents managed.

'Okay Dad, you win, we'll go now.'

'Do you always win?' Zoe asked Riordan.

'So far, but I'm not holding out much hope for the future. It won't be long before he's running rings around me.'

After Zoe had waved them off, she sat back on the sofa, feeling exhausted. She hadn't slept much the night before and it was starting to catch up. An early night would be the sensible thing.

She left Luna in her basket and went upstairs. Just as Zoe was drifting off, she heard a soft whining and felt a wet nose pressing into her hand. Luna had come up the stairs and crept into the bed. Zoe knew that Luna should sleep on a beanbag or it would become a habit, but she was just too tired to move and the soft, warm body lying next to her was comforting.

Zoe was deeply asleep when her mobile rang. She jerked awake, heart racing. It was the hospital.

Mary had gone into labour and was asking for Zoe to be present at the birth.

Chapter Nine

This was one mercy mission Zoe wasn't looking forward to.

Zoe was unfamiliar with Leytonsfield General Hospital and had to ask twice before she found the Maternity Unit and then the correct delivery suite. Two midwives were in the room, working with calm but urgent efficiency. One of them came over as Zoe loitered in the doorway.

'Can I help you?' she asked.

'I'm the patient's GP, Dr Zoe Angelos. Mary asked if I could be here at the baby's birth.'

The woman's demeanour changed as if by magic. 'Oh, you're Zoe? We've been hearing good things about you from Dad. I'm Josie O'Connor.'

Of course, Dan's only daughter. 'Pleased to meet you. How's Mary doing?'

'She's doing fine. But she's only four centimetres dilated so there's still a long way to go.'

It was going to be a long night; she could be in labour for hours yet.

'We've been talking to Mary about how much the cervix dilates and what it looks like,' said Josie. 'I was telling her how I learned it when I was a student. One centimetre is the size of a blueberry; two the size of a cherry; four a lime slice—which is what Mary is now. Isn't that right, pet?'

'Yeah,' said Mary, who didn't sound a bit impressed with the fruit analogy.

'Then,' Josie went on undeterred, 'six centimetres is a chocolate chip cookie; eight is an orange slice and then—bingo! When you reach ten centimetres you're nearly there. That's a bagel.'

'Why do they always compare the body to food?' said the other midwife, who was older and grumpier. "Coffee grounds for haematemesis and so on.'

'What's that?' asked Mary.

'Blood in the vomit,' said the midwife without looking at her.

'Yuk,' said Mary.

Zoe decided it was time to change the subject. 'Hi, honey, how are you?' What a stupid question, but Zoe felt completely out of her comfort zone.

'I'm glad you're here, Doctor.'

Zoe squeezed her hand. 'I'm not going anywhere, don't worry.'

Hannah from the women's shelter arrived and Zoe decided to get herself a coffee from the vending machine, trying not to think about coffee grounds. Whilst she was drinking it in the waiting room, Josie came over and asked if Zoe wanted a quick tour of the maternity unit.

She added, 'Don't worry, there's plenty of time and I'm on my break.'

Although it was the last thing Zoe needed, she didn't want to appear rude, so smiled and nodded.

Josie was friendly and doing her best to explain the best features of the maternity unit; she took her job seriously and loved being a midwife. Zoe tried to look and sound enthusiastic too. The last time Zoe had been in a maternity unit was the worst day of her life.

'And this is our latest acquisition,' said Josie. 'The Jasmine ward, named after a kind woman whose baby was stillborn and she had to spend the night on the ward with all the mothers who had their babies with them. She raised money so we could have somewhere for bereaved parents and their families to be together.'

'Oh ...' Zoe could feel a blockage in her throat.

'Zoe? Are you okay?' Josie moved closer and put her hand on Zoe's arm.

'Yes, thanks, but ...' Zoe could hardly get the words out. 'I need to see how Mary is doing.' She turned and fled, leaving Josie staring after her.

*

Zoe stayed at Mary's side after that, focusing on her patient and pushing away negative thoughts. Hannah retreated to the waiting room, saying that Zoe would be more use in this situation, but she'd stay until the baby was born. Josie returned to work.

Zoe caught Josie throwing puzzled looks her way, and Zoe wished she could apologise for her behaviour. But what would she say? If Zoe tried to talk about it, she'd break down and be no use to Mary. So Zoe refused to think about anything but the young girl lying on the bed, groaning and huffing and puffing at each contraction.

Zoe mopped Mary's brow, talking gently to her, saying she was doing a great job. Mary clenched her hand tight and begged Zoe not to leave. Zoe's heart went out to the girl. She was nineteen and young to be having her first child. Alone in the world with no family, and now no supportive partner. Life could be so hard for some people.

But women were strong, they had to be. With the support of Hannah and Nina, the wonderful women who ran the refuge, and the friendship of the other women in the house, Zoe had no doubt that Mary would be okay.

Time seemed to slow down for Zoe and stretch out like elastic. Her whole world shrank to this room and the patient on the bed, the warm stuffy atmosphere filled with strange aromas, and Zoe trying to bring Mary some comfort while the midwives flitted in and out periodically. Zoe just wanted it over. She could feel her heart beating too fast and her stomach performing acrobatics.

The worst thing was the memories filling Zoe's head with more pain, and the gargantuan effort required to keep them at bay.

Mary got to the point where she didn't want to talk anymore, so they spoke only to count the length of her contractions. Zoe tried to avoid looking at the clock on the wall, the hands seeming scarcely to move. She saw an opportunity to nip out of the room to get more coffee, although it tasted disgusting.

As Zoe was leaving, Josie came in. They stopped and looked at each other. Zoe had to say something.

'Josie, I'm sorry about the way I behaved earlier, I'm sure you think I'm terribly rude, it's just ...'

'Did you lose a baby?' Josie's soft voice and the pity in her eyes nearly caused Zoe to break down.

'I can't talk about it,' Zoe muttered and hurried away to the toilets.

Zoe leaned on the washbasin and stared at her reflection. She looked like shit and felt like it as well. This couldn't go on. There would be more babies to look after in the surgery, more pregnant women to help and ... yes, there would be deaths. That was life in the medical profession, it was unavoidable. Zoe needed to *do* something. Either leave medicine—which was not an option as it was her life and always would be—or do something to stop this massive, intractable pain that caused Zoe to act like a mad woman every time she saw a baby, or a pregnant woman. Perhaps she *was* going mad?

Oh, pull yourself together, you stupid woman.

She took deep breaths and tried to empty her mind. I can do this. I *can* do this.

Zoe washed her hands, then went to buy yet another cup of coffee.

*

More waiting. More coffee. Mary was now eight centimetres dilated—an orange slice, moving steadily and painfully towards the bagel. Zoe wished there was music, or something to distract her.

Suddenly the room was full of people. The SHO had come in first, and then the registrar had been called. The midwives were still calm and efficient, but there was no more joking or idle chit-chat. Monitoring showed that the baby was beginning to display signs of distress. Mary needed an emergency caesarean, and fast.

Zoe felt helpless. She could do nothing but stand and watch.

'What's happening?' Mary asked her. Before Zoe could gather her thoughts to give Mary a reassuring answer, the older midwife was leaning over the bed.

'We need to get baby out, darling. We are going to do a caesarean. Nothing to worry about. We'll be taking you to theatre in a minute.'

Mary had an epidural, a line inserted for fluids, antibiotics, and antiemetics, all in the blink of an eye. From time going slowly, Zoe now felt that someone had pressed fast-forward and it was speeding up like a crazy cartoon.

Mary would be awake for the procedure, so Zoe was allowed to stay with her. The theatre seemed full of people and Zoe counted them; Josie was there, the registrar and SHO, the anaesthetist, a paediatrician and her team, an anaesthetic nurse, a scrub nurse, and two theatre nurses. With all those people, medically trained and standing by, a patient would be forgiven for thinking that nothing could go wrong. But Zoe knew that the opposite was true. Anything could go wrong and sometimes did. Again, she was conscious of a familiar dread; sometimes a vague feeling and at other times a smothering tsunami.

There was a lot of noise in the room with all those people and Zoe wanted to tell them to be quiet. She was listening intently for the baby's first cry. Only then would she be able to lose the tension that made Zoe want to scream.

Mary was looking at her, needing reassurance, so Zoe smiled and nodded as if everything was going swimmingly. She held the girl's hand and stroked her knuckles gently. Hurry up! Deliver this baby! Zoe wanted to shout at them to get on with it.

Then amongst a flurry of activity and relieved voices, she heard the baby cry.

'Oh, thank God!' Zoe hoped that she hadn't said that aloud. Luckily no one heard as the baby was attended to by the army of medics, all waiting to do their thing.

'Is he alright?' Mary asked anxiously.

'Yes, he's gorgeous,' said Josie, placing the slightly cleaned-up new edition to the world in Mary's arms. 'Just a quick cuddle and then we'll have to take him to let the doctors finish up.'

'What d'you think?' asked Mary, turning a beaming smile in Zoe's direction.

'I think he's wonderful and you've done remarkably well. I'm proud of you.'

'Thanks.'

'What are you going to call him?'

'Elliott.'

'That's lovely.'

Then it was all over. Mary was taken back to the ward and the baby was being looked after. Zoe went to the ward to make sure Mary had everything she needed, and then left as soon as she could.

Outside the hospital Zoe was amazed to find that it was still dark. It was cold, but crisp and there was a layer of ice on the windscreen. She scraped it off after starting the engine and putting the heater on full.

Driving home, Zoe tried not to think about babies, or hospitals. But instead of feeling relaxed and comfortable, Zoe felt wired from all the coffee and the adrenaline surging around her body for the last few hours.

Luna greeted her exuberantly and Zoe wondered if the dog thought she was being abandoned again. Zoe gave her a lot of fussing and cuddling, telling Luna what a good dog she was.

Luna wagged her tail so hard it thumped the side of the sofa in a steady rhythm.

Zoe built the fire up again and the room was warmed by the cheerful blaze. When the dog had calmed down, she snuggled up to Zoe on the sofa, and Zoe buried her face in Luna's fur.

'Oh, Luna, it was awful,' she said, tears streaming now. 'I feel so helpless, I don't know what to do.' Luna licked her tears away and Zoe clung to the dog as if Luna was her last hope for survival.

Zoe knew she shouldn't do it; she was in far too fragile a condition to cope but felt compelled to look at him again. She went upstairs and took a box from the bottom of the wardrobe. Then, as the bedroom was too chilly, she brought it back downstairs to the warmth of the fire. Zoe opened the box and took out an envelope containing the precious memorabilia. It was all that was left of him, her baby, her precious little son. There were two cards with tiny hand and footprints, a small blue teddy, and a photograph of Zoe holding him.

She stared at these for a while until Zoe's vision blurred like a windscreen full of rain. Then she heard a sound like an animal in pain. A guttural, agonising, hopeless sound. It took Zoe's befuddled brain seconds to realise that *she* was the one making the noise. Then she let fly, crying, thumping her fists on the sofa. Luna was whining in distress, but Zoe couldn't stop—she had to let it out or she'd burst. Zoe sat and cried hysterically for what seemed like hours but was probably only a matter of minutes. Her throat and eyes were sore, and her head ached until there were no more tears left.

Luna crept back up to the sofa and laid her head carefully in Zoe's lap. Zoe stroked her and muttered, 'I'm sorry, girl, so sorry. Forgive me.'

Zoe wasn't really apologising to the dog, but to the dead child. Despite reassurances that it wasn't her fault and Zoe couldn't have prevented it, she still felt deeply responsible. She was his mother, meant to protect and bring him into this world safely, and Zoe had let him down.

Exhausted now and empty of all feeling but sadness, Zoe fell into a light sleep, waking only when the doorbell rang. It was seven o'clock and still dark. Zoe ignored it and tried to shake herself awake, wanting the visitor to just go away.

Whoever it was, they were persistent, and the bell kept ringing.

There was nothing else for it; she'd have to answer the door.

Chapter Ten

'Hi, Zoe, can I come in?'

'Dan? What are you doing here? Is something wrong?'

'Yes, my dear, I think there is. Josie rang me as soon as she'd finished her shift. She's concerned about you. I know it's early and I apologise for that, but I think we need to talk.'

'Come in. I'm having tea, do you want some?'

'I'd love some.'

'Go in and sit down, I'll bring it through.'

Of course Josie would have told her father. Zoe acted so strangely on the maternity unit; Josie was right to be concerned. And Zoe *did* want to tell Dan, so now was as good a time as any. She made the tea, rehearsing in her mind how to word the coming conversation. Zoe didn't want Dan to think she was a liability; not up to the job he was offering, but she had to tell him the truth and he could interpret it any way he liked.

When she carried the tray with the tea things into the living-room, Dan was holding the cards and the photograph. He looked up, revealing the depth of compassion in his expression.

'Is this him?

'Yes. Samuel. His heart stopped beating at thirty-two weeks and I had to be induced. As you can see from the photograph, he was perfect. Well, physically. Just not … alive.'

'Zoe, I'm so, so, sorry.' Dan sat there holding the cards and photo.

Zoe sipped her tea, and then heaped more sugar into it. She needed energy to fight the black hole slowly sucking her nearer and nearer towards it.

'It's not that I don't like babies, you see. In fact, I love babies, always have. My nieces and nephews are precious gifts. All babies are precious. It's just that …'

'Zoe, you don't need to explain.'

'Oh, but I do, I mean, I want to. I need you to understand. I'm not mad, but every time someone mentions "mum" or "maternity" or "baby" or …' Zoe was crying again, silent tears that rolled down her cheeks. Luna, once again, had her head on Zoe's lap, as if she had just worked out that this was her new role in life. Zoe stroked her and let the tears fall.

'My dear girl, please stop apologising. How long ago did you lose Samuel?'

'Eighteen months.'

'That's no time at all. And did you have counselling after-wards?'

'Yes, but it didn't help. I only went twice. It was too pain-ful to keep talking about it.'

'I think that's because it was too soon. Maybe now it would be more use to you?'

'No, I don't think counselling helps.'

'Are you willing to try again?' he asked softly.

'Is that what you recommend?'

'Yes, I do. You lost a child. That's not something you can get over. Most parents never do. What you need to do is learn how to live with the memory.'

'Right.'

Dan smiled. 'You're right to be sceptical, I would be too. But it works. I promise you. I know this doesn't compare with what you went through, but Eloise had a miscarriage at eight weeks, two years before the twins were born. I'm a medical man and I thought I could cope with anything, but losing that baby hit me for six. Oh, I told myself there were all kinds of medical reasons why the pregnancy wasn't viable, but it didn't alter the fact that one of our children died. That's how I look at it anyhow. I can't even begin to imagine what you're going through, my dear.'

'That's the problem, I think. No one knows what I'm go-ing through and I don't know how to explain. Oh, people are very sympathetic, kind even, but they haven't a clue. How could they?'

Dan asked, 'What about Samuel's father?'

'We're not together. He never wanted a baby and told me I should have an abortion. I haven't seen him since we split up.'

'And your family? Are they supportive?'

'They try to be. I can't rid myself of the thought that I've robbed my parents of another grandson, and my nephews and nieces of a cousin.'

'You feel responsible.' It wasn't a question, so Zoe didn't try to think of a response.

Dan went on, 'It seems to me, Zoe, that you are carrying a lot of guilt as well as grief. Natural in bereavement, of course, but I think you *do* need to talk to someone. Will you?'

'If you think it'll help. I do feel as if I need help. Providing you still want me to work with you, of course.' She tried to smile, but it was a poor effort and Dan took her hand.

'Nothing's changed as far as I'm concerned. I want you in the team, and I'm sure the others would feel the same if they knew.'

'Are you going to tell them?'

'No, it's up to you whether or not you want them to know.'

'Thanks, Dan—for everything.'

Dan got to his feet and Luna stood up too as if to escort him to the door.

'Right, I'll give a colleague a ring. His name's Dr Joe Moreton and he's helped people close to me. I think he'll be able to help you.'

'A psychiatrist?'

'Yes, is that a problem?'

She shook her head sadly. So, it had come to this. But if Joe Moreton could help her, Zoe would take it.

*

The ward round was nearly over without too many problems. Riordan and his team had yet to visit Jack Dempsey in the coronary care unit. Jack was well enough to be discharged but was still refusing to go anywhere but back home. He had rejected the suggestion of a convalescent home and was also refusing to discuss it with anyone but Riordan—and the ward needed Jack's bed urgently.

'How are you feeling, Mr Dempsey?' Riordan asked the standard question.

'Fit as a flea, I am, I don't know why I'm in here, to be honest.'

'You had a heart attack, Mr Dempsey,' said the sister helpfully.

'I know that, woman.' He glowered at her. 'I'm not stupid.'

Riordan kept his expression blank. 'We'll have to see what we can do about getting you back home.'

'I'm not going in a home; you can't make me. Bloody awful places. No, I'd rather die in here.'

'Not a home, Mr Dempsey, *your* home,' Riordan raised his voice slightly. 'We'll see if we can get you back into *your own home.*'

'Alright, you don't have to shout, I'm not deaf.'

Riordan smiled and walked away. He glanced at Sister, who raised her eyes to the heavens.

'He's deaf as a post,' she muttered.

When Riordan returned to his office, he logged into Mr Dempsey's details and saw that Dan was listed as his GP. A number of his father's patients had been passed over to Zoe, Riordan was pleased to see that his father was decreasing his workload. He picked up the phone and dialled the surgery. A receptionist promised to get Zoe to return his call after finishing with a patient.

Ten minutes later, the phone rang.

'Riordan O'Connor.'

'Hi, Riordan, it's Zoe. How can I help you?'

'I've got a patient who I need help with. Mr Jack Dempsey. Came in after an MI and now we're discharging him, and there's some concern about how he's going to manage. The team are putting together a care package for him, but I wonder if you could see him with an eye to offering some assistance?'

Riordan could hear the click of nails on computer keys, as Zoe accessed the patient's details.

She said, 'Yes, it seems Bilal saw him, and Mr Dempsey told him to F-off and that he didn't want strangers in his home. He said he could manage very well alone, and no one was going to tell him what to do.'

Riordan laughed. 'Yes, that sounds like him. Anyway, he does need help and, if Mr Dempsey wants to stay in his own home, which is his only wish, he's going to have to accept it.'

'I agree. Leave it with me, Riordan, and I'll see what I can do.'

'Great.' Riordan felt strangely reluctant to end the call. He was rather enjoying listening to Zoe's voice. 'How's Luna?'

'Luna's fine, thanks. I bet Tom's looking forward to getting his puppy.'

'He talks of nothing else.'

'Bless. Right, better go.'

'Yes, me too. Thanks again, Zoe.'

'My pleasure.' She rang off.

Riordan put the phone down, and then stared into space wondering what pleasure with Dr Zoe Angelos would be like. It was a long time since he'd felt a strong attraction to any woman. Riordan always deliberately fought those feelings. His heart wasn't strong enough for another beating, and he had no intention of getting involved like that again. Still, Riordan missed the company of a woman; someone to talk to, share interests with, holidays and the like. Could he have that and not get involved? Was he brave enough to try finding out?

Chapter Eleven

It was dark when Riordan left the hospital and headed towards Leytonsfield Town Centre. His mother had asked him to pick up a few items on the way home.

To avoid driving around looking for a space, Riordan pulled into the car park of an office block, a place normally used by clients. Or in this case, the patients of Joe Moreton. Joe shared office space with accountants, lawyers and a couple who advertised themselves as private investigators. Joe didn't mind Riordan parking there when he was short on time.

After doing his shopping, Riordan hurried back to find that someone had parked next to him and was walking up to the doors. Riordan watched as she pressed the intercom and was buzzed in, an appointment card clearly in her hand.

Zoe disappeared inside the building, and Riordan started his car and drove home, lost in thought.

*

Zoe left Joe Moreton's office and headed to her car. Her first session had gone well. Joe was easy to talk to and younger than she had expected. The hour had flown by and Zoe had surprised herself by telling Joe all about Samuel and the endless pain of his loss that she didn't know how to deal with.

Joe reassured Zoe that it would get easier, but everyone was different, and the healing process was never linear. He had praised her for making the first positive step and Zoe left the appointment feeling optimistic.

Zoe strode towards her car, head down, hands deep in her coat pockets, engrossed in her thoughts. She didn't notice the man leaning nonchalantly against the driver's door until he spoke, making her gasp and stop abruptly.

'Zoe, hi. It's me, Toby. Sorry, did I startle you?'

'Yes, you did. What are you doing?' He stepped forward with his hands outstretched.

'It's okay. I'm sorry I frightened you. I was waiting for you.'

'How did you know I was here?' Her heartbeat was slowing down, returning to normal. He'd given her quite a jolt, appearing out of the gloom like that.

'I recognised your car.'

'Have you been waiting long?'

'No, not long.' He pointed to the other end of the carpark. 'My car's over there. I've just been late night shopping and when I spotted your car I wondered if you fancied a quick drink.'

He smiled and Zoe felt foolish at being so jumpy. If she hadn't been staring at the ground, lost in bad memories, she'd have spotted him sooner. But she really wanted to get home to Luna.

Toby was watching her, waiting for an answer.

'It's a nice thought, Toby, but ...'

'Just one. There's a decent wine bar around the corner. How about it?' His grin was hard to resist, and Zoe found herself grinning back.

'Oh, okay then, but just one as I do really need to get home.'

They strolled out of the carpark and onto the main road.

The wine bar was warm and inviting, with the heady aroma of alcohol. Toby bought them a glass of red wine each and they found a table next to the window.

It was a young person's place and groups of women, dressed for a night out, talked and laughed loudly. Some of them stared brazenly at Toby. He was unaware of it or used to that kind of attention. Either way, he ignored them.

'Cheers,' Toby said holding his wine glass up.

'Cheers,' replied Zoe and they clinked glasses.

'Not a bad drop of Shiraz,' said Toby.

'Are you a wine connoisseur?'

Toby laughed. 'Not really but I know what I like, put it that way.'

'Nothing wrong with that.'

Zoe was curious about Toby but didn't want to appear too nosy. He looked around the wine bar then back at her.

'It's busy in here tonight. For a weekday.'

'Is this one of your favourite places to drink? It's very nice.'

'If I said I drank in most of the pubs and bars in Leytonsfield, would that make me sound like an alcoholic?'

'No, of course not. You obviously have an active social life. Alcohol is part of that.'

'And what about you, Zoe? How's your social life?'

Zoe laughed and sipped her wine. 'Practically non-existent. But I haven't been here long, I'm still finding my way around.'

'If you ever need someone to show you the best places, just give me a call.'

'Thanks, that's very kind of you.' They were flirting. Subtle but unmistakable. Zoe felt shy suddenly and blurted out the first thing she could think of. 'How do you know Dan O'Connor? You said everyone knows him.'

'I went to school with Riordan.'

'Were you friends?'

'No, not really.' Toby turned away and gazed out of the window as if he didn't want to talk about it.

'Sorry, I didn't mean to pry.'

'It's okay. I was friends with Sally, not Riordan. I met her in London, at university.'

Toby was restlessly playing with a cardboard coaster, flipping it over and catching it again. She sat in silence, sipping her wine.

Toby said, 'Sorry, it's just that Sally and I were close and losing her like that was difficult.' Toby drained his glass.

'I'm sure. Let's talk about something else.'

'Would you like another drink?'

'Oh no, in fact,' she looked at her phone, 'I should be going. Luna's been on her own all day.'

'Let me give you a lift home. You can pick your car up tomorrow.'

'No, I'll drive home. I need to be in early. But thanks for the offer.'

'We'll have to do this again sometime. Go on a pub crawl and I'll introduce you to all the dens of iniquity this little town has to offer.' He smiled and Zoe was aware of how handsome he was. She imagined most of the women in the place would love to be in her shoes, and all she wanted to do was go home.

'Okay, you're on.'

*

'Dad, how about a pint?'

'On a school night?' asked Eloise.

'Just a quick one,' said Riordan.

His mother studied his face and then, realisation dawning, said, 'Ah, you want to talk to your dad alone? Why didn't you just say so?'

'Still fancy a pint though,' said his father, standing up and stretching.

'Well, don't be late, you two,' she said.

'Yes, dear.'

'Yes, Mum,' said Riordan.

'Let's walk, then we can feel less guilty.'

'Good idea,' Riordan replied.

The Dog and Partridge was the nearest pub. It was also one of the oldest and best-loved in South Leytonsfield. Traditional, but popular with the younger punters, it served good food, good beer and it had a corner table near the open fire that Riordan and his father always gravitated to if they could, especially when a serious chat was needed.

Riordan bought the drinks and carried them to the table. His father sat, his arms folded, dozing. He opened his eyes as soon as Riordan sat down.

'I wasn't asleep, I was just resting my eyes.'

'I didn't say anything.'

They took a pull on their pints, then put the glasses on the table. It was quiet with the only sound being the murmur of conversation. There was no music, pin-ball machines or one-armed bandits, and Riordan felt himself relaxing.

'So, Riordan, what did you want to talk to me about?'

'There was something, but I don't want you to take this the wrong way.' Riordan chose his words carefully.

'Go on, spit it out.'

'When I was coming back from the shops, I saw Zoe going in to see Joe Moreton. I just wondered if you knew?'

'If I knew what?'

'Oh Dad, don't be obtuse. Zoe's likely seeing him for some problem or other. And before you say she could be visiting Joe on a professional basis, there was an appointment card in her hand.'

'You've noticed a lot. Are you sure it was Zoe?'

'I'm sure of it.'

His dad picked up his pint and took another mouthful.

'You know I can't confirm or deny anything. Patients trust us not to blab about their private affairs.'

'Zoe's not a patient though, is she?'

'Doesn't the same principle apply to our colleagues?'

'Of course, and I agree completely. Dad, I'm not asking because I'm a nosy bugger or want to cause trouble for her, you must know that. I'm just concerned, that's all.'

'Concerned about what?'

'About you, of course. Zoe is supposed to take the weight off you, but if she's going through something like I did, then she'll be in no fit state to help anyone. I couldn't work for months, remember?'

'I know, son, I remember.' His dad's voice was gentle. 'Me and your mum were the ones who looked after you and Tom, and we were happy to do it. And we kept it private, within the family.'

'I know you did. I wouldn't have survived without you guys, and the whole family. I'll never be able to repay you ...' Riordan felt his throat closing and put his head down.

'Well, that's in the past now, so you can put it behind you. No need to thank anyone. That's what family's for.'

They were silent for a while, his father giving Riordan time to get himself together. They drained their beer and Riordan stood up and took the glasses to the bar for a refill. A quick pint always meant two.

When he returned his dad looked as if he had something to say, so Riordan kept silent.

'Riordan, I'm not going to talk about Zoe, but I will say this. She understands me. She knows that I'm not the kind of man to sit at home with a newspaper and slippers. I have to work, it's important to me. And Zoe has embraced the ethos of the type of medical centre I've been trying to set up for years. She understands the patients' problems and knows the best approach to take. She's a damned good doctor and I don't want to lose her.'

'Okay, I get all that. But will you promise me something?'

'Depends what it is.'

'If you feel the slightest twinge, or excessive tiredness, or any of the other symptoms, you'll tell me.'

'Of course, goes without saying.'

'You didn't say anything the *first* time,' Riordan reminded him dryly.

'Well, I've learnt my lesson. You're never too old to learn.'

'Okay then.'

'I love you, Riordan, as I love all my kids and my two beautiful grandchildren. And the best wife a man ever had. Do you really think I'm in a hurry to leave you all?'

'No, I imagine you're not.'

'Well then.' Dan sounded as if he'd won an argument. Riordan let him, because he'd still be keeping an eye on his father regardless.

And on Dr Zoe Angelos.

Chapter Twelve

'Oh, it looks lovely, Doctor,' said Mavis, clapping her hands and gazing around at the decorated hall.

'It does, doesn't it?' said Zoe. 'Now all we need are people to come and dance.'

Zoe and a dedicated group of elderly ladies—most of them patients who had promised to attend the keep fit classes—had adorned the walls with posters Zoe had brought. They'd pushed the tables to the edges of the hall and covered them in gingham tablecloths. In the centre of each table stood a small vase containing an artificial flower. When everything was to their liking, they swept the floor.

'Don't you worry about that, Millie's coming and so is Beryl, and they're bringing some ladies from the WI. You'll soon have a class full.'

'What about the men, Mavis? I do hope we get a few males to balance the numbers.' Zoe busied herself with moving a small table into the corner and putting her CD player on it. The Medical Centre budget didn't run to extra computers and they had to make do with the old-fashioned way of playing music.

'We don't *have* to dance with them though, do we?' Mavis looked worried. 'I've not danced with a man for decades. The last one stepped on my big toe. It didn't half hurt.'

'No, that's the beauty of line dancing and why I chose it. You can do it anywhere and on your own. I'll soon have you hot-footing it up your hallway when no one's looking.'

Mavis chuckled. 'I used to love dancing in my younger days. And Millie. We turned a few heads in Leytonsfield once upon a time, I can tell you. *And* we went to clubs in Manchester.'

'I bet. Well tonight's your chance to strut your stuff.'

Zoe had sent an email to patients inviting them to the class and pinned a brightly coloured poster on the notice board in the waiting area. She also left flyers on the reception desk. No one was expecting a huge turn-out, not on the first week. These things took time to get going.

'Right, is everything ready in the kitchen?' She was offering tea, coffee, fruit juice and biscuits. As this was a weight loss exercise the biscuits seemed a bit self-defeating if everyone stuffed themselves on chocolate hob-nobs straight afterwards, but the women of the WI would feel slighted if they weren't offered refreshments after all their hard work on the dance floor.

'Yes, we're all ready. The boiler's on and the mugs are laid out.'

'Great. Thanks, Mavis, you're a star.'

Mavis blushed and beamed at the same time. 'There we are, Doctor—here's the hordes coming in now.'

The "hordes" consisted of Louis, who had promised to back Zoe's weight loss classes, Millie and two friends, Beryl and three WI ladies, Shelley and two girls from the refuge, and Andrew, the young man who had put his name down for a puppy.

'Welcome everyone. I'll just check the music and then we'll make a start.'

Twelve. Zoe had been hoping for more, but twelve wasn't bad for the first class. If everyone enjoyed themselves and spread the word, hopefully there would be twice as many next week. Of course, if she included herself, there were thirteen. Zoe hoped nobody was superstitious.

*

'How do I look, Mum?' Josie did a twirl in the middle of the living-room.

'You look lovely, dear, I wish I was coming with you, but someone's got to have these two.'

'I'll stay behind next week and look after the kids,' said Lexi. 'So you can go and join in the fun.' Lexi was wearing an oversized T-shirt and leggings. She and Casey had announced their pregnancy, having passed the third month, and Lexi took every chance she got to show off the tiny bump.

'Mum, I'll look after them instead, if you want to go this week,' Riordan said quickly, sensing an opportunity.

'Aunty Josie? Are you a cowboy?' asked Jade, examining Josie's clothing with envy. She wore a cream cowboy hat, skin-tight black denim jeans with calf-length leather boots, and a red cropped top with fringes that showed off her flat belly. Riordan wondered when Josie had got her bellybutton pierced without telling him. Probably in Australia.

'No darling, a cow*girl*.'

'Dad?' asked Tom with a frown. 'Where's your costume?'

'Yes, Riordan,' said Josie grinning. 'With you being the king of costumes, I'm disappointed you haven't got into the spirit of the thing.'

Riordan ignored the jibes. 'I thought it was a weight loss class?' He looked over at his father who had just wandered into the room.

Dan said, 'Zoe thinks that if we put the emphasis on having fun rather than losing weight, more people will come to the classes. I think she's right. So we're doing line dancing, Riordan, and the music is going to be country and western. Hence your sister looking as if she's an extra on the cast of Bonanza.'

'Grandad, what's Bonza?' asked Jade.

'It was a TV programme, way before your time, sweetie.'

Riordan thought about Zoe dressed up as a cowgirl in tight jeans, a shirt tied across her midriff, and he decided the class might be enjoyable after all.

'Okay then, will everyone who wants a lift please get in the car and let's go.' Riordan hurried them along. They were late already, and he hated to be late for anything.

'I wish I was going,' said Tom. He looked sad and even though Riordan knew he'd be spoilt rotten by his Gran, Riordan felt a twinge of guilt that he wasn't spending the evening with Tom.

Riordan knelt and hugged his son. 'We'll do something special on the weekend, okay? You have a think and tell me tomorrow what you'd like to do.'

'Okay, Dad,' said Tom, brightening and flinging himself onto the sofa, and grabbing the remote control. 'Let's see what's on TV, Jade.'

Jade, who had idolised Tom from the minute she set eyes on him, ran to sit next to him.

'See you all later. Have fun!' shouted Eloise.

They all waved goodbye and Riordan shepherded them, still talking, out of the house and into the car.

When they walked into the community hall, Riordan felt his spirits lift. Zoe was talking to the people and explaining the steps. She looked the part in blue denims, ankle boots with a heel, and a pink shirt over a white vest top. She had a cowboy hat on, and her dark hair was loose and tumbled over her shoulders.

'We're not late, are we?' asked Dan.

'Dan! Welcome. No, of course not, we haven't started yet. Hi everyone!'

Zoe was beaming and hugged the four of them in turn. When it was Riordan's turn, she looked at him with shining eyes, and he held on tightly for a few seconds. Zoe's hair smelt of coconut and Riordan was reluctant to let go.

'It's great to see you, Riordan, I'm so glad you've come. There are now four men, which is perfect as you can make up the corners.'

'Oh, I'm not sure I'm going to dance. I just gave these guys a lift.'

He suddenly felt shy in front of Zoe. Not that he wasn't a good dancer—Riordan was surprisingly light on his feet for a tall man. Sally had loved dancing and was always the first one onto the dance floor and the last to leave it. She wouldn't take no for an answer and dragged Riordan up protesting all the way. That was the way their marriage had been. Sally led and he followed.

'Don't listen to a word,' said Josie, grabbing Riordan's hand and pulling him towards the group waiting in the middle of the room. 'He's playing hard to get. Aren't you, Riordan?'

'Who me?' he asked with mock innocence.

Zoe called, 'Okay, let's start. If the gentlemen would be good enough to make up the corners and the ladies stand in two lines between the gentlemen, I'll run through the moves quickly. All the action is in the feet, so you can put your thumbs through the belts of your jeans, or on your hips— whatever you like.'

As Shania Twain's "Any Man of Mine" started up Riordan watched as Zoe demonstrated the moves. He wanted to impress Zoe and get everything right. Why he should want Zoe's admiration, he couldn't really say. It wasn't as if Riordan was attracted to Zoe—apart from in an obvious kind of way—and didn't need her approval or respect. But ... something, maybe pride, was urging Riordan to make up for the embarrassment of the gladiator costume, and to show that he could be a good sport.

Luckily, it didn't take long to pick up the moves. Or at least for Riordan. When he glanced down the line and saw the tangle of elderly ladies, turning in the wrong direction, bumping into each other and not knowing their right from their left, Riordan had to smile. His father was conducting himself well, despite an unfortunate habit of counting out loud. The other two men were doing well too.

Of the women, Josie was one of the best, looking as if she had been line dancing all her life. She was a bit like Sally in the way that Josie threw herself into new experiences with enthusiasm. Sally, however, took risks and eventually paid with her life for the recklessness. Riordan forced thoughts of Sally out of his mind.

He had moved on and needed to keep the past in its place, if he was going to have any peace.

He watched some of the other women. Lexi was concentrating hard and staring at Zoe's feet. Shelley was dancing as if no-one was watching. The others, especially the older ones, were stumbling and holding on to each other for support. But everyone was having fun and exercising, so—a result.

When the song ended, Riordan noticed Zoe watching him.

'Nice moves, Riordan,' she said with a grin.

'Thank you kindly, ma'am,' he replied in a bad cowboy accent. Riordan wished he'd worn a hat to doff like a real cowboy. Or at least, the television version of one.

After another two songs, the ladies were starting to get the hang of it, all except Mavis who got a stitch and had to sit out. But she clapped and cheered Millie and the rest of the dancers on. Beryl went to sit next to her shortly after, making a show of gasping and fanning her face.

By the end of the class, the men were still going strong and, in Riordan's opinion, had won hands down. Josie was still enjoying herself and looked as if she could have continued. Riordan gave her the thumbs-up at one point and she blew him a kiss. His father was also doing well, but looked a bit breathless, causing Riordan to watch closely.

'Okay!' said Zoe as the music faded. 'That's the end of the first class. Well done, everyone, you should be proud. Did you enjoy yourselves?'

They all shouted yes, some promising to be back the following week. Andrew was chatting to Shelley and, when they were joined by Lexi and Josie, the four of them decided to skip the tea and biscuits and head off to the pub.

Mavis, Millie, Beryl and their friends headed into the kitchen to make the drinks.

Riordan went over to Dan and asked if he was alright.

'I'm fine, son, why shouldn't I be?' He sounded defensive.

'You seem a bit short of breath, that's all.'

'Of course I am, I've just been dancing my socks off—haven't done that since before you lot were born.'

'No chest pain?'

'Riordan, if you're going to watch me like a hawk all the time, then you and I are going to fall out, son.'

Riordan lowered his voice as Zoe wandered over, saying quickly, 'I'm concerned, that's all. I'm just looking out for you.'

'Because I'm too old and stupid to look out for myself, I suppose?'

'No, of course not, it's just that—'

'Let me tell you what I told this young lady here ...'

Zoe had joined them and smiled, and Riordan knew he was in for one of his dad's lectures.

Dan went on, 'I'm not dead yet, and until I am, I have every intention of living life to the full. And if that includes dancing, then I'll dance. Got it?'

Riordan had no choice but to nod.

'Good. Right, I'm off home. Same time next week, Zoe?'

'Looking forward to it.'

'I'll give you a lift,' Riordan told Dan.

Riordan was hoping to stop for the refreshments and have a chat to Zoe but didn't want his father over-exerting himself by walking home after all the dancing.

'Are you coming back next week, Riordan?' asked Zoe.

He grinned. 'Wouldn't miss it for the world.'

Chapter Thirteen

When Zoe got home, congratulating herself on how well the class had gone, Luna wasn't at the door to greet her as usual but was in the special "nest", which consisted of a large cardboard box filled with soft towels, and with part of the front cut away to get in and out easily.

According to Toby, the nest should be in a quiet spot of the dog's choosing, safe and private. Zoe had no idea that dogs were so particular about where they gave birth. Fortunately, Luna was quite happy in a corner of the living room where Zoe could keep an eye on her.

Luna was in some discomfort. She kept standing up, turning around and collapsing down again. She was also licking more than usual.

'Are your puppies coming, my darling?' Zoe asked gently. The dog looked at her with pain-filled eyes and Zoe tried to remember what Toby had said. There were certain signs to look out for when a dog goes into labour. Luna *had* been off her food for a day or two, seemed restless and couldn't settle.

Zoe carefully took Luna's temperature. It was lower than normal. If the puppies hadn't been delivered within twenty-four hours, then a vet should be called. Zoe wasn't going to wait that long.

She dialled Toby's number, but it went to voicemail, so she sent him a quick text.

Zoe made herself a coffee and sat on the sofa, watching Luna. She suspected it was going to be a long night, so she left the coffee machine on in readiness. Zoe was pleased with her coffee machine. She had spent a lot of money on it and loved decent coffee. The machine had all the dials and levers, and stainless-steel milk frothing arm that a coffee lover needed. If she ever got tired of being a GP, or the clinic decided Zoe was too unstable to be around pregnant patients, she could always be a barista.

Her mobile rang, the cheerful ring tone pushing away negative thoughts.

'Toby, hi, I think she's started. What do I do?'

'Wait for me. I'll be there in about twenty minutes. Oh, and put the kettle on.'

'Do we need hot water?' They always needed hot water in movies, but through medical school, obstetrics training and her own tragic experience of giving birth, Zoe had never discovered why.

'No, but I'm gasping for a cuppa. See you soon.'

Zoe smiled, sipping her coffee. She looked over at Luna. 'It's going to be alright now, sweetheart, the cavalry is on its way.'

*

Toby was as good as his word and arrived in twenty minutes. A cup of tea was waiting for him with a red velvet cupcake.

'Oh brill', thanks,' he said, stuffing it into his mouth. 'I'm starving.'

'Have you been working?'

'No, day off today.'

'I'm sorry if I interrupted anything.'

Toby grinned. 'Just going to wash my hands, then I'll ex-amine her. Don't worry, I was with a friend, but I told her I might have to leave urgently. She's used to me dashing off on some mercy mission or other.'

'Girlfriend?' Damn. Zoe hadn't meant to ask *that*.

'Casual,' answered Toby, and wandered off to the kitchen. Zoe remembered Riordan calling Toby a stud. A man as at-tractive as Toby must have a different girl every night. She examined her feelings, looking for any signs of jealousy and was surprised to find none. She liked Toby and was grateful that he was willing to give up an evening to help. But that was as far as it went.

'Right, let's have a look at her.'

Toby examined Luna with the utmost gentleness, talking quietly to the dog the whole time. The examination was quick, then Toby went back to the kitchen to wash his hands again.

'What's the verdict?' called Zoe from the sofa.

He came back, drying his hands on a piece of kitchen towel. 'She's started; dilated and ready to go. We wait now for the first puppy.'

'How long does it take?' Zoe felt frustrated. She knew nearly everything there was to know about human pregnancy, but nothing about dogs.

'About ten to twenty minutes. Then we wait for the placenta. Each puppy has one. Luna could rest for up to an hour between each birth.'

They sat side by side on the sofa, not speaking, watching Luna who was panting heavily and whining.

'I feel so helpless,' said Zoe, 'I wish I could help her.'

'Most dogs don't need help, but I'm here if she does. Try not to worry. If you want to go to bed, or do something else, I'll stay here.'

'Oh no, I wouldn't dream of it. I want to watch the puppies being born. She's my dog, I feel responsible.'

'It could be a long wait,' Toby warned.

'I'm not leaving her.' Zoe suddenly felt tearful. Luna had been treated so badly by people and deserved the best care now.

Toby asked, 'Have you got any takers for the puppies?'

'Yes, all four have got homes to go to.'

'What if she has five? Four was just an estimate.'

'Do you think she will?'

'We'll soon find out,' said Toby, going over to the nest. He knelt just as a small, slimy, blue-coloured sac was delivered. 'Good girl,' said Toby, as he retrieved the placenta and watched Luna lick the puppy all over.

Zoe crept forward and knelt a short distance away. She didn't want to startle Luna or interfere, but the process fascinated her, and she was desperate that all the puppies survived. Zoe couldn't bear it if one of them died.

'Is it alright? Should we do something else?'

Toby laughed and looked at her. 'Luna is in charge; we don't need to interfere. She's doing a great job.'

Just then the puppy made a high-pitched squeak and Zoe gasped. She hadn't realised she'd been holding her breath.

Toby was busy cutting the umbilical cord and wiping the end with iodine as Luna worked on her puppy. Zoe sat back, leaning against the sofa, and tried not to hyperventilate. One down, three to go.

As Toby put the puppy to one of Luna's nipples, Zoe asked, 'Is that one male or female?'

'Male.'

'Right. I hope they're all as easy as that.'

Luna rested for forty minutes before giving birth to number two. During the time they waited, Zoe made Toby a sandwich and another mug of tea. She was too nervous to eat.

Three hours later, worn out from the effort, Luna gave birth to the fourth puppy. Two males and two females.

'Right, that's the lot. She's done well.'

They both sat near the nest and watched as the puppies suckled. They were tiny, with closed eyes and little pink noses. Zoe could have sat and watched them for hours. Luna looked exhausted and Zoe sympathized—and she was too excited to sleep. Luna made giving birth look so easy and Zoe was in awe. She was indebted to Toby, who had gone above and beyond the call of duty.

'I can't thank you enough,' Zoe said, realising how inadequate that sounded.

'No need. I'm glad it's worked out well.'

'Were you worried? You didn't seem to be.'

'I wasn't worried at all. To be honest, I love being present when puppies are born. I'm thinking of breeding dogs one day. I think it's something I could get really involved in.'

'Go for it, although I wouldn't want to go through it again, it's far too stressful.'

Toby laughed. 'Nonsense. It's natural. The most natural thing in the world.'

Zoe managed a smile, her thoughts going to her lost baby.

Birth *was* natural, but sadly, so was death.

Chapter Fourteen

'I don't want strangers nosing about in my home,' said the old man.

Zoe sighed. 'Look, Mr Dempsey, we *want* to keep you in your home for as long as we can, but the only way we can do that is if you accept a bit of help. Carers can assist with basic tasks like washing and dressing. Meals on Wheels will leave a cooked meal each day.'

'I do my own cooking, I'm not dead yet.'

Zoe looked around the living room of Jack Dempsey's terraced house. There were no photos in sight. There was a television and a pile of books sat on the coffee table. The room looked uncluttered and remarkably dust-free. In fact, it looked neater than Zoe's living room.

'Does anyone come in to see you during the day?'

'No, and I don't want anyone either. You can all keep away, all you do-gooders. I'm fine as I am.'

'What about your medication? Are you taking it regularly?'

'Of course I am. Go and look in the kitchen, it's all there written down, how much to take and when. I've got all my faculties, you know.'

Zoe went into the kitchen, which was sparse but clean, and saw the bottles of tablets in a row on the side with a piece of notepaper containing a list of his medication, how much to take, and how many times a day. It was very organised, and Zoe was impressed. She opened the fridge to shelves stocked with cheese, butter, eggs, things in cartons and plenty of milk. There was fruit as well and two small tubs of yoghurt. She closed the door, satisfied.

'Okay,' she said, back in the living room. 'We'll keep things as they are for now, but please ring the surgery if there is anything you need, okay?'

Jack Dempsey grunted and wouldn't look at her.

'I'll pop in and visit again, just to see how you're getting on. Goodbye, Mr Dempsey.'

'Shut the door on the way out,' he said.

When Zoe returned to the medical centre, she fired a quick email off to Riordan.

Just seen Jack Dempsey. He appears to be managing remarkably well but I'll keep my eye on him over the coming weeks. By the way, Luna had her puppies. Please feel free to bring Tom over to meet them.

The rest of the day passed quickly and uneventfully. She couldn't help worrying about Luna and her pups as it was the first day she had left them alone. But when Zoe got home, Luna was lying on her side on the clean, fresh towels put there that morning, and the puppies were suckling busily, making little squeaking noises, their tiny paws pushing at Luna's side to extract more milk.

Zoe had no sooner taken her coat off than the doorbell rang, and Riordan and an extremely excited Tom arrived, standing grinning on the doorstep. Riordan was clutching a Tupperware dish, no doubt containing one of his mother's offerings. It seemed Eloise O'Connor still didn't trust Zoe to feed herself properly.

Then Zoe thought of Jack Dempsey's fridge, compared it to hers, and realised Eloise was probably right.

*

As soon as Riordan had told Tom that the puppies had been born, Tom was searching for his shoes and coat. Persuaded to have his tea first, Tom ate so fast it had barely touched the sides. He was so excited, chattering all the way to Zoe's about names and what colour the puppy would be, and asking whether his mum had liked dogs. Whatever Tom fell in love with, he always wanted to be reassured that Sally would have approved.

'Come in, come in,' said Zoe. She took the dish that Riordan somewhat sheepishly held out. 'Thanks, what is it this time?'

'Home-made rhubarb crumble. It's good.' Riordan felt the need to justify the food gifts to avoid Zoe feeling patronised. Eloise wanted to look after everyone who moved into her orbit, and Zoe all alone in the cottage was a natural candidate. Riordan remembered that his mother had done the same thing when Louis joined the practice.

Zoe said, 'I'm sure. I'll have some later.'

Tom was already kneeling by the cardboard box, gazing at Luna and the pups. He was speechless and Riordan felt his throat constrict. He should have let Tom have a puppy before this. And paid more attention to his son and his needs.

'Is it okay for him to be that close?' asked Riordan.

'Yes, it's fine.'

'Just look, Tom, don't pick them up, they're too little yet,' Riordan said, looking at Zoe, and she nodded.

'Coffee?' she asked.

'Please.'

Zoe went into the kitchen and Riordan joined Tom. The puppies were tiny little things, wriggling and making high-pitched noises.

'Aww Dad, look at them. Aren't they wonderful?'

'They certainly are. We'll have to ask Zoe some of the questions we thought about, won't we?'

'You ask,' replied Tom, without taking his eyes off the puppies.' I just want to look at them.'

'Okay.' Riordan got up and put his hand on his son's head, but even that didn't distract Tom from his vigil.

Riordan sat on the sofa and waited for his coffee. Zoe returned and sat down next to him.

Riordan said, 'Thanks. Did the birth go to plan?'

'Everything went amazingly well. Toby was here and didn't leave until first light. He's coming back in a few days to check on them. He couldn't have been more helpful.'

I bet, thought Riordan. His gut twisted at the thought of Toby being in the house all night.

'Dad ...' Tom looked over at them.

'Oh yes,' Riordan said, remembering questions needed to be asked. 'We have a few things we need to know.'

'Okay, I'll try and answer, but if not I'll ask Toby.'

'Well, the first question is, do you know the genders yet? Tom wants a boy dog.'

'Yes, I can answer that one.' Zoe stood up and crept closer, pointing out the two male puppies to Tom.

'Oh cool,' he said, 'I liked this one straight away. Can I have him?'

'Sure, he's yours.'

'Oh, yeah!'

Tom seemed so happy and Riordan wished he could keep things this way forever; shielding Tom from the pain of growing up and being a responsible adult. Pain that Riordan still fought every single day.

'Next question?' asked Zoe.

'How old do they have to be before you can let them go?'

'Toby says a minimum of eight weeks. But if they don't look ready to go, then I'll keep them a few weeks more.'

'How will you know?'

Zoe frowned. 'I've absolutely no idea. I'll get back to you on that one.'

Which meant she would ask Toby, naturally.

'Okay. I think we'll have more questions nearer the time.'

'Of course,' said Zoe with a smile.

'Thanks for the email, by the way, about Jack Dempsey. I'm glad he's coping.'

Zoe said, 'Yes, I'll keep my eye on him, but he seems to be doing fine so far.'

Riordan nodded, wondering how he could make the conversation friendlier. He wasn't good with small talk, and Zoe also seemed reticent. Maybe she just wanted them to go and leave her in peace? He'd make sure not to outstay their welcome.

'Did you enjoy the dancing?' she asked, sipping her coffee.

'I did, and everyone else seemed to as well. Looking forward to the next class.'

'You're pretty good, Riordan. I was watching you out of the corner of my eye. You've got natural rhythm and picked it up straight away. Have you danced before?'

'Yes, my wife wanted us to have lessons. We did the lot over the years; ballroom, Latin, jive … she even tried to make me go to zumba, but I drew the line at that. There's a folk club here and they have barn dances with *ceilidh* bands. They hold them monthly on a Saturday night. Sally and I never missed those. They were a good laugh.'

He stopped. Why was he talking about barn dances, for goodness sake? Zoe wouldn't be interested in anything so provincial. She was a glamorous lady, well-travelled and sophisticated. She probably went to the ballet or opera. It was a pity that Riordan didn't like either. Zoe was watching him, and he felt hot under the open scrutiny.

She said, 'Tell me to mind my own business, but … how long ago did Sally die? Dan told me you were a widower.'

Riordan sat forward and pretended to watch Tom. Really, he was travelling back to the time he lost Sally. It was still hard to talk about, even with his family.

'Nearly seven years ago. Tom was two.'

'That must have been so hard. Do you mind me asking how she died?'

Riordan put his head down and eased the tension in his neck. 'It was a climbing accident. In the Lake District. She fell, and it took the rescuers hours to reach her. Sally was still alive when they took her to hospital, but never regained consciousness.'

'Oh, Riordan, I am so sorry. Were you there too?'

'No, I was at home looking after Tom.'

Where his wife should have been. The resentment resurfaced. Sally had no right to go climbing in winter and knew the dangers but went anyway. Even though Riordan had pleaded with Sally not to go.

His hands were clenched into fists and Riordan breathed deeply, relaxing his body limb by limb as he'd been taught.

'What was she like?'

Riordan wasn't expecting that question and hesitated, unsure how to answer. 'She was a physio, very fit, active, into extreme sports and pushing herself.' He stopped before adding that Sally was obsessed with danger, living on a knife edge. Fine when you're a young woman, single and unencumbered. A married woman with a child should have put family first.

Zoe was watching his face, expecting more.

He said, 'She was beautiful, an extrovert, restless, always wanting to be better, run faster—she ran marathons—climb higher, she loved speed.'

One of the biggest rows they'd had, after Tom was born, was over a motorbike. Sally wanted one and tried to get Jay on-side. As a bike rider, Jay extolled the virtues of motorbike riding, but Riordan wasn't convinced. Usually, in the face of his wife's demands, Riordan gave in, but that time hadn't, and in the aftermath, Sally left and went to stay with a friend. Riordan was convinced he'd lost her, the argument was so acrimonious, but Sally came back two days later and carried on as if nothing had happened. Motorbikes were never mentioned again.

'So, you went back to stay with your parents, right?'

'When Sally died, I couldn't cope on my own with Tom. I moved back so they could look after both of us. I owe them a lot.' Riordan wasn't going to tell Zoe about his mental health issues. Even now, he hated talking about it.

'That's what families are for, Riordan. To support each other, be there for each other.'

'Is that what your family does?' Riordan was thinking that maybe this was the time to broach the subject of Joe Moreton? Find out why she was seeing him.

Zoe said, 'Yes. We're both lucky that we have people who care about us. And Tom's lucky that he has a father like you.'

'And I'm lucky that I'm going to have a puppy!' said Tom. Riordan sometimes forgot that young children have ears like bats and never miss anything, even if they don't always understand what they are hearing.

'And I think,' said Zoe, getting up and walking over to Tom. 'That the little puppy is lucky to have such a kind, loving boy to look after him.'

Tom smiled shyly and Riordan silently agreed.

Chapter Fifteen

By the time the pups were two weeks old they were starting to open their eyes and gaining in strength. Tom was visiting them daily, sometimes with his father and other times alone. This was one of the evenings on his own. Riordan was working late and would collect Tom on the way home. Andrew and Simon, the two patients who had also staked their claim, had visited once and promised to come back again before the eight weeks was up.

'Have you decided on a name yet?' asked Zoe. Tom gently picked up his puppy and stroked its tiny head.

'Yes, I'm going to call him Solo. Not 'cos he's the only one, he's got two sisters and a brother. Dad got it straight away. He's in *Star Wars*. Han Solo. He's a pilot from the planet Corellia.'

'That's a good name.'

'Yeah, we think so.'

Zoe was relaxing with her feet up. Surgery had been busy, with the usual winter colds, flu and bronchitis. Mary had brought Elliott in for a check-up. This time Zoe managed to hold and examine the baby without freaking out and crying hysterically. A small step forward to be reported to Joe.

Another visit to Jack Dempsey had prompted his usual unwelcoming self. He was eating well and mobilising around his home, and managing all his activities of daily living, so Zoe was satisfied. She knew Mr Dempsey's gruffness hid real fear that he'd be forced out of his home; the house shared with his wife until her death ten years previously, and the place he felt safe. Zoe would do everything in her power to stop that changing. For an introverted, antisocial man, a nursing home was the worst nightmare.

Tom was talking to the puppy, something about a visit from Aunt Martha. Zoe's curiosity got the better of her.

'Who's Aunt Martha, Tom?'

'She's not a real aunt, but she is my Godmother. She's Dad's friend from university. Aunt Martha's coming to stay at Easter. I love her, she's great fun. I can't wait for her to see Solo.'

'That's nice. Is she a doctor like your dad?'

'Yeah, she goes all over the world. She always tells me stories about the places she works in. I want to travel when I grow up. Just like her.'

'Do *you* want to be a doctor?'

'Maybe, but I might be a photographer and take pictures of places. And animals,' he added.

'You can take pictures of Solo, if you like.'

'Can I? That'd be cool. Then I can send Aunt Martha a picture.'

'Does she like dogs?'

'Sure. Aunt Martha likes everything that I like.'

How convenient. Aunt Martha sounded as if she knew how to win the hearts of all men, of whatever age. Zoe asked herself, was she jealous? The jury was out on that one.

Zoe again couldn't help herself. 'Is Aunt Martha married, Tom?'

'No. She doesn't have any children either.' He was quiet with his head down, deep in thought. 'I wish ...'

'What Tom? What do you wish?' Zoe held her breath.

'I sometimes wish she was my mum.' He turned anxious eyes to Zoe. 'Does that make me a bad person? I don't re-member my real mum.'

'Oh no, my darling, of course it doesn't. It's natural to want a mother. And Aunt Martha is someone you love, isn't she?'

Tom nodded. He still looked worried and Zoe's heart bled.

Her mobile rang, and Zoe was tempted not to answer it, but Tom was talking to Solo again, taking a photo on his phone. She smiled at the name on the screen.

'Toby, hi. How are you?'

'Good and you? How's Luna and the puppies?'

'We're all fine, thanks. They're thriving and Tom is here, giving them all a cuddle.' She smiled at Tom, and he grinned back and gave a thumbs-up.

'Excellent. I rang to ask if you were doing anything next Thursday.'

Zoe went into the kitchen where a calendar hung on the wall. She wrote all her appointments here to be reminded whenever she was making coffee.

She frowned and said, 'Valentine's day?' Surely Toby had a hot date for *that* night. Maybe he got the date wrong.

'Yeah, I know. I don't know about you, but I dread it. For those of us without a significant other, it can be a minefield.'

Zoe laughed. 'Oh right, so you don't know which of your numerous girlfriends to ask out, is that it?'

'I'll have you know I don't have numerous girlfriends. I don't even have one.'

'Friends with benefits?'

'Something like that. The thing is, Zoe, I have no intention of settling down any time soon. There are too many things I want to do with my life first. So I wondered, if you didn't have a date already, would you fancy a few drinks with me? We can talk about puppies, if you like.'

Zoe laughed again. The idea of going for a few drinks with a handsome young man, on an occasion that she, too, hated with a passion, was tempting. And this time she would be more sociable and not ask upsetting questions. 'Okay, it sounds like an evening too good to miss. I'd be delighted. And we can talk about you, and your dreams and ambitions. I'd love to hear all about them.'

'Oh God, I'm coming across as a conceited prick, aren't I? Sorry.'

'I'm teasing, Toby. Seriously though, I'd love to spend an evening with you—as friends. You've been so good with Luna, I can't thank you enough.'

'Like I said before, it was my pleasure. Great! I'll pick you up about eight then.'

'Looking forward to it.'

Zoe ended the call and ambled back into the living room to stretch out on the sofa again. She couldn't help grinning. She liked Toby, he was an uncomplicated man with a free and easy attitude to life, although he was a consummate professional when it came to animals. Zoe owed him one anyway. Without him and his calm but caring approach to the birth of the puppies, Zoe would have been a nervous wreck.

And now, when people asked how she was celebrating Valentine's Day, Zoe could tell them she had a date.

Riordan arrived just before Tom's bedtime to collect him. Zoe brushed her hair and put on lipstick before he arrived. She felt a mixture of emotions in his presence. He was the opposite of Toby; what you saw is what you got with him. Riordan, however, was deep. He was shy, that much was obvious, and could be quite brusque, but he adored his family, cared for his patients passionately, and had been deeply hurt by his wife's death. Still waters ran deep with Dr Riordan O'Connor.

'Coffee?' she asked as always. Making coffee gave her something to do when Riordan hovered in the hallway like he always did, as if he wasn't sure where to put himself.

'Just a quick one, thanks. It's nearly Tom's bedtime.'

'Do you ever relax that rule?' She was teasing, but he frowned anyway.

'Not if I can help it. Children need routine. And they need eight hours sleep, minimum.'

'What about holidays?' She was being provocative, but something about Riordan's stiff manner made Zoe want to keep pushing to see if he would bend.

Tom said, 'Dad lets me stay up a bit longer so I can read. I'm reading Harry Potter again. It's my favourite.'

Zoe smiled at Tom. What a lovely, loyal child. She wondered, as always in the presence of a boy, what Samuel would have been like. Would he have been kind and gentle like Tom? Or more like his father, Andy, who was a total extrovert and, Zoe suspected after Samuel died, one with sociopathic tendencies and who didn't seem to care when Zoe lost the baby and, in fact, appeared more relieved than sad. Zoe had shouldered the burden of losing their child alone, and in some ways had felt just as alone ever since.

The memories overwhelmed her, and she put her hands over her face.

'Zoe? Are you okay? You look pale. You should sit down.' Riordan tried to steer Zoe towards the sofa. She mentally shook herself.

'I'm fine ... sorry, I'll get you that coffee now.' She took Riordan's hand and held it, smiling and trying to show how okay she was. When Zoe looked into his eyes, the depth of his concern threw her off balance.

He said, 'I don't need coffee. Come and sit down.'

They went to the sofa and Zoe sat, still holding his hand, not wanting to let go. His touch was strong, but gentle too, and warm. It was comforting and Zoe started to feel better.

'I'm fine now, really. Maybe I just need to eat something.'

'You *do* know that you can talk to me anytime, don't you?' His voice was low and had a husky break that Zoe thought sounded sexy. But she figured Riordan was using his professional bedside manner, so sexy shouldn't come into it.

'What about?' she asked cheerfully.

'Anything at all.'

For a brief second Zoe wondered if Dan had told Riordan about the baby. But he wouldn't, would he? Dan was serious about confidentiality, and Zoe had asked him not to. Perhaps Riordan couldn't switch off from doctor mode.

'Thanks, but there's nothing wrong. Listen—would you and Tom look after the pups while I let Luna out into the garden? The poor thing must be bursting.'

Riordan said, 'Tom, look after the pups for us, please? We're taking Luna outside.' Zoe raised her eyebrows at him, and Riordan whispered, 'I want to ask you a question.'

'Oh, right,' she whispered back.

While Luna ran around the garden, piddled on the lawn, and then continued an exploration of all the interesting scents, Zoe and Riordan stood and watched.

Riordan was frowning, and Zoe hoped he wasn't going to mention her lapse again.

'So?' she looked at him, but Riordan seemed reluctant to meet her eyes. 'What did you want to ask me?'

'Well, the thing is, next Thursday I'm taking Tom and Jade to the cinema. Not sure what we're going to see yet. Something that Jade will like, and Tom will put up with, I imagine.' He laughed nervously.

'Yes, it must be hard to cater for two kids who have different tastes.' She still had no idea where this was going.

'Yes, compromise is the key.'

'Valentine's Day, isn't it?'

'Exactly. Casey and Lexi are going to Rocco's—you know, the Italian restaurant in the precinct? It was where they had their first date, although they still argue about whether it *was* a proper date.'

'I've heard of it, but never been.'

'It's good, you should try it sometime.'

'I will … and?'

Zoe wondered why it was taking Riordan so long to get around to it.

He said, 'My parents are also having a night off and a romantic date night. Although I'm an adult I still find it hard to think of my parents in that way, but still …'

Zoe had heard enough. 'Riordan, what do you want to ask me? I think Luna wants to get back to her family and it's past Tom's bedtime.'

Riordan ran his fingers through his hair, so it stood up in spikes. 'Sorry, yes, I'm not very good at this type of thing. Would you like to come to the cinema with us?'

The last sentence came out in a rush and Zoe was tempted to ask Riordan to repeat it.

'You want me to come to the cinema with you and the kids?' She tried to keep the laughter out of her voice. Not because it was a ridiculous idea, but because Zoe had been asked out twice in one night whereas before she had hardly ever had a date on Valentine's Day.

'Oh God, I'm so stupid. You've probably got a hot date lined up. Ignore me. Sorry. Of course you wouldn't; you'd be bored out of your mind. As I probably will be.'

'Riordan—no, and I wouldn't be bored, honestly. But the thing is that Toby has asked me to go for a few drinks. Nothing special.'

'Right, of course, Toby.'

He turned away and started walking back to the kitchen door. She called Luna, who came bounding up, tail wagging harder than ever.

Hurrying after Riordan, Zoe said, 'Riordan, we're just friends. Toby's been good with Luna and I feel I owe him.'

'It's okay, you don't have to explain. I hope you have a good evening.'

'It was a lovely thought though, maybe another time?' Zoe had to almost run to keep up with him.

'Maybe.' When they got to the house, he marched straight into the living room. 'Come on Tom, let's go.' The barriers had come back up and Zoe knew she'd get nowhere with Riordan now.

''Bye then,' she waved them off.

Although Tom waved back with a big grin, Riordan didn't look at her.

Chapter Sixteen

Riordan skipped breakfast and arrived at the hospital early. He couldn't face any longer the Valentine cards and bouquets of flowers littering the dining table at home. His parents still gave each other cards; funny ones usually featuring geriatrics being amusing.

Eloise received her usual mystery card. Someone had sent her an unsigned card every Valentine's Day for the past twenty years. At first everyone in the family thought it was their father having a joke, but as the years went on and the cards kept coming, the novelty started wearing a bit thin and it was obvious that Eloise had an admirer after all. Riordan couldn't help wondering if his mother knew who it was but enjoyed the mystique. If she did know, Eloise wasn't telling. Dan had taken to ignoring it altogether.

Sally had always made a big thing of Valentine's Day. Before Tom was born, they went away for the weekend to somewhere impossibly romantic like Paris, Venice, or the Isle of Man. The last one was Riordan's attempt to think up something original for his beloved wife. He booked them on the five-kilometre Noble's Park run, and then a romantic evening at a sushi restaurant that offered a five-course tasting menu. Sally loved every minute of it. That weekend was one of the happiest of Riordan's life. Before everything started to go wrong.

'Morning, Riordan, Happy Valentine's Day,' said the sister on the cardiology ward.

'Morning,' he muttered, before striding away to see one of his patients who was having a pacemaker fitted that day. Riordan quickly forgot about cupids and roses as he reassured the lady that life would become much easier once the pacemaker was fitted.

'Is it heavy, Doctor?' asked the elderly woman. 'Will I feel it?'

'No, not at all. It's a tiny electronic device, and you won't even know it's there. Its purpose is to monitor how your heart is beating and, if necessary, produce an electrical signal that makes your heart beat regularly.'

'Oh ... I see.'

Riordan wasn't sure if she understood and offered more reassurance.

'All you need to know is that the symptoms you were experiencing of feeling faint, short of breath, and tired all the time, will go, and you'll be able to get on with your life as normal.'

'Oh good, thank you, Doctor.'

'I'll come and see you after your surgery, okay?'

'Okay.' She put her glasses back on and went back to a magazine. Riordan moved on to his rounds.

Some of the patients seemed eager to talk and Riordan's quick ward round took twice as long as usual, making him late for morning clinic. He was striding down the corridor to the outpatients department when his mobile rang. There was no time to answer it—they would have to leave a voicemail. Riordan glanced at the screen and changed his mind when he saw Zoe's name. He moved off the main corridor and into a quieter area.

'Zoe, good morning.'

'Good morning to you, Riordan. I hope I'm not interrupting anything?'

'No, nothing. What can I do for you?'

'I'm ringing to find out if your offer of the cinema still stands?'

'Yes, of course. What happened to the hot date?' Riordan's heart leapt at the thought that Zoe wasn't seeing the love rat after all.

'It was never a hot date, just a couple of drinks between friends, but Toby has had to swap shifts with another vet. So I'm free and would love to go to the pictures. I haven't been for years. As long as the offer still stands, of course.'

Riordan's mood lifted like sunshine after the rain. 'The offer definitely still stands. The kids will be delighted, especially Tom, he's taken quite a shine to you.'

'Really?'

Riordan detected genuine pleasure. 'Yes, really. He likes the little chats you have when he's alone with you.'

'Well, that's lovely. He's a great kid, a real credit to you.'

Riordan stepped back to allow a porter pushing a trolley full of bags of dirty linen to go past. 'Thank you. We're having pizza first, but you don't have to come for that, if you don't want.'

'I love pizza, and I'd love to come.'

'Great. Well then, how about we pick you up about five? The film starts at six, which gives us an hour for tea.'

'Five is fine. Looking forward to it.'

'Me too. See you later.' He rang off and stood staring into space for a few seconds. Then Riordan realised that he was now *really* late for clinic and better hustle. Thoughts of movies, pizza, and gorgeous young doctors with dark brown laughing eyes would have to wait.

Riordan took off down the main corridor again, this time with his head held high and a spring in his step. He noticed more people smiling and wishing him good morning. Valentine's Day was turning out to be a good day after all.

*

Zoe was on duty for the morning clinic and managed to get away at four, which gave her less than an hour to get ready. After a quick shower she rifled through clothes to find something appropriate. Smart casual, but how smart and how casual? When she went to the cinema, Zoe wore old jeans and trainers. She had a fine collection of plaid shirts to be worn over white tank tops. This date, however, called for something a little smarter than that. It was still cold, and it looked like rain, so ankle boots with pink jeggings and a long white T-shirt would do. She had a black leather jacket with zips and a tailored waist, but trying the outfit on, Zoe wasn't happy with the jacket and changed it for a suede coat that was comfortable and fashionable.

'Don't wait up,' she told Luna after giving her a cuddle.

Zoe had just enough time to let Luna out in the garden and feed her, before Riordan arrived with two excited children in the back seat. She hadn't noticed before, but Riordan drove a maroon-coloured Jaguar XF, the same car that her father drove. Great minds think alike.

'Ready?' asked Riordan, who looked happier than normal. He was such a serious man, and Zoe would make it a mission to get Riordan to laugh tonight.

'Ready and raring to go,' she grinned, and he smiled shyly. *Oh well, it's a start.*

'What film did you guys decide on in the end?' Zoe asked, as she put her seat belt on.

'The latest Toy Story,' answered Tom.

'Good choice,' she replied, turning to smile at Tom and Jade. The little girl was clutching a tatty rag doll with a blue dress.

'Are you familiar with the Toy Story films?' asked Riordan.

'I've seen the first three. I used to babysit for my brothers and their wives, and we always had movie night. Toy Story was a favourite.'

'Which character do you like best?' asked Tom.

'Oh, let me think … probably Woody.'

'I like Buzz Lightyear.'

'Me too!' shouted Jade.

'Jade likes everything I like,' Tom explained.

'No I don't! I don't like carrots.'

Riordan glanced at Zoe. 'Are you ready for this?'

'Bring it on,' she said. 'I've been looking forward to it all day.'

And she had. Strangely, the thought of spending an evening with Riordan, Tom and Jade watching an animated film held more appeal than spending it drinking in a local pub—even though it would have been in the company of a gorgeous-looking man and made Zoe the envy of every woman in the place.

She glanced across at Riordan as he drove steadily through the streets, checking the mirror periodically to make sure the children were okay. Riordan was good-looking in a quieter, more mature way. His hair was thick, and he wore it short and swept back off his forehead. His features were good with fine cheekbones, and his glasses made him look studious and intelligent. He had a glorious smile—but didn't smile enough. His eyes were a lovely grey that sparkled when he was amused.

Zoe decided that she got the better deal for any Valentine's Day date.

*

Pizza First was packed. Riordan managed to find them a table that looked out onto the High Street. People bustled passed, some peering in, others shuffling along, gazes glued to their smartphones.

'I want the pineapple one,' said Jade. Then, noticing Riordan's expression, added, 'Please, Uncle Riordan.'

'Good girl. Tom, what would you like?'

'Pepperoni please.'

Zoe said, 'I'm happy to share with Jade, I don't imagine she'll eat a whole one, will she?'

'They have children's sizes, but you're right. Neither of them will eat the whole thing.'

'So why don't we get one to share, and eat what the kids leave?'

'Sounds good to me. You choose the topping.' Riordan would have been happy to eat anything. He was just grateful that Zoe had chosen to spend the evening with him and the children.

When they had ordered, Riordan sat back and listened to the conversation between the three of them, which consisted mainly of the latest new character in the Toy Story franchise.

Riordan's concentration wandered and his gaze settled on the crowd of people congregating outside the Crown and Anchor, directly opposite. A group of girls, out on a hen night, had pink body parts and lewd signs hanging around their necks. A few couples wandered in through the main doors, arms around each other, oblivious to everyone else. Then he spotted a man he recognized; Toby, with a young woman. An extremely attractive young woman. And they had their heads close together.

He glanced at Zoe, but she was still engrossed in the conversation with the kids and hadn't noticed anything. Riordan debated pointing Toby out. But to what purpose? It might upset Zoe. Or she might already know and that's why she was there waiting for pizza and not with Toby, getting drunk on cider or something.

'Dad, the pizza's here,' said Tom.

'Great!' Riordan rubbed his hands. 'Thanks,' he said to the waiter.

'This looks good,' said Zoe, and took a slice.

The children were eating theirs noisily, the sound of happy munching reminding Riordan of why they were there. It was a treat for the kids, and to give parents and grandparents a break. Still, Riordan's curiosity was getting the better of him.

'So, Toby's working tonight, is that right?'

'Yes,' she swallowed quickly. 'He swapped with another vet so he could take his wife out for Valentine's Day.'

'Right.'

'He's kind like that.'

'Sure.'

'Why?'

'No reason.' Should he tell her that Toby Dean had lied and was, at this very moment, ensconced in the Crown and Anchor with a gorgeous blonde?

'Where have your parents gone?' Zoe took another slice.

'Their usual date night consists of my mother cooking one of Dad's favourite meals, a couple of drinks in the Dog and Partridge, then home to bed. What they do after that I wouldn't really like to dwell on. Probably just sleep.'

'I hope, when I'm their age, I'm still having hot sex.' Her eyes flashed at him, sending a message, and Riordan glanced nervously at Tom and Jade, who were otherwise engaged and hadn't heard. Tom was explaining why the Hulk turned green when he was angry.

'With anyone in particular?'

'No one in particular.' Zoe put her head down and concentrated on the pizza. This was a perfect opener and Riordan wasn't going to waste it.

'You can tell me to mind my own business if you like, but …' *Approach with care*, he told himself. 'Well, a woman as attractive as you must have left a string of broken hearts behind in Manchester. Did you have someone special?'

A shadow passed across Zoe's eyes and for a second Riordan wished he'd kept quiet. The last thing he wanted to do was ruin an enjoyable evening. Zoe was quiet for a long time.

'There was someone. His name was Andy and he was a police officer. But he turned out not to be the man I thought he was.'

'I'm sorry.' *Cryptic.* He was tempted to probe further, but this wasn't the time or place.

She said, 'Thanks. Anyway, how about you? Have you had any significant others since …?'

'Since Sally died? No.' He wasn't going to elaborate either. Keep it light-hearted, for the kids' sake as much as their own. If Riordan could pluck up enough courage to ask Zoe on an actual date, there'd be plenty of time for serious conversations. One careful step at a time.

'Dad? Can we have ice-cream?'

'You can, but if you do, you won't be having popcorn.'

Jade looked affronted and ready to burst into tears. 'Awww … no popcorn?'

'You can have popcorn, sweetie, but not ice-cream as well. You have to make a choice.'

Tom was smiling and, revealing surprising logic, leaned over to reassure Jade. 'It's a no-brainer. Think about it, Jade—popcorn is far better than ice-cream. We can have ice-cream *any* time. But when we watch movies, what do we eat?'

'Popcorn!' she shouted, causing people on the nearby tables to look over and smile.

'I think you've made a very good choice,' said Riordan. *And learnt a good lesson for life.* Rather than trying to have it all, appreciate one thing and be grateful.

He looked across at Zoe who had listened to the conversation with amusement. The one thing Riordan wanted at that precise moment was to know more about the enigmatic woman who sat opposite. She had a secret; something that had rocked her world, he guessed. Was it to do with this Andy character? Whatever it was, it was bad enough to see Joe Moreton about it. And Riordan knew, from personal experience, how bad that might be.

Chapter Seventeen

The Scala Cinema in the town centre was very different from the multiplexes in Manchester. It was a small, compact, red brick structure in the Baroque style with arches and curlicues giving the front of the building a unique appearance.

When they entered the theatre, after buying popcorn and soft drinks, Zoe gasped in amazement. She moved automatically towards the single seats at the back but eyed the luxurious ones at the front with envy. There were purple seats upholstered in soft, plush material with gold filigree drinks holders. The *pièce de résistance* were the sofas for two.

Zoe was so engrossed in looking around that she hadn't noticed the other three making their way to the sofas. She hurried after them.

'Wow! You are pushing the boat out tonight.' She sat next to Jade as Riordan and Tom were sharing a sofa. Zoe felt as if she'd wandered into some multi-millionaire's mansion.

'I'm sorry it's so comfortable and luxurious,' said Riordan, not meeting her eyes. 'I understand that you were probably expecting cramped, hard seats that numb your bum within half an hour and litter all over the floor. Or that's what it used to be like when I was a kid.'

'Same here. This is wonderful, Riordan. I love it. You must let me pay my share.'

'I wouldn't hear of it. Anyway, I'm a member and I got the tickets at a reduced price.'

'A member?'

'Yes.' He looked at Zoe before reaching into the carton he was sharing with Tom for some popcorn. 'We're here quite a lot. Both of us love movies.'

Tom nodded enthusiastically.

Zoe ran her hand over the upholstery and drank in the atmosphere. Cosy and intimate, but still a public theatre.

The adverts came on and a hush descended. The kids were soon engrossed. Zoe shared a carton of popcorn with Jade, who quite often forgot it was there; probably full from all the pizza anyway, so Zoe just kept eating until she started to feel a bit sick, having eaten more in one evening than a normal day. It was a good job there was another line dancing class coming up, or she'd balloon like Mr Blobby.

After fifteen minutes, Jade asked in a whisper if Zoe would take her to the toilet. So they walked back up to the entrance, past people staring at the screen and shovelling pick-n-mix, popcorn and drinks into their mouths as if their lives depended on it. As a GP, Zoe thought about bad cholesterol, but otherwise she loved it.

Zoe took the opportunity to use the facilities then they both washed their hands. She studied Jade as the little girl frowned with concentration, making sure her hands were washed thoroughly. With a nurse for a mother and doctor for a father, it should be no surprise the child knew how to wash her hands properly.

They returned to their seats, and the antics of Woody and company.

Half an hour later, Jade announced in a loud voice that she wanted to sit next to Tom. So Riordan and Tom swapped over and Zoe found herself sharing a small, cosy pink sofa with a man who, at six feet two, could only sit with their legs touching. Suddenly the sofa, which had seemed spacious with Jade next to her, felt like a child's toy.

Zoe was aware of every move Riordan made. She could hear his breathing, even over the film. He balanced the carton of popcorn on his knee and every few minutes he dipped his hand in. He ate neatly and even crunched quietly. Everything the man did was considered, deliberate. Zoe wondered what it would take for Riordan to be spontaneous, crazy, utterly off-the-wall.

He offered Zoe the popcorn. She smiled and shook her head. She couldn't eat another mouthful. Instead, she drank some cola. Her throat was very dry.

From the moment Riordan sat next to her, to the time the credits rolled, Zoe couldn't have said what the film was about. She had completely lost concentration and any interest in the film. Riordan's closeness, his proximity, was messing with her mind. Zoe wanted Riordan to put an arm around her which was, of course, the purpose of the sofas in the first place. Knowing Riordan wasn't going to do anything so reckless made Zoe want it more.

She pretended to watch the film and wondered if Riordan was doing the same. Then she got a wild impulse to laugh out loud at the ludicrousness of the situation. But perhaps Riordan wouldn't see the joke and think she was mad. Maybe she *was* mad.

Just as an experiment, she gently pressed her thigh a fraction harder. He stopped eating, then coughed and tried to move away.

He muttered, 'Sorry.'

'It's okay. There's not much room, is there?'

'No,' he said. His voice sounded hoarse and he smelled of popcorn. He passed the carton over to Tom who tipped the leftovers into Jade's carton and continued to munch happily.

Then Riordan didn't know what to do with his hands, so he laced his fingers and let them hang loose. He shifted in his seat, put one elbow on the arm of the sofa and rested his head on his hand. His other hand was on his knee and it was obvious, by his fingers restlessly drumming, that he wasn't comfortable.

Not comfortable at all.

The trouble with being spontaneous is that the other person might not react in the desired fashion. Zoe didn't care anymore. She reached over and grasped Riordan's hand. She remembered how comforting holding hands with Riordan had been and Zoe wanted to feel that again. She put their palms together and linked fingers.

Riordan sighed deeply and moved closer to her. 'I've been wanting to do that all evening,' he whispered.

'Me too.'

They sat like that for a while, then Zoe felt bereft when Riordan slowly removed his hand. Her whole being smiled as he put his arm around Zoe's shoulders, and they moved even closer to each other. She noticed Tom glance over, and thought he smiled, but wasn't sure as he was stuffing his face with the last of the popcorn, tipping the carton up to get the last few pieces.

Zoe put her head on Riordan's shoulder, and he rested his head on hers. Sitting together like that, such a simple position, spoke volumes to Zoe. Riordan *did* like her after all. He was attracted. He was shy, but responsive.

She realised the movie must be winding down to the finale. Zoe wished it was just starting and they could sit like this for a few more hours.

Then it was over. Riordan removed his arm and stood up as the house lights came on and children came awake, blinking at the light. Jade was sleepy and Riordan carried her. Tom and Zoe trailed after him, and she put her arm on Tom's shoulder. He looked up and smiled. His smile was the image of his father's. She wondered what Sally had looked like. Beautiful probably. Tom was an attractive boy.

They headed back to the O'Connor's and Jade fell asleep in the car. Tom was quiet too, so Zoe obliged and sat in silence. Besides, it was comfortable silence. There wasn't any need to fill it with meaningless chatter.

When they arrived back, Eloise and Dan were in the kitchen, talking and drinking tea. Riordan carried Jade upstairs and Eloise put her to bed. Then he came straight back down again.

'Bed now, Tom. Wish Zoe goodnight and thank her for coming.'

Tom did as his father said and Zoe put an arm around Tom and hugged him. He hugged back briefly, said goodnight to Dan and made his way up the stairs.

'Enjoy the film?' Dan asked them.

Zoe said, 'I enjoyed the whole night. It was lovely.'

'Good. Right, I'm for my bed. 'Night all.' Dan followed Tom up the stairs.

'I'll run you home,' said Riordan.

When they got back to Rosemary Cottage, after a journey again spent in silence, Zoe turned her brightest smile on Riordan.

'Would you like to come in? You haven't seen Solo for a while. The puppies are three weeks old and changing all the time. He's grown.'

Riordan's expression was unreadable, and he got out of the car. Zoe did the same and Riordan carefully locked it before following her to the front door.

'Coffee or tea?'

'Tea please. I'll just go and say hello to the dogs.'

She made tea and took it into the living room.

Riordan said, 'You weren't kidding, he has changed. His tail is wagging. Tom'll be pleased.'

'I'm going to try them with a bit of proper food at the end of the week. Toby said their canines and incisors will be cut by now and then the back teeth in about a week or so.'

'Toby ...'

Something about his tone made Zoe look at him closely.

'You don't like Toby, do you?'

'What makes you say that?'

'Just a feeling.' She sipped her tea and looked away. She sat on the sofa with Riordan next to her, keeping a good distance between them.

He said finally, 'My only concern is how *much* you like him. I wouldn't want you to get hurt, that's all.'

'He's just a friend. We're not romantically attached and not likely to be either. And, anyway, I'm a big girl who can look after herself.'

'Good.' They fell silent, drinking their tea and not looking at each other. Zoe could feel the good vibes of the evening slipping away. The intimacy of the cinema had gone, and Riordan was being polite but distant again. Which seemed to be his default setting.

'I'd better go. I need to work tomorrow. Then I promised Tom I'd spend the afternoon with him.'

'Thank you for tonight, I really did enjoy it. *All* of it.' Zoe said the last bit so there could be no mistaking her meaning. She enjoyed Riordan putting his arm around her and wanted him to know that. But he either chose to ignore it or didn't pick up the message.

'Good. Right. See you next week at the line dancing.'

'Okay. Glad you're still enjoying it.'

'I am. 'Night, Zoe.'

She saw him out after he stroked Luna and Solo and watched Riordan striding down the narrow path to the gate. Then he fired the car engine and was away in seconds.

Zoe went back inside and sat on the sofa, again watching Luna and her pups. What would Luna think when all the pups had gone? Would she miss them? Would she cry for them? Zoe didn't think she could bear that. Maybe she'd keep one pup so Luna wouldn't lose her whole litter.

The cottage was quiet, and Zoe felt lonely after such an enjoyable evening. She had to keep busy, to fight her loneliness, and the misery that still ate away at her heart. Joe had warned that it would take time. Possibly years. The best way Zoe knew to avoid dwelling on her pain was to help others in need. Apart from her work as a GP, there was the battered women's shelter and the other charities the WI helped.

Maybe in helping them, Zoe would heal herself.

Chapter Eighteen

A week later, Valentine's Day was all but forgotten and the Easter cards and chocolate eggs had appeared in the shops. Zoe spent her lunch break in the High Street stocking up. She felt more than a bit guilty that she hadn't been back to Manchester since moving to Leytonsfield. She would buy eggs for her nieces and nephews, and cards for the grown-ups, before returning home for a weekend.

Zoe had picked suitable cards for her parents, and a humorous one for Markos and Jacinda, when her mobile rang. She pulled it out of her pocket and, seeing it was from Riordan, moved to a quiet corner of the shop.

'Hi, Riordan, how's things?'

'Good. How are you?'

'Fine.' There was a lot of background noise and she could hardly hear what he was saying.

'I can't hear you very well. Are you in the hospital?'

'Yes, the canteen. Hang on, I'll go somewhere else.'

Zoe sighed. She didn't get long for lunch and had plenty of things to buy yet. But Riordan never rang unless there was a good reason, so she waited patiently.

'Is that better?'

'Much better.'

'Right, I'll be quick, I'm sure you're busy. Um, you said you'd never been to Rocco's?'

'That's right.'

'Okay, so … would you like to go? Next Friday? I'm not on call and could get away early.'

Part of her wanted to squeal with excitement. 'Let me just check my diary.' Not that Zoe needed to; she knew what was in it—almost nothing.

'Of course, do you want to ring me back?'

'Oh no, that's okay, it's right here.' She screwed her face up, took the blank diary out of her handbag and looked at the date anyway. 'That'd be the 28th?'

'Correct.'

'Well, I've got no prior engagements, so yes, thanks, that would be lovely.'

Zoe thought she heard Riordan sigh down the phone. 'Great. I'll be in touch nearer the time. 'Bye Zoe.' He rang off. No doubt dashing off somewhere. As she should be.

*

The puppies were four weeks old, the age at which their socialisation should start. Toby had advised Zoe to get them used to as many people as possible, and at five weeks they could meet other dogs. The problem was, Zoe was out all day at work, lived in an isolated cottage and didn't know anyone else with a dog. Toby said not to worry as she was doing fine, but Zoe suspected he was just being nice.

The night of her date with Riordan, the puppies seemed particularly boisterous, as if they were growing too big for the cardboard box nest. They were playing together, rolling around and biting. They also performed their toilet away from the nest and Zoe had spread sheets of newspaper all over the floor to protect it. They were too young yet to be taken out to the garden.

As Zoe got ready, she kept one eye on Luna and her brood. They were being left for too many hours a day, what with her working long hours at the medical centre, then enjoying such a mad whirl of a social life. *Yeah, right!* Zoe smiled as she applied mascara. This was only the second "date" since arriving in Leytonsfield and both had been with Riordan. Not that she was complaining, having enjoyed the cinema night immensely, but the thought of being alone with Riordan, just the two of them, in an Italian restaurant, being wined and dined … well, it didn't get any better than that.

This occasion called for a special effort, so Zoe had put on a little black dress. Short and sleeveless with a low neck that showed off her cleavage, it was perfect for Rocco's. An updo to display the drop earrings, and smoky eyes and red lipstick. She looked in the mirror. It had been a long time since Zoe had dressed up and she hardly recognised the woman staring back. It was time to get back out there and enjoy life.

She waited for Riordan's car to pull up outside and smiled when he was right on time.

''Bye Luna and puppies,' she called, pulling on a smart black coat and slipping into high heels.

Zoe opened the door just before Riordan could ring the bell. She was glad he got out and came to the door. So much better-mannered than staying in the car and beeping the horn, or sending a text to say he had arrived, like a taxi driver. That had been one of Andy's more annoying habits.

'Hi,' Riordan said, smiling and holding out his arm to take. Yes, he was definitely a gentleman. Zoe locked the door quickly, then the two of them strolled down the path to the gate which Riordan held open, then he hurried to the passenger side of the car and opened the door too.

'You look lovely,' Riordan said, and Zoe felt warmth spreading all over.

'Thanks,' she said.

They were silent until they reached the car park at the back of the restaurant. Why was she feeling tongue-tied? Riordan had that effect on her. She wanted to appear intelligent and witty but recalled feeling this way at age sixteen on her first date; awkward and stupid.

'Are you okay?' That concerned tone again. Zoe needed to get her act together or Riordan would never ask her out on another date.

'I'm fine, Riordan, thank you. Shall we go in?'

'Yes, let's.' He locked the car and offered his arm again. Zoe felt good as Riordan escorted her into the restaurant. She was a feminist; always had been, and always would be. She believed emphatically in equality for everyone. However, to be treated as Riordan was treating her now, as if she mattered, as if he was proud to be seen with her, was an uplifting and affirming experience.

The restaurant lived up to its reputation, at least in appearance. It was modern, classy and sophisticated. Two storeys linked by a spiral staircase, soft lighting illuminating the tables which were dark wood and chrome. The mixed aromas hit Zoe as soon as they walked through the door, making her stomach growl. There was garlic, lemon, the delicious smell of meat cooking, and a bouquet of perfumes and aftershave from the clients.

When they were seated, Riordan read the menu and Zoe took the opportunity to study him. He looked good enough to eat wearing a dark blue suit, pale blue shirt and a tie that looked as if it was a design of the night sky. Zoe remembered Tom saying how he and his dad loved anything to do with space, especially movies like *Star Trek* and *Star Wars*.

Riordan closed the menu with a snap and looked over at Zoe, catching her out.

'Are you ready to order?' Riordan asked.

'No, I can't decide. What are you having?'

'Steak. It's very good here, always cooked to the customer's specifications. And *gamberoni* to start.'

'Right.' Zoe went for something with cheese—her favourite food in all the world. 'I'm having the *melanzane,* then *gnocchi* with clams.'

'*Limoncello?*'

'Oh, yes please.'

Riordan gave their order to the waiter and pronounced the Italian with ease.

'Do you speak Italian?'

'Only enough to order food and greet people. I did it as an extra subject at school, but I haven't kept it up. Do you speak any other languages?'

'A bit of Greek that my grandparents taught me, and the French we all did in school.'

'Tell me about your family.' Riordan smiled and Zoe realised he was genuinely interested, not just making polite conversation.

'Okay. Well, the Greek line is from my mother's side. I lost my Greek granny quite recently. They lived in Manchester and ran a restaurant until my grandfather died, then my grandmother went back to Greece. They gave the restaurant to my eldest brother and his wife to run and they're doing a great job. I loved my gran, she meant the world to me.'

'I know what you mean. I was close to my grandmother too. What about the other set of grandparents?'

Zoe thought of her father's parents who were quite protective of their only child and never really approved of her mother, a hard-headed businesswoman.

'We don't see them very often. My parents still work. My father is a bank manager and my mother an accountant.'

'I seem to remember you saying you had three brothers?'

'Yes, there's the twins, Caleb and Damon. Caleb and Jo have two girls, Emma and Avis. Emma's second name is Daphne, which is my mother's name. And Markos and Jacinda's oldest son, Michael, has his grandfather's name as his middle name.' She laughed, seeing Riordan's eyes glazing over. 'It's complicated. Some Greeks keep up the tradition, but not all.'

The waiter put the first course in front of them and Zoe tucked in. She was ready for this after deliberately starving herself during the day to do justice to the meal.

She said, 'Um, this is delicious. How's the prawns?'

'Good,' said Riordan. 'So, is cooking a family tradition?'

'It was, but it ended with me, I'm afraid—I can't cook to save my life. I'm just hoping that one of the younger generation is interested enough to keep the restaurant going.'

'So, my mother's food gifts have proved useful after all.' Riordan was eating his prawns as he usually did everything—fastidiously. Zoe, however, had nearly finished the starter. She took a sip of wine.

'Does Tom see his other grandparents much?'

Riordan was still for a few seconds, put down his knife and fork, and sat back and wiped his mouth with his napkin.

'No, I'm afraid they cut all ties with our family after Sally died.'

'Oh no, that's awful. But why? Tom is their grandson, don't they see him at all?'

'It's me they hate, but they seem happy to take it out on Tom.'

Zoe was silent, mulling over Riordan's words. How could grandparents hate their son-in-law so much that they miss out on their grandchild's life? She looked at Riordan, who was frowning, deep in thought.

'I don't want to go into it too deeply,' he said. 'But I'll just tell you briefly that Sally was in a coma and the EEG showed that she was brain dead. The consensus of opinion was, rightly in my mind, to turn off the ventilator and let her go.' Riordan stopped and put his hand over his eyes.

'I'm so sorry, Riordan.'

Riordan shook his head as if he didn't want platitudes, so Zoe didn't say any more, giving him time.

The waiter came and removed their plates. Riordan seemed to have steadied himself and he smiled sadly.

'Sally's parents were against the idea and refused to give their permission. The consultant involved in her care tried to explain the situation, but they wouldn't listen. As Sally's husband and next-of-kin, it came down to me to make the final decision and I told them to turn the ventilator off. She died a couple of hours later.'

'Oh God, that's awful. And her parents blame you.'

'Yes. I can understand their attitude to me. They lost their beloved daughter, but what I can't defend is cutting Tom out of their lives. I'm just glad he has my parents in his life.'

'Is that the reason you still live at home?' She wasn't sure if that was an appropriate question, but Riordan was confiding in her, so she felt it was okay to ask.

'I know it must seem strange, a man of my age still living with his parents, but for a long time I needed them for practical reasons as well as emotional. I work long hours, and sometimes I don't spend quality time with Tom for days. I don't know what I'd do if they weren't around to support us.'

'They're lovely people, your parents. We're both lucky, I think, with our families.'

'Agreed.'

The waiter brought over the main course and Zoe decided to try shifting the conversation to safer ground. Riordan had confided a painful event in his life and might expect Zoe to do the same. But she wasn't ready to tell him about Samuel yet.

'And friends, what about them? Tom said you have a friend from university coming to stay over Easter?' Zoe didn't really want to hear about the wonderful Martha, but it might help to know more about the competition.

'Martha,' Riordan said with a big smile, transforming his face, 'Yes, she's probably my closest friend. She works for *Médecin Sans Frontières* and is abroad a lot. When she does come home, however, Martha stays with us for some of the time.'

'What's she like?' *Please don't tell me she's blonde and gorgeous.*

'Martha is someone you need to meet. I couldn't begin to describe her. She's devoted her whole life to helping others. I'm in awe of her.'

'Really?' Zoe couldn't imagine Riordan being in awe of anyone. Martha must be quite a gal. Now she *was* jealous.

They ate silently but again, the silence was comfortable. Riordan wasn't a man who needed to talk about himself all the time and show off, as Andy had been. When Andy had come home, he was full of stories of getting one over on someone or arresting a dangerous criminal. He gave the impression the police force couldn't exist without him.

'This is nice,' she said. 'How's the steak?'

'It's good.'

When they finally put their knives and forks down, Zoe was feeling replete. But there was always room for a dessert. She had cast her eye quickly over the dessert menu and one or two had appealed. The *pannacotta* with cherry and hazelnut in particular seemed to have her name on it. But when Zoe looked up to ask Riordan what he was going to choose, he was staring past her and scowling. Zoe turned around and saw Toby with an attractive woman entering the restaurant.

She turned back to Riordan, who was clenching his jaw and glaring. Zoe was at a loss at the complete change of mood.

Why on earth did Riordan hate Toby so much?

Chapter Nineteen

The evening had been going so well. Riordan managed to tell Zoe about Sally without the usual feelings of despair and anguish. He'd lived daily with the sense of sadness and loss from Sally's death—and everything that had gone before—and desperately wanted to move on with life, for Tom's sake as well as his own.

Zoe was great company, beautiful, intelligent and bright. Riordan wanted to get to know her better. And the meal was delicious. Then it all changed.

Toby Dean strode into the restaurant as if he owned the place. Riordan could see women eyeing Toby up, despite the blonde beauty on his arm again. Toby attracted the attention of women wherever he went.

Puzzled slightly, Zoe was watching Riordan, and he tried to relax and rid himself of the anger, not wanting to ruin a perfectly good evening because of that scumbag.

'Riordan, what's wrong?' Zoe leant over and took his hand. Her touch calmed him, but then, out of the corner of his eye, Riordan saw the pair heading in their direction. He took his hand away.

'Hi, you two,' said Toby.

Zoe stood up and kissed Toby on the cheek. 'Hi yourself.' She looked at the woman, who smiled.

'This is Melissa,' Toby said. 'She's just joined the practice and I'm showing her around. She's like you, Zoe, a stranger to Leytonsfield.'

Riordan stood up too, as he didn't want to be the only one not standing and appear rude, even though he was feeling far from sociable and just wanted Toby Dean to leave them in peace.

'This is Dr Riordan O'Connor,' Toby continued.

After they had all shaken hands, Zoe turned to Toby. 'Why don't you guys join us? Although we've only got dessert left.'

Riordan held his breath, silently begging them to say no.

'Melissa? What do you think?' asked Toby.

To Riordan's dismay, she nodded, and the couple settled themselves at the table. This was a nightmare for Riordan. He couldn't sit there making polite conversation, it was beyond him. Riordan didn't know what to do, except cut short the evening somehow. Zoe wouldn't understand, and he'd have to brazen it out, be polite but noncommittal and let the others talk. Toby Dean had spoiled the evening.

How much longer was Riordan going to let Toby affect him like this?

The waiter, who had been hovering nearby during the introductions, took their orders. Then returned with water and beer for both of them.

'Well, this is nice,' said Zoe, looking over at Riordan for his support.

Riordan asked Toby. 'Are you running many marathons these days?'

Toby shook his head. 'No, I don't seem to have the time at the moment.'

'What about rock climbing, or abseiling? You seemed keen on those at one time.'

Zoe was frowning, but Riordan wasn't going to let this worm off the hook. He wanted to see Toby squirm.

Toby put his elbows on the table. 'We're expanding the practice, Riordan, and our every waking moment is taken up with work. Isn't that right, Melissa?'

Melissa, who seemed to be a woman of few words, nodded and said, 'Yes.'

'Toby's been marvellous with my dog and her pups. Has he told you the story?' Zoe asked Melissa, who shook her head. Zoe explained to Melissa about the car late at night and finding Luna in the ditch.

'He's been wonderful. Coming around to check on the pups and giving me free advice. I must owe you a lot of money by now, Toby.'

'Oh, don't worry,' Toby laughed. 'I'm still working on the bill.'

They all laughed except Riordan, who didn't think he could stomach much more.

'Have you got homes for them all?' Melissa asked.

'Three of them, but I'll probably keep the fourth. I couldn't bear the thought of poor Luna losing all her babies in one go.'

Toby smiled. 'Zoe, you're making the classic mistake of attributing human feelings to an animal. When a bitch has whelped, as far as she's concerned, she's done her bit. Luna will be glad to see the back of them.'

'Really?'

'Yes, dogs live in the moment and have short attention spans. If Luna met her pups in the future, she probably wouldn't even recognise them.'

'I'd never thought about it like that.'

'You're the one she loves. So long as you give her plenty of time and affection, Luna'll be fine.'

'You could also get her a soft toy to replace them,' said Melissa. 'I had a dog once who took all my daughter's soft toys when her puppies were homed. She took them into her basket and slept with them.'

'Doesn't that prove that some dogs *do* miss their puppies?' asked Riordan. He didn't believe a word that Toby uttered, the man was a fool. An arrogant fool.

'Not really, Riordan, there is always the exception to the rule.'

Riordan wanted to argue with him. That wouldn't help the situation. He needed to be the adult.

And ignore the obnoxious ...

'Riordan, shall we order dessert?' asked Zoe.

'Of course. What would you like?'

'What are you having?'

He'd lost his appetite and couldn't eat anything. He glanced at Toby tucking into his starter and Riordan felt ill.

'Just coffee.'

'Oh.' Zoe sounded disappointed. Riordan realised he was coming across as a miserable party pooper.

'But you have something. Didn't you want the *pannacotta?*'

'Actually, I don't really want anything either. And we can have coffee at my place. Shall we go?' She said this quietly and Riordan could have hugged Zoe in gratitude.

'Of course, I'll just settle the bill.' Riordan walked to the bar to pay and, by the time he'd done so, Zoe was standing behind him with her coat on.

'I've said goodbye for you.'

'Thanks.'

She walked ahead to the car, the warmth of earlier having turned as frosty as the night sky. Spring seemed a long way off.

As soon as they were in the car, Zoe turned to Riordan, her eyes flashing.

'Okay, now you can tell me what all *that* was about.'

'All what?'

'You know damned well, Riordan, your rudeness to Toby. Why do you hate him so much? Tell me, because I don't understand.'

Riordan started the car and turned out of the car park.

He said, 'You don't know him the way I do.'

'So? Is that any reason to be so bloody rude? What's he done to you that was so bad?'

'He lied to you. When he said he was working in another vet's place on Valentine's Day, he lied.'

'How do you know?'

'I saw him and Melissa going into the Crown and Anchor. When we were in Pizza First. I didn't know, of course, Melissa's name then.'

'You didn't say anything.'

'No, I debated telling you, but I thought you'd be upset. I didn't want to ruin the evening.'

'So what about now? I'm more upset *now* than I would have been, if you'd just been honest and told me at the time.'

Riordan wanted to stop the car and talk properly, but they were nearly at Rosemary Cottage. He couldn't look at Zoe properly, keeping his eyes on the road, and wanted to take Zoe in his arms and explain how he felt.

'I'm sorry, the last thing I wanted was to upset you. You must believe that. Toby isn't trustworthy, I don't want you to get hurt.'

Zoe said, 'You've said that before, and I've told you that I can look after myself. And as for lying to me on Valentine's Day, perhaps he did. Maybe Toby wanted to take Melissa out, but was trying to spare my feelings—so he lied. It's no big deal. Toby is just a *friend*, but you don't seem to want to believe that, Riordan. Whatever he's done to you in the past, you need to let it go. It's affecting your judgement and you're coming across as cynical. I'm sure you're not like that really.'

Riordan didn't know what to say. He stopped the car outside the cottage and turned off the engine. 'I'm sorry. I hope I haven't spoilt the evening.'

'No, but if you don't mind, I'm not going to invite you in for coffee after all. I'm feeling a bit wound up and would like to relax before going to bed, otherwise I'll never sleep.'

'I'm sorry,' he repeated. The last thing Riordan wanted was Zoe to feel upset after their date. Riordan wanted to ask about going out again sometime, but was afraid Zoe would say no.

Zoe said, 'Thanks for tonight, I enjoyed most of it.'

'Me too. Sorry again.'

'Goodnight, Riordan.'

He watched Zoe walk up the path to the front door, then go inside the cottage. She didn't look back. Riordan believed he'd had one chance with her and blown it—messed it up. There was no one but himself to blame.

Feeling worse than he'd felt in a long time, Riordan headed for home.

Chapter Twenty

The following Wednesday, the line dancing class were doing Latin American. Zoe's favourite music *ever*, she said. As it was a complete beginner's class, starting off slowly with some simple steps, the Lambada would be a good one to begin with. Those who weren't too steady on their pins could miss out the turns and just concentrate on the basics. The rest could swirl and wiggle for all they were worth. Then the class could progress to Cha-Cha, Salsa, Mambo, Rumba and even have a go at Merengue and Bachata.

The classes were slowly growing and becoming the highlight of the week for several people, including for Zoe. She loved the teaching and helping patients to lose weight and have fun at the same time.

The only fly in the ointment was Riordan. Zoe hoped the disastrous ending to their meal the previous Friday wouldn't make him stay away. They needed to be friends, if nothing else. He was Dan's son and Tom's father. Zoe had a lot to do with the O'Connor family and wanted everyone to get on. Perhaps she should apologise—having said some harsh things. Maybe Riordan had good reason to hate Toby? Or perhaps Riordan was jealous. Whatever the reason, they needed to clear the air.

People started coming into the hall and Zoe watched anxiously to see if Riordan was amongst them.

Right at the end, just as Zoe was convinced Riordan had stayed away, the O'Connors trooped in; Dan, Eloise, Josie, Lexi who was showing her bump proudly now, and Riordan.

'Hi everybody,' she called. 'Get yourselves in line and we'll make a start. Okay, we're doing the Lambada, so watch carefully as I demonstrate the steps ...'

*

At the end of the class, Eloise came over to Zoe and took her hands. 'That was wonderful. I don't think I've had so much fun in ages. Thank you for these classes, Zoe, you're doing a good thing here, and if I can get one of my sons to babysit, I'll be back next week. And I must tell you,' she leaned closer to whisper. 'Dan is losing a bit of weight and has more energy than he's had for a long time, so thank you for that too.'

Zoe laughed. 'It's a pleasure. Glad you're enjoying them.'

She noticed Riordan hovering in the background, waiting.

Eloise said, 'Right, we'll be off then. Come on everyone.'

As Eloise attempted to gather the family together, Riordan sidled up to Zoe.

'Zoe, can I have a word?'

'Of course, but I think it would be better if you came to the cottage later.'

'Fine, I'll see you in about half an hour.'

Zoe cleared up quickly with the help of Mavis and Millie, who were humming the Lambada tune completely out of key and wiggling their bottoms as they packed things away. The boiler had broken down, so there was no coffee and tea. No doubt the younger dancers would head off to the pub anyway, which had become their routine.

It all took longer than Zoe expected. By the time she arrived home, Riordan's car was outside the cottage.

'Come in.' She unlocked the front door and went ahead, switching on the lamps in the living room. Luna came over to greet them, pushing her nose into their hands, tail wagging lazily. 'Hello, gorgeous,' said Zoe, stroking her head, then she asked Riordan, 'Right, are you staying long enough for a drink?'

She was determined to be matter of fact and unemotional, but when Zoe caught sight of Riordan's expression and the haunted look in his eyes, her heart melted.

'If it's not too much trouble,' he said quietly.

'No, of course not. I'll make a pot of tea.' She went into the kitchen and Riordan went over to stroke the puppies.

When Zoe carried the tray through, Riordan was sitting on the sofa. He sprang up and took the tray off her, putting it down on the coffee table.

She said, 'Thanks, did you enjoy the lesson tonight?'

'I did, but then I enjoy all the lessons. You're a good teacher.'

Zoe poured the tea and handed Riordan a mug. He took it and murmured thanks, then fell silent. Zoe figured she'd have to make the first move.

'I need to apologise to you, Riordan, for the things I said—'

'You have nothing to apologise for. I behaved like a child and spoilt a perfectly good evening. I want to explain.'

'Okay.' Zoe curled up on the sofa and tucked her feet under, sipping the tea and waiting.

'Just before she died, I found out that Sally was having an affair and I have a strong suspicion it was with Toby.'

'Oh, God, I'm sorry.' Zoe was not expecting *that*. She was speechless, mulling over the implications.

'I have no solid proof, and Sally denied having an affair, but I know.' Riordan's voice was emotionless, as if this was a script much-rehearsed beforehand.

'How do you know, if she denied it?'

Riordan sighed and drank some of his tea.

'Sally was a member of a club. It was one of those unofficial, word-of-mouth type of things. They were very particular who they let in, and security was tight.'

Zoe was intrigued. 'What kind of club?'

'It was called TAO—Try Anything Once—and they indulged in dangerous sports and unusual activities. They took an ordinary sport, for example skiing in the Alps, and upped the ante, never sticking to the recommended slopes, but skiing off-piste and taking risks. They were crazy.'

'Did you ever go with them?'

'Me?' Riordan laughed. 'They wouldn't let me into their precious club even if I'd wanted to join. I was far too staid and boring for them. I never take risks; at least not intentionally.'

'Was Toby in this club?'

'He was. Toby's from Leytonsfield originally but went to university in London. He moved back here when Sally and I got married.'

'You mean, Toby followed Sally here?'

'Again, I can't prove it, but I think so. Sally was a Londoner. That's where TAO originated. They met in London.'

Zoe poured them both another mug of tea, trying to make sense of it all.

'But … what makes you think they were having an affair?'

'Toby was with Sally when she fell. They always climbed in pairs for safety, ironically.'

'I still don't understand why you think they were having an affair. They could have been just friends, if they were in a club together.'

Riordan said quietly, 'I found a note listing the activities of the club. Sally had left it lying around. I had a few seconds to read it, but I remember every word. I've been blessed—or cursed, depending on how you look at it—with an excellent memory in that regard. Everything Sally had done, or was scheduled to do, Toby was there too. His name cropped up all the time.'

'How many people were in this club?'

'I've no idea. They didn't like anyone knowing their business, even spouses. Especially spouses who didn't approve—as I didn't.'

'So even though Sally knew you didn't approve, she still took part?'

Riordan drained his mug, placing it carefully on the coffee table. 'Sally did what Sally wanted. I only realised how totally self-centred she was after we married. To be more accurate, after Tom was born. I begged Sally to stop putting her life in danger, and she laughed at me. Called me boring and old-fashioned. Made jokes about old men. She once bought me a beige cardigan for Christmas as a prank. I had to open the present in front of my family and pretend to laugh along, but I was mortified. Sally made me feel about an inch tall. She said that it was only the freedom of being a member of TAO that made the rest of her life bearable—meaning her husband and son.'

'Oh, Riordan.' Zoe was close to hating Sally. 'You're not boring in the slightest. You're one of the most interesting and intelligent men I've ever met.'

Riordan smiled and put his hand over Zoe's. 'Thank you for that.'

'But I still don't think you can assume they were having an affair. Toby doesn't strike me as someone who would do that.'

'Toby Dean introduced Sally to the club in the first place. And Sally once told me that Toby was her idea of a *real* man, always comparing us and finding me wanting. After the fall, when Sally was lying in the coma, I checked her phone messages—I had to know. Somehow, the phone survived the fall. Sally had Toby's number on speed-dial. She told him she loved his company and lived for their trips away. There was more … it proved they were having sex.'

'Oh Riordan. I don't know what to say. He seemed such a nice man.'

Riordan moved closer to Zoe on the sofa and she held his hand, wishing for a way to do more, but nothing Zoe said would make any difference. Riordan had lived with this for too long.

He said, 'The weekend she died, I begged Sally not to go. There was a bad weather warning for the Lake District. Sally just grinned and said it made it all the more exciting. I should have tried harder to convince her, but Sally was determined. She was obsessed, always wanting more. More adventures, more danger, more excitement, more of everything I couldn't give her.'

A determined lady and a selfish one, thought Zoe. She squeezed Riordan's hand, and he turned. She put an arm around him.

Zoe said, 'I understand now. And I'm sorry. If there's anything I can do …'

Riordan cupped Zoe's face. His grey eyes held a world of pain and Zoe wanted to take it all away, so she kissed him gently, feeling Riordan respond. His mouth opened and she deepened the kiss. Their tongues touched and locked, Riordan stroked her hair, then pulled away and kissed Zoe's forehead, cheeks, and lips again. The kiss became more urgent and Zoe could feel Riordan's heart beating strongly. He carefully ended the kiss, leaned back, took her hands and kissed Zoe's knuckles.

'Zoe, I really like you and would like another chance at a date. So long as Toby Dean isn't in the vicinity, I can act like a civilised human being.'

Zoe laughed. 'I'd like that too.'

'Good. I'd better go, Tom'll be wondering where I've got to.'

'Okay, it'll soon be time for Solo to go to his new home. Are you ready for that?'

'Tom certainly is, he talks of nothing else. He's already bought a bed, toys and a lead. Yes, Solo will be welcomed with open arms.'

Zoe said, 'Toby will be here to check the puppies for one last time. Sorry about that, but I'll have to let him in.'

Riordan smiled. 'Of course. You have no argument with Toby, I understand that. And he *is* a good vet.'

'So long as we understand each other.'

He kissed Zoe again, gently and tenderly. Zoe kissed him back as if she never wanted the kiss to end.

Riordan whispered, 'Oh yes, I'd say we understand each other.'

Chapter Twenty-One

As February turned to March, the weather turned with it. There was torrential rain, gale-force winds, and the temperature plummeted. The number of people attending surgery dropped, and those patients who requested phone consultations or home visits increased.

The practice had only just got around to organising the phone consultations due to the mountain of work Imelda needed to get it up and running. Now the idea had caught on and the majority of the patients were eager to try it.

Zoe found herself on the phone for at least half the day, talking through patients' problems. With some it was practical; those who were articulate and could explain things. For others, however, it was a struggle. The elderly and hard-of-hearing found it particularly difficult. Other patients used it as an excuse for a chat, and Zoe couldn't stop them from nattering away about everything under the sun *except* their medical complaints.

Then a patient told Zoe that Jack Dempsey hadn't been seen for a couple of days. He always ventured out for a short walk to get his paper, or for a quick pint in The Old Oak. Zoe, realising it was probably down to the bad weather, decided to visit anyway. Better to be safe than sorry.

There was no point attempting to use an umbrella. The wind whipped it inside-out instantly, and Zoe was afraid of being carried off over the rooftops like a demented Mary Poppins. Instead, she wore a cagoule with the hood tightly fastened, and knee-length boots.

Zoe rang the bell at Jack Dempsey's terraced house and waited, her head down to avoid the driving rain blowing into her face. Any sounds from the house were masked by the force of the wind howling down the street.

After what seemed an age, the door opened a crack and Jack's face appeared.

'Mr Dempsey, are you okay?'

'What?'

Zoe raised her voice. 'I said, are you okay?'

'Yes, I'm fine. I didn't call a doctor.'

'Right, only Mrs Bannister said she hadn't seen you for a few days.'

'What? I can't hear you.'

Zoe pleaded, 'Can I come in, just for a few minutes?'

He reluctantly opened the door and stood back to let Zoe into the hall. He shut the door abruptly.

He said, 'I won't ask you in as you'll drip all over the floor, and I've just done it.'

Zoe could detect the tang of lemon furniture polish, and the hall floor shone.

'That's okay, I just wanted to check you're alright. I didn't know whether you'd be able to get out much in this weather. Mrs Bannister was worried.'

'Her from number twenty-four?'

'Yes, she sees you going for a paper sometimes.'

'Nosy old cow, what's it got to do with her?'

'I think she's just concerned, as we all are.'

'Well, tell her to mind her own business. You can see I'm fine. I've got food in the freezer, beer in the cellar. What more do I want?'

Zoe nodded. 'Yes, I can see you're managing very well. I'll leave you in peace then.'

'Aye, you do that. And mind how you go. You're so skinny that wind'll have you over.'

Zoe couldn't help smiling. It was the first time she heard Mr Dempsey express any concern for another person.

'I will. Goodbye, Mr Dempsey.'

''Bye then.'

Feeling lighter in mood, Zoe fought her way back to the car. At least one of her patients was unaffected by the weather. Tough old boy, he seemed to be coping better than a lot of people. Her thoughts automatically turned to Riordan and Sally.

Driving back, Zoe thought over Riordan's story. What had Riordan and Sally ever seen in each other? They appeared to be chalk and cheese. Sally, loving dangerous sports and craving excitement, and Riordan quiet, studious and thoughtful, wanting only to be a good husband and father. They said opposites attract, but to what extent? Zoe found it hard to believe.

Back at the medical centre, Zoe sent Riordan a quick text about seeing Jack Dempsey. *"How are you liking this weather?"* she put at the end.

He replied, *"Not at all, but don't worry it will blow over soon."*

*

Riordan was wrong. It took three weeks before the rain stopped, and the winds died down. When the sun made an appearance, Zoe decided to take advantage of it. Luna had been going stir-crazy inside the cottage with the puppies for so long, and Zoe took her for a short walk into the woodlands bordering the cottage. She marvelled at the flowers that survived the battering March weather. Hyacinths, crocuses and daffodils were in abundance, and they cheered Zoe with their beauty and the colours heralding the start of spring.

'It's going to be okay, girl,' she told Luna. 'Once three of the pups have gone, it's just you me and the last puppy and we'll have such fun. We'll go for walks and I'll throw a ball for you to fetch, and …'

Luna suddenly stopped listening and started barking, straining at the lead. Zoe stopped and saw a man leaning against a tree, grinning at them. Her heart raced until Zoe recognised him.

'Toby ... you scared me. What are you doing lurking in the woods?' Her voice shook slightly.

'Sorry, but I love listening to people talk to their pets. You can tell a lot about their personalities by the way they treat animals.'

He came over and knelt to fuss Luna, who began licking Toby's face and whining. Toby hadn't answered the question of why he was alone in the woods, but perhaps like Zoe, Toby was enjoying the first decent day of the year and was just out for a walk.

He stood up and put his hands in his jacket pockets.

'Whilst I'm here, I could look the pups over, if you like. If it's convenient.'

'Yes, it's convenient. If you don't mind, that would be good. Tom is bursting to have his puppy and luckily Solo is the biggest of them all, so he must be ready to go by now.'

'Right, let's go then.'

They walked back to Rosemary Cottage and Zoe wondered what to say—if anything. If what Riordan had said was true, then Toby wasn't the man Zoe thought. Just like Andy had turned out to be so different from Zoe's original assessment. Maybe she was just a rotten judge of men?

'So, you and the good doctor, are you an item now?'

'No, we're just friends.' Zoe didn't want to admit that she and Riordan were getting closer. Then Toby might assume that Zoe had heard all about Sally and TAO. After Toby checked the pups, Zoe would only see him on a strictly professional basis. She owed Riordan that much.

'Good. So, would it be okay if we tried again?'

'Tried what again?'

Toby laughed, and Zoe knew he was laughing at her. 'Us. Having a date. Just a drink to start with, if you like.'

'What about Melissa?' She didn't mean to blurt it out. Being so close to Toby was making Zoe nervous.

'What about her? She's a vet at the practice, just a colleague.'

'Are you always in the habit of wining and dining your colleagues, or is it only the blondes?'

Toby stopped and stared at Zoe. She suddenly felt uncomfortable and started walking on with Luna, eager to get home.

'Hey, wait!' He caught up and took her arm, swinging Zoe around. 'What's going on, Zoe?'

'Nothing's going on.'

'You start spending time with Riordan O'Connor and suddenly you're the ice princess. What's he been telling you?'

'Only that you were with Melissa on Valentine's Day night, but you were supposed to be working. You lied, and I don't like being lied to.'

She started walking again and he kept pace.

'How do you know that?'

'Riordan saw you going into the Crown and Anchor.'

'Right. Okay, I *was* with Melissa and yes, I lied to you, but only because I was saving your feelings. If I'd said I'd had a better offer, you would have been upset, right?'

Zoe said pointedly, 'If you'd said it like *that*, I would have been angry. But if Melissa was just a colleague, new in town, and you wanted to make her feel welcome, I would have understood. If that was really the case.'

'What do you mean, "if"? Don't you believe me?'

'I don't know, Toby, I'm not sure what to think.'

'I see.' His voice had lost all warmth and Zoe just wanted him to check the puppies and leave. 'I thought you liked me. We seemed to be getting on okay. Are you sure it's not something Riordan said?'

'Like what?' Zoe wasn't going to mention Sally, and if Toby did, she'd act dumb and pretend not to know anything.

'Well, I know he doesn't like me. Has he been trying to turn you against me?'

'No, of course not, and I'm perfectly capable of making my own mind up about people. Now, let's just be friends and see to the puppies. I'll make you a cappuccino.' Zoe smiled, hoping he would take the hint and drop the argument.

He smiled back and shrugged. 'Sounds good. Zoe—I really like you. I just want you to know that.'

'Thanks.'

They had reached the cottage and Zoe hurried inside, took Luna's lead off and her own coat, throwing both over the back of the sofa to sort out later. The living room smelt of dog pee and looked as if something large and hairy had trashed it, instead of four small puppies. Toby didn't seem to notice as Zoe hurried into the kitchen and turned the coffee machine on.

Half an hour later, the puppies had been declared ready for their new homes, the coffee had been drunk, and Zoe was wondering how to get Toby out of the cottage without her appearing rude.

When Toby's phone rang, Zoe sighed with relief. The conversation sounded serious and Toby ended it quickly and put his jacket on.

'Sorry, needed back at the surgery.'

'Thank you for everything, and you must let me pay you for your trouble.'

He walked over and cupped Zoe's face. She tensed and Toby dropped his hands and stepped back.

'It was no trouble, Zoe. Don't forget what I said. I don't give up easily.'

When Toby had left, Zoe collapsed on the sofa and was grateful when Luna crept on too and cuddled up. She put her arms around Luna, who licked Zoe's face.

'What do I do, Luna?' Luna wagged her tail. 'If he'd said that to me a month ago, I would have thought it was charming. A man who wanted me so much he wasn't prepared to give up. But now …'

Luna whined.

'Well, between you and me, I think it's just creepy.'

Chapter Twenty-Two

Riordan had a rare and precious weekend off and intended to make the most of every minute. It coincided with Tom becoming the proud owner of Solo. When Zoe brought the puppy to the house, she sat Tom down and they had a serious conversation. She explained in great detail about vaccinations and how important it was that Solo wasn't exposed to any infection, such as places where foxes or badgers had been, and other dogs who may not have been vaccinated. Tom had listened with wide eyes and a frightened look.

'How do I stop him getting sick?' he asked. 'Do I have to keep him in the house until he's had his jabs?'

'Well, no, because he needs to be socialised.'

'How do I do that?'

Riordan had listened without interrupting, even though he'd already researched all the information on the internet. Zoe had no doubt been briefed by Toby Dean, which was unavoidable. Riordan tried not to feel the familiar resentment at the thought of Toby being anywhere near Zoe.

This was Tom's dog and his son needed to take full responsibility. Riordan was pleased to see Tom was doing exactly that by asking the right questions. And, once all the pups had been homed, Zoe didn't need to see Toby again. There were other vets in Leytonsfield after all.

Zoe was saying, 'You'll have to carry him, I'm afraid. That's the only way to ensure he isn't exposed to anything harmful. At least until he's vaccinated.'

Tom turned to Riordan who tried to hide a smile.

'Dad, we've gotta carry him.'

'I know, which is why I've brought you a present.'

'For me?'

'You and Solo, yes.'

He gave Tom a shopping bag and watched his face light up, taking a pet carrier out of it. 'Oh wicked!' Tom quickly slung the carrier around his shoulder, so the bag was at the front, and picked up his pup. 'He fits—look at that!'

'That's great,' said Zoe. 'Now you can take him for walks without Solo being at risk of infection. I think I'll recommend these to the other two potential owners.'

'Dad, will you take a photo of me and Solo?'

'Sure.' Riordan took Tom's phone and snapped a picture.

Zoe said, 'I hope you two are coming on the first weight loss group's spring walk. We're going to stroll along the canal, the part that goes through the woodland. If you bring Solo, you can start the socialisation. He'll be able to smell all the scents, hear all the noises, and see the sights from the comfort of his carrier.'

'Yeah, we'll be there, won't we, Dad?'

'We will, and I believe Casey is free on Sunday, so I'll drag him and Jade along too.'

'Zoe? What kind of things do I need to show Solo?' Tom was so happy his face positively glowed.

'Well, he needs to be comfortable around people, fields, woods, birds … everything will be new to him.'

'It's exciting isn't it, Tom?' said Riordan. 'You've always wanted a dog and now he's yours.'

'Yeah, thanks, Dad—and you, Zoe.'

Zoe said, 'You're more than welcome. Right, I better be off. See you on Sunday then. We're meeting at two outside Rosemary Cottage. It gives some of the group the chance to attend church first.'

Riordan said, 'And gives me a chance to have a lie-in.'

Zoe smiled and, when Tom wasn't looking, she blew Riordan a kiss. He took it to mean Zoe would like to be with him lying-in. There was nothing Riordan would have loved more.

*

Zoe couldn't have wished for better weather. Weak spring sunshine in a pale blue sky dotted with white fluffy clouds, and a slight breeze, all made it perfect for a walk. Zoe locked Rosemary Cottage and went to join the group already milling around eager to be on their way.

'Afternoon,' she called.

There was a chorus of answering voices accompanied by big smiles. Most of the people who did the line dancing were there, as well as some who looked as if they could teach Zoe a thing or two about walking. They were decked out in serious walking boots, thick socks, cagoules, and fingerless gloves. Some had binoculars slung around their necks.

'Morning, Bob,' Zoe said, as an elderly man pointed out a flock of redwings flying over. 'I'm honoured. I never expected we'd be joined by members of the Leytonsfield Birders. Welcome, and I hope you all enjoy your walk.'

'Morning, Dr Angelos. When Beryl told me you were going to do a canal walk, I thought it was an opportunity too good to miss.'

'I didn't know you liked bird-watching, Beryl.'

'Oh aye, I used to go with Gordon every weekend until he passed. We went all over the country. Every summer we travelled to the Scilly Isles and winter in East Anglia. I don't know what I'd do without the bird-watching club. I've got my notebook and pencil ready to list the ones we see today. I might even get to add something to my lifer's list.'

'Good for you.' Zoe moved towards the people at the back, stopping to let them fuss over Luna whose tail was wagging hard at all the attention. Luna had been cooped up for so long with the pups, she would benefit from a good long walk as much as any of them.

Riordan and Tom hadn't arrived yet, and Zoe didn't want to leave without them. She'd give them another five minutes or so.

Bob was telling anyone who listened the species of birds they were likely to see. Millie and Mavis were eating sandwiches because they didn't have time for breakfast, and Zoe was growing more anxious as the minutes went by. She had been looking forward to this walk all week, but more than that, had been daydreaming about spending a few restful hours with Riordan. She longed to get to know Riordan better, and a relaxing walk in the sunshine was just the tonic they both needed.

Then, as Zoe was about to lead the group off, Riordan's Jaguar arrived and parked neatly in front of the gate. Tom got out first, wearing the carrier with Solo safely ensconced in it, and a huge grin on his face.

'Hi, Zoe,' he called. 'We're ready to go.'

She laughed and went over to the car. Luna straight away tried to jump up to reach Solo and the two dogs sniffed each other. Luna licked Solo's face and Zoe's heart turned over.

Riordan said, 'So much for a certain vet's advice. They obviously recognise each other.' He locked the car and came strolling towards her.

'You're right. Ready for this, Riordan?'

He bent and kissed Zoe on the cheek. 'We are, but I warn you, there's trouble brewing back there.'

'Why, what's wrong?'

They looked back at the car. Jade stood with hands on hips and confronting Casey. Her voice carried clearly.

'I want a puppy. It's not fair that Tom has one and I don't.'

Casey looked across at Zoe helplessly. 'I don't suppose you've got any left, have you?'

'You give in too easily,' said Riordan, grinning.

'Come on, Jade, let's go. We can talk about it on the way. We don't want to hold up these people any longer do we?' Casey was struggling, and Riordan stepped in to help.

'Jade? Are you going to walk with Tom? You can point out any interesting things you see that Solo might like to see too.'

Jade glared at her father, then stomped away to stand beside Tom.

'Sorry Zoe, I think we're ready now,' said Riordan with a smile. He looked much more relaxed—relaxed and handsome in a green Barbour jacket, jeans and walking boots.

Zoe had checked people's footwear surreptitiously to make sure no one was wearing anything inappropriate. She didn't want to treat any blisters or twisted ankles today.

'Right, let's go!' She led the group off and Riordan fell into step next to her. Tom, Jade and Casey followed closely behind.

Riordan asked, 'Have you homed the rest of the pups yet?'

Zoe said, 'I've got one left. I'm wondering now if I should let Jade have that one. It's a female and the smallest of the litter. I was only keeping it really for Luna's sake, but if Jade wants a puppy it would be nice to keep them all in the family.' Riordan listened without interrupting. He nodded thoughtfully but said nothing. After waiting a moment Zoe asked, 'What do you think?'

'If you're not bothered about keeping one of them, then it would be a nice gesture and let Casey off the hook.'

'I'll talk to him after the walk.'

They fell silent and Zoe could hear the conversation the kids were having. It made her smile. Jade was pointing out everything from the stones on the path, to the common bindweed clinging to a wire fence, bordering the railway line. Tom was being kind and faking interest in some things and praising Jade for spotting others that Solo would find interesting. The puppy was wagging his tail inside the carrier and Tom was talking to him the whole time.

'Do you miss the pups?' Riordan asked Zoe.

'Surprisingly, not as much as I thought I would. It's nice to have my living room smelling sweet again, and anyway, Luna and I muddle along well together.'

'Do you ever get lonely, Zoe?'

Wow, that was out of left field. Zoe wasn't sure how to answer.

'No, why do you ask?'

'You come from a big family with siblings, nieces and nephews … I just wondered if being away from them and living in such an isolated spot was sometimes a bit hard.'

'I miss the family, it's true, but I can easily get back to Manchester for a night or two, if I wanted. So much has happened since arriving in Leytonsfield, I just can't seem to find the time. But I'm going back for a weekend soon. Before Easter.'

'Good, family are important.'

'You're a big family man, aren't you, Riordan?'

'I wouldn't have survived without them,' he said quietly.

'Do you think you'll ever marry again?'

He was silent for a long time, thinking. Zoe had been warned about this. Riordan wasn't ignoring her. He sighed and looked round to where Tom and Jade were involved in a serious conversation about dogs. Casey was nearby talking to Shelley.

'Heron!' shouted Bob, and Tom took a photo of the bird as it stood like a statue on the far bank of the canal.

Riordan said, 'If you'd asked me that a few months ago, I would have said no. Emphatically. But now, the thought of being able to trust again is appealing. After Sally, I didn't think I'd ever trust another woman. I'm not sure I'm ready yet, but maybe one day. What about you? Are you open to the idea of marriage?'

'Trust is a difficult one, isn't it?'

Zoe couldn't complain—she'd walked right into this. She was struggling to find the words. The truth was that she wasn't scared of marriage, just getting pregnant again. Zoe could never risk losing another baby. It would kill her. The only way to avoid it was not get pregnant. Or find someone who already had children, or a child. Someone who didn't want any *more* children.

Riordan asked, 'Was it the policeman? Is he why you can't trust men now?'

'Yes, in a way. I don't think I'm a very good judge of men. I've got a bad habit of picking the wrong ones.'

'Does that include me?' Riordan was smiling. Zoe wasn't sure if he was serious. There was so much about this man Zoe didn't know but was eager to find out.

She said, 'No, I didn't mean you.'

'I enjoyed our evening at Rocco's. I'd like to do it again, if you're willing.'

'I am willing, thanks, I'd like that too.'

They came to a bend in the path. Three canal boats were lined up and tied to the bank, their bright blues, reds and greens shining in the sunlight. A young man stood at a bow with a dog by his side.

'Dad,' called Tom. 'Can I let Solo meet that dog?'

'If the owner says it's okay, but don't let them touch.'

'Okay.'

Tom and Jade walked to the boat and Zoe watched closely. Riordan had stopped a short way along the path, and he too kept a close eye on things. Zoe loved the way Riordan allowed Tom to do things for himself, rather than always stepping in. Riordan was a good father and seemed to have achieved the right balance of allowing Tom the freedom to learn and grow, and Riordan still provided help and support when it was needed.

The two children returned.

'Mission accomplished,' said Tom. 'And another thing I can tick off the list.'

'You're doing well,' said Riordan.

The short stop had given the stragglers the chance to catch up and the group was, once more, united.

They carried on after a quick drink from water bottles and flasks of coffee and came to a beautiful spot where a bridge stretched over the canal. Weeping willow trees dangled their branches in the water. It was an old, brick bridge with graffiti sprayed at one end. Zoe thought it was such a shame that a lovely structure had been vandalised. She was all in favour of street art, but here in this peaceful spot, these inane scribblings just looked ugly.

'There's Canada geese, coot and moorhen near the edge of the water,' said Bob. Everybody looked except Zoe, who was watching three small boys on the bridge. One of them, the youngest, looked as if he was climbing the wall.

'Daddy,' said Jade. 'Look at that naughty boy.'

They were all watching now, some holding their breath as the lad straightened to stand unsteadily with his arms out.

'Oh no ...' said Zoe.

'Dad, he's going to fall,' said Tom.

'Shit!' said Casey, seeing the boy lose his balance and plummet into the water.

Jade screamed. Casey and Riordan started running.

Chapter Twenty-Three

Casey stripped off his jacket and left it on the bank, plunging into the water before Riordan even reached where the child had gone in. Riordan took his coat off too and handed it to Tom who, despite being encumbered with carrying Solo, had run after them.

Casey reached the child in a few powerful strokes and began swimming on his side, back towards the bank, keeping the boy's head above the water. Riordan did a quick risk assessment. Casey couldn't check the child's breathing or heartbeat. Riordan needed to be ready to perform resuscitation. He turned and saw Zoe on the phone, calling for an ambulance.

'Tom, would you make sure people don't crowd around when I look at the boy, please?'

'Yes, Dad,' he said with a shaky voice.

'What can I do?' asked Jade, who seemed quite calm.

'You help Tom, sweetie.'

'Okay.'

Riordan waded out to meet Casey, who had slowed down considerably on the return swim. Riordan instantly realised why—the water was freezing, and trying to move in sodden, cold clothing was hard.

Without a word, Casey handed the boy to Riordan, who carried him to the bank. He laid the boy flat on the grass and checked for a pulse and breath. He found neither. Damn. The worst-case scenario. He started mouth-to-mouth, watching the small chest rise. Nothing. He then started chest compressions, taking care to avoid the boy's ribs. He was a small child, but Riordan guessed he was over eight years old and performed CPR as if for an adult—it was a different technique for a baby or young child.

Then he changed back to mouth-to-mouth, then back to CPR. Riordan kept this going, using the same rhythm and timing. He focused completely on the task, hardly noticing that Casey and Zoe were kneeling with him, ready to take over.

'Are the other boys still there?' Casey asked.

'Long gone,' answered Zoe.

Riordan could hear Jade's bossy little voice telling people not to get too close as her daddy and Uncle Riordan were saving the boy's life. How easily kids had faith in adults. He kept going, even though Riordan felt slightly dizzy and fatigued. He wasn't going to lose this boy, even if he had to stay like this, administering CPR all day.

'Do you want me to take over?' asked Casey. Riordan saw Casey was still panting from his exertions. Although Casey had been a champion swimmer, it was an entirely different thing to swim fully clothed in icy water.

Riordan shook his head.

Then suddenly the boy moved, coughed, and Riordan quickly turned him on his side as the child spat out canal water. Then he vomited.

'Hooray!' shouted Tom, and Jade mimicked him. The children high-fived each other. The group broke into spontaneous applause, with cries of "well done".

They could hear the ambulance siren in the distance, and Riordan slowly began to accept that the boy was safe. For now. The boy needed to get to a hospital.

'Here comes the cavalry,' said Casey, and collapsed on his back on the bank.

'Daddy, don't go to sleep,' said Jade. 'Your clothes are all wet. Mummy'll be cross.'

*

The excitement was over, the boy had been taken off in the ambulance, and the group stood around undecided what to do next.

Riordan couldn't control his shivering and Casey, trying to calm an excited Jade, was shaking too. Riordan wanted a change of clothes, a hot shower and a mug of tea, pronto. All he could do was stand and shake, trying to gather his thoughts.

Then Zoe took charge.

'Bob? Could you lead the group please? It would be a shame for you all not to finish the walk, and you know so much about the canal and its history.'

'It would be a pleasure, Dr Angelos,' said Bob.

'Can I be second-in-command?' asked Beryl.

'Of course.' Bob smiled at her, and Beryl's face turned an attractive shade of pink.

Zoe called, 'Good, but can someone come back with us and take Tom and Jade home? I need to get these two heroes inside Rosemary Cottage before they catch their death of cold.'

'We will,' said Shelley. 'Andrew gave me a lift. Is that okay?'

'No problem,' Andrew said, and they all started walking back the way they had come. Jade had to run to keep up.

They quickly arrived back at Rosemary Cottage. Riordan was desperate to get his wet clothes off and he was sure Casey felt the same. When they got to the gate, Zoe hurried up the path and unlocked the front door. The others said their farewells, bundling the children into Andrew's car.

Riordan waved. He couldn't trust his voice not to shake.

Then, at last, they were inside Rosemary Cottage.

Zoe told them, 'Right, you two, upstairs and have a hot shower. Leave your wet clothes outside the bathroom and I'll put them in the tumble dryer. They'll be dry in no time. There's bath sheets in the airing cupboard and I'll get duvets for while your clothes are drying.'

'Yes ma'am,' said Casey, and went up the stairs.

'Your floors are going to get awfully wet,' Riordan said. He realised what a sight he must look. Drowned rat didn't even begin to cover it—even though it was only from the waist down for Riordan. Poor Casey was thoroughly soaked.

Zoe placed her palms on either side of his face. 'I don't care about the wretched floors. I just want you to be warm and dry again. After what you and Casey did today … well, you did a wonderful thing.'

Riordan shook his head. 'Casey was the hero of the hour. We don't even know how the boy is. I'll phone the hospital later, see if I can get any information.'

'Whatever the outcome, both of you were amazing.'

'We did what we've been trained to do, that's all.'

'No, it's *not* all, Riordan. Take the credit when it's due to you.' She kissed him gently on the lips. 'Now go, before your brother takes all the hot water.'

When he got to the bathroom, he found Casey wrapped in a bath sheet.

'That was quick,' Riordan said, stripping off.

Casey said, 'Listen, I don't want to cramp your style. I'll leave the two of you together.'

'I think Zoe would prefer you wait until your clothes are properly dry. And there's no style to cramp.'

'Don't give me that, I've seen the way you look at each other. Mum'll be pleased,' he said with a cheesy grin. 'She worries about you, you know.'

'I know.'

Riordan stepped under the hot water and breathed a sigh of relief. Casey was right. Both their parents worried about him. But Riordan needed to move at his own pace, not before he was ready. He liked Zoe a lot, and was strongly attracted, but they needed to know each other much better before things went further. And Riordan wanted to know why Zoe was seeing Joe Moreton. Zoe plainly had secrets. Riordan had told Zoe his story; well, most of it, and deserved to hear hers.

By the time Riordan padded down the stairs, wearing a bath sheet and a duvet, he was feeling a hundred times better. Casey was sitting on the sofa with a mug of coffee. Zoe was in the kitchen.

'Tea, Riordan?' she called.

'Yes, please,' he replied, then joined Casey. They looked like a pair of ancient Romans in a bath house.

Zoe came into the living room carrying the clothes which were now warm and dry. 'I'm afraid your shoes are still sopping wet.'

'No matter. I've phoned for a taxi and it'll be here in ten. Thanks for everything, Zoe.'

'You don't have to rush off,' said Riordan, 'I'll give you a lift back.'

'No, I wouldn't hear of it. Anyway, I'm worried about the picture that Jade will be painting for Lexi. She has a vivid imagination, my daughter.'

'Only if you're sure …' said Zoe, not convincingly.

Riordan saw Zoe wink at him as Casey ran up the stairs to get dressed.

'If I didn't know better,' Riordan said. 'I would think you were trying to get rid of him so we could be alone.'

Zoe grinned. 'It's not often, if ever, that I have the pleasure of a semi-naked man sitting on my sofa. The possibilities are endless.'

'The possibilities? For what, exactly?'

Zoe's grin widened. 'Wait 'til he's gone, and I'll show you.'

Chapter Twenty-Four

Casey left and Zoe waved as the taxi moved away.

Zoe returned to the living-room to find Riordan sitting on the sofa with his phone in one hand and a packet of condoms in the other. His jacket lay next to him. He looked up at her with a bemused expression.

'I ...'

'Well, Dr O'Connor, aren't you full of surprises.' She smiled at him and he shook his head.

'No, I ...'

'I was all ready to seduce you, but you've beaten me to it.'

Zoe wasn't in the habit of seducing men. They always came to her. This time it was different. Riordan was shy, and still suffering from his wife's betrayal and death. The man was cautious, tentative, and over-thought everything. He was also sitting on the sofa and wearing only a bath sheet, having pushed the duvet off his shoulders in the warm, cosy living room. Holding a packet of condoms. That was a clear enough signal that he wanted her. Zoe shivered with need.

Zoe wanted him—more than any man before. The first time she had seen him, in that gladiator costume, she thought Riordan was a fine figure of a man. Next to him in the cinema, Zoe had felt drawn physically as well as mentally, and when they had kissed, something awakened within her that had been long dead. Now, moving slowly and seductively towards Riordan, all she wanted to do was to remove the towel and have her wicked way.

Zoe knelt in front of Riordan. His legs were spread, hands resting on his thighs. Hardly moving, his breathing growing more ragged, chest rising and falling fast.

Riordan never took his gaze away from Zoe's face.

She put her hands on his knees and slid them up, underneath the bath sheet, to the top of his thighs. Riordan's muscles tensed and the hairs on his legs felt springy. When he stopped Zoe's fingers from reaching their destination, she felt a pang of disappointment. She looked up and, keeping eye contact, leaned forward and kissed his mouth. Riordan moaned softly so she deepened the kiss. Riordan cupped Zoe's face and the kiss became hot, hungry and urgent. She pulled the towel away.

'Zoe ...' he whispered, and she murmured his name. She ran her hands down Riordan's body, starting with his shoulders, then his chest with a mat of chest hair, down his stomach, taking the time to admire his six-pack and then further down to where he was erect and ready. He was beautiful and Zoe wanted to taste him, taking him in her mouth.

Riordan cried out as she took him deeper and she glanced up to see his head was thrown back, eyes tightly shut, fingers reaching out to wind in her hair. Zoe cupped him and squeezed gently as her mouth and tongue brought him swiftly to orgasm, and his whole body spasmed.

Zoe got up and sat next to Riordan on the sofa and putting her arms around him. He was panting and groaning softly, hugging Zoe tightly.

'That was …'

'Wonderful?'

'Unexpected … and wonderful.'

'Why unexpected? Don't you like oral sex?' Zoe's wide eyes feigned innocence.

'Don't I like—are you kidding me? That was about the best thing that's happened to me for so long, I can't begin to explain how good that was.'

Zoe wanted to ask if Sally had ever done that, but stopped herself, instead silently stroking his hair.

'Shall we go upstairs?' he asked.

'Would you prefer the bed to here?'

Zoe was a bit disappointed, preferring to stay where they were without the disturbance of having to walk up the stairs and get into bed. It would break the mood. But if Riordan wanted it, then she wouldn't argue.

'No, I just want to make love to you. I don't care where we are.'

'Right answer,' she said, and kissed him.

'Now I intend to take all your clothes off so we're on an equal footing. I feel a bit strange being naked while you're fully clothed.'

'Really? I rather like it.'

'Is that one of your fantasies, Zoe? To have naked men waiting on you hand and foot?'

'What makes you think I have fantasies?'

'Everyone has them, sexual or otherwise.'

'Okay then, you go first. What's your sexual fantasy?'

'Oh, I have hundreds.' Riordan smiled and started to un-button her shirt. 'One of them is that a gorgeous GP of Greek heritage with beautiful brown eyes and the sexiest mouth on the planet, lets me strip her naked and kiss her all over.'

He took off the shirt, draping it on the back of the sofa. Zoe said nothing, and just let Riordan position her as he wished. He stood up and pulled Zoe to her feet, where she found herself staring at his chest. He took off Zoe's bra and cupped her breasts, before bending and kissing one, then the other. He undid the button on her jeans, and then unzipped them. He knelt and pulled them down. She put a hand on Riordan's shoulder for balance, stepping out of them. He moved unhurriedly but capably, and soon Zoe was naked too. Then Riordan swept Zoe up and laid her gently on the sofa. He sat next to her.

Zoe had one arm behind her head and the other resting on her thigh, without a care if she looked sexy and alluring, or just plain silly. She waited, her heart doing a fandango.

Riordan was smiling shyly, almost as if he couldn't believe his luck, and drinking Zoe in as if she was a painting or a sculpture. He wasn't wearing any glasses and Zoe idly wondered how bad his eyesight was and got the urge to giggle.

Riordan leaned down and kissed her navel. It tickled and Zoe squirmed slightly. He kissed all the way up her body to her breast. Zoe tangled fingers in his hair. Thick, strong hair that smelled of her coconut shampoo. He took a nipple in his mouth and sucked. Zoe felt the connection right through to her toes. She was wet; had been for some time, and the awakening desire that had been dormant so long was springing to full life. Riordan was growing aroused again as well. Good recovery, she thought.

He moved on, across to her other breast and repeated the process. Riordan had said he wanted to kiss Zoe all over, so she let him, giving in to the sensations of his lips, soft and caressing, his tongue giving little licks, and occasionally she felt his teeth, but never sharp, just enough to make Zoe jump slightly. He stroked, using the back of his fingers, on the inside of her arms, down her sides and over Zoe's stomach. It was erotic and she wanted more, a need that had to be met. Zoe didn't want to wait any longer, she wanted Riordan inside her. Now.

'Riordan?'

'Um?'

'Please …'

'Soon.'

He moved down and spread her legs gently, placing one over the back of the sofa and the other over his shoulder. Riordan placed his hands under Zoe's buttocks and lifted, so she was exposed. Then he licked her clitoris. Zoe nearly came straight away and cried out with the sensation of soaring like a bird in flight, circling ever upwards towards the sun, gloriously out of control, the pleasure roaring through her body making Zoe feel alive, vital and powerful.

All thoughts dissolved and disappeared into nothing as Riordan brought her to orgasm. Zoe cried out, loudly and unashamedly as a climax ripped through her. It lasted forever and she wanted it to never stop.

She heard, as if from a great distance away, Luna barking. Zoe returned to earth to see Riordan sitting on the floor watching her. Luna was sitting next to him, also watching. They looked so funny together that Zoe burst out laughing.

'That wasn't the effect I was aiming for,' Riordan said, pushing his glasses up.

'When did you put your glasses on?'

'When I was waiting for you.' He smiled. 'You orgasm beautifully even though you're a screamer. You frightened Luna.'

'Sorry Luna,' Zoe called out. Luna wagged her tail and came towards the sofa to make sure Zoe was okay. 'Maybe we better go to bed after all? Don't want the dogs disturbed, do we?'

'Certainly not,' said Riordan, who looked perfectly comfortable sitting on the carpet. He had his knees bent, hiding a sizeable erection.

'Riordan? How bad is your eyesight?'

'Bloody awful,' he said cheerfully. 'Can't see a thing without the specs.'

'So, when you were kissing me all over ...'

'I was relying on instinct and touch. I enjoyed the touching.'

'So did I.'

'Yes, I heard.'

'I don't remember ever screaming that loudly before.'

'I'm flattered.'

'Shall we go to bed?'

Riordan grinned and leapt up, scooping Zoe into his arms.

Chapter Twenty-Five

Riordan couldn't believe how light Zoe was. Carrying her made him feel masculine and in control. It had been a few years since he'd had sex, and never with a woman like Zoe.

He put Zoe down on the bed and took the box of condoms from her. She'd remembered to quickly grab them, and his phone, which set her off giggling again. This time Riordan had joined in. He'd found the condoms in his jacket pocket when he was searching for his phone. He hadn't put them there, but he knew who had. Casey. Riordan would thank him later, but for now, he was planning to put them to good use.

Riordan clambered into bed and lay on his back, waiting for Zoe to make a move. She turned over and cuddled up.

'This is nice. I like snuggling.' He sighed, putting an arm around Zoe, drawing her in close.

'Good, most men don't.'

'I'm not most men,' he said.

'I'm beginning to realise that and I'm glad. Most men can be arrogant so-and-so's. You're not, Riordan.'

'What am I then, Zoe?'

'You're a gentleman.' She kissed his chest.

'I'll take that.'

She moved slightly, fingers lightly stroking his chest and abdomen down to his navel. He groaned loudly.

'Do you like that?'

'Yes, it's one of my hot-spots.'

'Lovely. In that case, I'd better find the rest—no, don't tell me, I want to discover them for myself.'

'I wasn't going to tell you. That'd spoil the fun.'

They took their time, exploring each other's bodies. Caresses, strokes, and feather-light touches. They learnt what the other liked, what made them close their eyes and moan softly, squirm in ecstasy, and what left them completely unmoved. By the time they had finished the sexual inventory, they were hot for each other, panting, desperate with longing. Riordan, not able to wait any longer, opened the box and took out a condom.

She asked, 'May I see?'

He handed the box over and Zoe checked the contents while he slipped the condom on. He asked, amused, 'Okay?'

'A new box. Five left. Perfect. If there hadn't been six I would have been jealous thinking about who was the lucky recipient of the missing one.'

'You have absolutely no reason to be jealous. Of anyone. I promise.'

'Likewise,' she murmured as he kissed her, slowly at first, then more urgently.

Zoe was lying underneath him, and Riordan was supporting himself on his elbows. She spread her legs and placed them around his hips. He guided himself inside and marvelled at how tight and hot she was. They seemed to fit perfectly. Riordan was average size; or at least that was how he had always thought of himself. Zoe was a small woman, and when he pushed slowly and carefully into her, watching Zoe's face for the slightest sign of discomfort, there was none. She was smiling, watching Riordan watching her—it was like finding his sexual soulmate. They were perfect together. He thrust into her and she moved her legs to his waist, so he could bury himself in her.

'Zoe!' He loved to say her name, just to hear the sound.

They moved, groaned, cried out, their bodies locked together, until Riordan's thrusts became faster and harder and they were both past the point of no return. He held Zoe and she moved with Riordan until she cried with a sound so animal and uninhibited, it caused Riordan to let go and he came hard after Zoe, pouring himself into her.

He felt drugged, in a wonderful floating way, as if the whole world was contained in this bed with Zoe—and everything beyond was unreal and unimportant.

'Oh, God,' she murmured.

'Umm,' was all he could manage.

Riordan didn't know how long they lay there in a semi-conscious state, but he was no longer erect and was still in Zoe. He moved slightly but it was an effort. Zoe's breathing was deep and slow.

'Zoe …' She didn't answer and he carefully pulled out.

He got off the bed and padded to the bathroom to dispose of the condom.

When he returned, Riordan took Zoe in his arms, her head on his shoulder.

He said softly, 'Thank you.'

'You don't have to thank me every time we make love. But you're welcome.'

'I do, Zoe. After Sally, I never thought I'd meet anyone who I could feel such a strong connection with. I want to thank you for that.'

'That's a lovely compliment, Riordan. I feel the same.'

'Good, I don't want there to be secrets. It's better that everything is out in the open, which is why I want to tell you something.'

Zoe turned on her side to see his face.

'Go on.'

He swallowed. This wasn't going to be easy. 'I loved Sally, passionately and completely. I always knew I wasn't the right man for her. We were too different. But I desperately wanted our marriage to work, especially after Tom was born.'

'That's understandable.'

'When she died, I didn't go through all the stages of grief—denial, anger, bargaining, depression and acceptance…'

Zoe moved again, watching him closely, and encouraged Riordan gently, 'And?'

'I got stuck on anger. I couldn't shake it. I was *angry* with Sally for risking her life when she had a child. She should have put Tom first. I was angry with her for having an affair, but I was angry for a lot more that I couldn't deal with.'

'I'm so sorry, Riordan.'

'I needed help, which is why I became a patient of Joe Moreton.' There, he'd said it. He didn't look at Zoe, waiting for her to admit seeing him too. She stayed silent.

'My problem, you see, was that most of my anger was directed inward. Joe helped me to see that. I was so full of self-loathing I couldn't function. I blamed myself for not being firmer with Sally. I should have insisted that she leave TAO when she had Tom. I should have grown a pair and manned up, and all the other cliché's that I used to beat myself up with.'

'Oh Riordan, that's awful. It wasn't your fault. She was obviously a very independent woman and headstrong ... I should imagine.'

Riordan gazed at her. Zoe's brown eyes looked as black as treacle in the fading light, and her expression was hard to read. He traced his finger over her eyebrows, nose, and lips, watching closely as if trying to memorise every feature. Then Riordan stared at the ceiling.

'Sally was my first and only love. I met her at a New Year's Eve party at university. I was twenty-one and I'd never been in love. Never even been close. She was drunk and a guy was hitting on her, so I told him to leave her alone. He was quite aggressive, and I had to be firm. Fortunately, he backed down. I'm not a fighter, Zoe, hate confrontation, but I hate bullies even more and he looked like a bully to me.'

'And Sally thought you were a hero.'

'No, Sally thought I was interfering and told me so in no uncertain terms. Told me she was perfectly capable of looking after herself. Then she threw up all over someone and I took her home. Sally lived in shared accommodation and the other three girls were all out. She fell asleep and I sat up all night to make sure she didn't choke on her own vomit.'

'Was she grateful?' Zoe's voice was low and sexy in the intimacy of the bed. Riordan wanted to make love again but needed to tell Zoe everything first.

'Not particularly. She did offer to buy me a drink as a way of thanks. That was our first date. We had absolutely nothing in common, but I fell in love with her.'

'And Sally realised what a gem you were and fell in love with *you*.' He was silent for a long time. 'Isn't that what happened, Riordan?'

'No—yes, she *did* say she loved me, but actions speak louder than words. When I asked her to marry me, she said she needed time to think about it. That took all the romance away. Although she finally said yes, I should have seen the signs that we weren't compatible.

Martha tried to warn me, saying Sally was damaged somehow, and had a kind of death wish. I didn't believe Martha, saying she was wrong and that the woman I was mad about was just young and was getting something out of her system.'

'Did Martha and Sally get on?'

'No. Martha was perfectly willing to be friends, but Sally wasn't interested. Sally didn't encourage Martha to visit or show any friendship whatsoever. Martha gradually stopped visiting, but we stayed in touch. I think Martha knew that I would need her one day. How right she was.'

Zoe moved on top of him, running fingers through his hair.

'You're very close to Martha?'

'When Sally died, it was Martha who kept me from going insane. And that isn't an exaggeration. She was the only one who understood. My family were wonderful, as they always are, but when they found out that Sally had been unfaithful, they thought it would mean I wouldn't mourn so deeply or miss her as much. Martha knew that it meant the complete opposite. The fact Sally had the affair just increased my suffering. I wanted to know *why*, and I couldn't ask her. I'll never really know.' He fell silent, feeling drained.

'I don't know what to say. Thank you for telling me.' Zoe lay still and Riordan stroked her back, wondering if he should say more. But he'd come this far, and it would be cowardly to back down now.

'The thing is, Zoe … I know you're seeing Joe as well. It's none of my business, but I just want you to know that I understand. Whatever is wrong, it might help if you told me. I may be able to do something.'

Zoe quickly rolled away and sat on the edge of the bed with her back to Riordan.

'How do you know?' Her voice was brittle, and Riordan's heart sank. 'Was it your father? Did he tell you?'

'No, I saw you going into his offices. Please don't be angry, I haven't mentioned it to anyone. I want to help you.'

'I can't talk about it. I'm sorry, but it's too soon.'

Zoe abruptly got up, put on a towelling robe and left the bedroom, closing the door quietly.

Riordan stayed where he was, wishing he'd kept his big mouth shut.

Chapter Twenty-Six

After closing the curtains and feeding Luna and the puppy, Zoe sat alone on the sofa. The house was quiet, Riordan hadn't come down the stairs after her. She had felt close to Riordan after his declaration, pleased that he had confided such deep and personal feelings. But only so Zoe would reveal her own problems? Or was she being too cynical?

Riordan saw Zoe visiting Joe Moreton and hadn't mentioned it, until now. Zoe didn't know what to make of that. At least it hadn't been Dan being indiscreet, keeping her secret— as Riordan would too, Zoe was sure. So what was stopping her from confiding in him? It wasn't that Zoe didn't trust Riordan, because she did. Something else was holding her back and Zoe needed to go with her instincts. Riordan would just have to accept that.

Zoe went into the kitchen, made two mugs of tea and carried them carefully up to the bedroom. Riordan was sitting up in bed, the pillows stacked behind him. He was on his phone.

'Thank you, that's wonderful news.' He smiled at Zoe. 'That was A&E. The boy has been kept in overnight, but all the signs are good. They're discharging him tomorrow. His parents want to talk to us, apparently.'

'Us, or you and Casey?' She put the tea down on the bedside table and sat next to him.

'All of us. We're all witnesses. Apparently, the older boys dared Jimmy—that's his name—to climb up onto the wall. He wanted to be in their gang and that was the initiation, apparently.'

'So, it was a case of boys will be boys, rather than bullying?'

'I'd say so. Thanks for the tea.'

'Riordan, I'm sorry if I was abrupt just now, it's just that something happened to me and it's painful ...'

He put a hand on hers. 'No, I'm the one who should apologise. I'm glad I told you about Sally, but there's no reason for *you* to disclose something so personal, if you're not ready. I understand completely.'

'I will tell you, I promise.'

'That's good enough for me.'

They were silent, sipping their tea and not looking at each other. She wanted to make love with him again, but there was a distance between them now. Zoe hoped she hadn't ruined everything.

She said, 'I've decided to let Jade have the last puppy. I'll ring Casey tomorrow and tell him.'

'Good, he'll be pleased.'

Slightly self-consciously, they sat drinking their teas.

He said carefully, 'Zoe, we have five condoms left, and it would be a shame to let them go to waste.'

She grinned, relieved that things were getting back on track. 'I never realised you were so romantic.'

'I'll bring flowers next time.'

She reached over and straddled him, rubbing against his groin. 'What makes you think there's going to be a next time?'

'If I had my way, there'd be a whole run of next times, stretching to infinity.'

Wow, Zoe thought. 'You have the soul of a poet.'

'And you have the body of a Venus de Milo, the eyes of Cleopatra, and the mouth of … ah …'

Zoe threw her head back and laughed. 'The mouth of what, Riordan? Potty mouth?'

'I was trying to think of something complimentary. When you went down on me earlier it was amazing. Whatever that skill is called, that's what I meant.'

'The skill is called being a woman. A woman who wants a man. Not just any man, but this man.' Zoe felt him grow hard. She was wet with desire and wanted to feel Riordan inside her, but this time, she was going to be on top.

He said, 'Okay, your wish is my command.'

*

Riordan started the week feeling on top of the world. By the end of the week, that had all changed. On Friday morning, Casey rang him from A&E to say they had one of Riordan's patients in Resus.

'Mrs Murgatroyd. It's not looking good.'

'I'll be right down.'

When he got there, the patient's bed was surrounded by staff. They had obviously been trying to resuscitate her. Casey came over to Riordan.

'She was brought in after having chest pains and then fainting. Her heart stopped in the ambulance and they managed to get her back, but she had another attack twenty minutes ago. We tried, Riordan.'

Riordan knew how much his brother hated losing a patient. They all did.

'Thanks Casey,' he said quietly.

Mrs Murgatroyd's daughter was sobbing in a nurse's arms.

'I'll speak to her,' he told Casey.

'You don't have to, I'll do it, if you like.'

'No, she was my patient.' He walked over to the two women. 'Would you like to come with me where it's a bit quieter?' The daughter nodded and followed him.

There was a small room where patients and relatives could go and be alone. Riordan explained, as best he could, that her mother's heart had been getting weaker and that a transplant had been the only chance. They hadn't received a reply from the transplant team in time. It was tragic, but there was no guarantee that her mother would have had a transplant anyway, even if she had been accepted.

The daughter said through her tears, 'Why? Why couldn't she have been given a new heart sooner? If she was so sick, she shouldn't have had to wait.'

For once, Riordan didn't know what to say. He should have quoted the facts and figures on heart transplants. The number of patients on the waiting list had reached a record high, doubling in just a decade. The average time on a waiting list is three years. Donations of hearts aren't keeping up with demand. But he couldn't. It wasn't what this poor, grieving daughter wanted to hear. She had lost her beloved mother who could never be replaced. Nothing Riordan could say would make the slightest bit of difference to the pain she was going through.

'I am truly sorry. I wish I could have done more.'

'It's not your fault, Doctor, I know that, but ... she was my mum and I loved her.'

She started crying again and Riordan sat in silence, feeling the weight of her grief pulling him down to a place Riordan never wanted to visit again. For Tom's sake as well as his own, he must never go back there. Riordan held out his hand and she took it, crying even harder. Eventually the tears dried, and she got up.

'Thank you for everything you've done. I just want to sit with her for a bit. The nurse said I could.'

'Of course.' Riordan escorted the daughter back to where her mother's body lay covered by a white sheet. He wished there was something he could say that would bring some comfort. All Riordan could think of were the usual empty platitudes. This poor woman deserved better. He left her sitting quietly next to her mother's body.

*

When Riordan arrived home, he was greeted by the sound of an argument going on in the living room.

When Tom saw Riordan, he said, 'Dad, tell her …'

Casey and Jade were sitting on the sofa. Tom was standing in the middle of the room with Solo in his arms. Eloise was hovering in the doorway. Riordan tenderly kissed her cheek.

'Tell who what, Tom?' asked Riordan, putting his arm around Eloise's waist.

'Jade … she's going to call her puppy Polo 'cos it's nearly white, although it isn't all white.'

'It so is,' said Jade belligerently.

'It so isn't,' said Tom, pale with anger. Like his father, Tom hated confrontation. 'Polo is too much like Solo. She's just copying me.'

Riordan looked at Casey, who shrugged and said, 'I said she could call the puppy any name she wanted.'

'And she wants to copy me,' said Tom, close to tears.

'Tom, come with me and we'll talk in the kitchen.' Riordan led him out of the living room. Jade stuck her tongue out as they left, but luckily Tom didn't see. 'Sit down.'

They both sat at the kitchen table. Solo squirmed in Tom's arms, and he cuddled the dog as if he never wanted to let him go.

'Okay, Tom. We have a problem.'

'I haven't got a problem, Jade has.'

Tom wouldn't look him in the eyes, so Riordan got up and filled the kettle with water. His mother always made a nice cup of tea whenever there was a problem to solve. Maybe it would work for him.

'Jade adores you and, yes, she does copy you. But you know the saying, "Imitation is the sincerest form of flattery"?'

'What does that mean?'

'What it means is that, if she didn't love and admire you so much, Jade wouldn't want to copy you.'

'But it's not fair. Solo is *my* puppy's name.'

'I know it's not fair, Tom, but you can't force Jade to call her puppy something else. Imagine if you thought up the name and then a boy at school told you his dog was called Solo, and you'd have to change your puppy's name. How would you feel?'

Tom looked up and frowned. 'But that's different. Me and the boy at school don't know each other. Jade knows how much that name means to me.'

Smart kid. 'Okay, yes, that is a good point.' His little son was already winning arguments. 'Look, Tom, if Jade isn't prepared to change the name, then we can't do anything. Just grin and bear it.' He hated giving Tom advice like that, but Riordan otherwise had no idea how to fix this.

'I'm not giving up on this one, Dad. I'll think of a way to persuade Jade to change it.'

'Right—well, run it by me first, okay? We don't want Jade to be upset, do we?'

'I won't upset her, I promise. I love her.'

Riordan felt his eyes tearing up.

Tom left the kitchen to run upstairs to his room. No doubt to think of a cunning plan. Riordan wiped the tears from his cheeks. Tom was a good kid, gentle, kind and loving. He was also bright, intelligent and had a powerful mind. He wasn't ten years old yet and was already a force to be reckoned with. What had he done to deserve such a lovely son?

Chapter Twenty-Seven

On Friday morning Zoe loaded her car with a small overnight bag, Easter eggs for the kids, and a few small presents she had bought for the adults. She fitted Luna with her new dog harness that attached to the seat belt and checked the cottage was locked.

'Okay,' she said to Luna sitting in the front passenger seat as if she couldn't wait to get on the road. 'Let's go.' Luna wagged her tail, apparently unconcerned about travelling in a car.

Once Zoe got on the motorway, she stayed in the slow lane and turned the radio on. Classical FM or Smooth FM? Did she feel upbeat, or nervous, and needed calming down? She kept the station on Classic FM and enjoyed Debussy's *Arabesque No 1*.

Zoe's thoughts kept returning to Riordan and the night they had spent together. They shared some of the best sex Zoe had ever had. Andy had always been impatient to get to the main event and couldn't see the point of foreplay. A lot of the time, this had made sex uncomfortable for Zoe, and left her feeling unsatisfied and frustrated. Riordan was the complete opposite. He had turned her on so much with his lips, tongue and fingers that Zoe had been on the verge of begging him to take her. She smiled at the thought of the orgasms that had resulted. Skyrockets indeed!

She was growing more than just fond of Dr Riordan O'Connor, despite promising not to get involved with a man again—at least not until becoming established in Leytonsfield. When Riordan walked through the door of the line dancing class on Wednesday, Zoe's heart leapt at seeing him again, barely containing herself from running up and flinging her arms around Riordan's neck. He had smiled his usual shy smile.

When Zoe next looked at the motorway signs it was a surprise to have reached the turnoff already. Thinking about Riordan had taken up all the time it took to reach Manchester. Was she becoming too obsessed? Maybe she should back off a bit? Realising how hard that would be, Zoe channelled her inner Scarlett O'Hara and decided to think about it tomorrow.

'We're nearly home, Luna,' she said, but Luna had fallen asleep.

Was it still home? Since Zoe had started seeing Riordan, Rosemary Cottage had begun to feel like home. But it would be lovely to see the family again.

*

The house Zoe grew up in was a five-bedroom detached in Heaton Moor. Here she had learned how to compete with three brothers, giggled with school friends, studied for exams, and decided to become a doctor.

She rang the doorbell and her mother answered.

'Darling, how lovely to see you again, come inside and I'll make coffee. I'm just having a quick break before returning to work.' Her mother was an accountant who worked from home.

'Mum,' said Zoe, holding her arms out for a hug. Her mother held Zoe for a few moments, then ushered her into the kitchen. She wasn't a demonstrative woman. How different she was from Eloise O'Connor, thought Zoe.

'Is it okay to bring Luna into the kitchen?'

'Of course. She looks sweet.' Her mother gazed down at Luna but didn't move to stroke her.

'Hi, Zoe,' said Jo, her sister-in-law.

Jo was sitting at the kitchen table and was trying not to draw attention to her pregnant state. Caleb had rung Zoe to announce they were pregnant again. Zoe had congratulated him, feeling happy for them—although she felt a twinge of envy, mixed with the underlying fear that things wouldn't go to plan. Zoe hated the thought of someone she cared about going through the same experience.

'So, how's the new job?' asked Jo.

'It's good. I'm settling in now and have this gorgeous girl to help with that.' Luna was sitting quietly. Zoe fondled her ears.

'Oh yes, the dog! Caleb told me you'd got one.'

Zoe told them the story, the three of them sitting around the kitchen table and sipping coffee.

'That vet sounds like a nice man. Is he good-looking?'

'Extremely.' Zoe didn't want to talk about Toby. She had been hoping to introduce the topic of Riordan but didn't want anyone to think they were an item. After all, Zoe had only spent one night with him.

'And? Has he asked you out?'

'Toby's a bit of a womanizer. Not someone I'd like to get involved with.'

'So that means yes.' Jo laughed as Zoe frowned. 'You can't fool me. I bet he *has* asked you.'

Jo shook her curls in a flirtatious way and Zoe couldn't be cross with her. Jo and Jacinda were two of Zoe's closest friends—she was so lucky. They had taken over from the people Zoe lost when they heard about Samuel. Friends who showed their true colours by disappearing off Zoe's radar, rather than staying around to help deal with her grief.

'Anyway, enough about me. What about you two and the littlest Angelos? How far along are you?'

Jo beamed at her. 'I'm so glad you're okay with it. The baby's due in August. We would like a boy, but obviously we don't really mind so long as the baby's healthy and everything goes …' Jo realised what she'd said. 'Oh, God, I'm sorry Zoe, that was so insensitive.'

Zoe was shaking her head and trying to keep a fixed smile. 'No, don't be sorry, it's okay.'

And everything would have been okay, if her mother hadn't spoken up.

She said, 'Of course it's alright to talk about your baby. The same thing isn't going to happen to you, I'm sure. And it was a long time ago, I'm sure Zoe doesn't expect people to watch what they say around her after all this time, do you dear? You must be over it by now.'

Zoe was speechless. 'No Mum, I'm *not* over it,' she snapped. 'And it *wasn't* that long ago.' She couldn't say any more, her throat clogged with unshed tears, and Zoe wanted to get out of the house. 'I think I'll take Luna for a walk, she'll be wanting to relieve herself.'

Zoe got up, shrugged into her jacket and left the house, heading towards a nearby park. So many childhood memories came back, but suddenly Zoe found herself thinking of the canal in Leytonsfield, and Riordan and Casey desperately trying to save the life of a child. Then Zoe remembered the moment she'd told Dan about Samuel, and his kind words— parents don't get over the death of their children, they just learn to live with the loss.

Her mother's words had been without malice and thought-less, but still cut deeply. Zoe didn't think her mother would ever understand.

Zoe stayed in the park for as long as she could, enjoying the unexpected warm spring sunshine, sitting on the swing she'd played on as a little girl, and visiting the bandstand that once provided shelter from unexpected rain. Zoe had been with a group of friends and Paul Somerton had kissed her. She'd been twelve, hated the kiss, and wondered what all the fuss was about.

The park held so many memories. Zoe often came here to be alone. When her first boyfriend dumped her, and when her grandfather died. Through all the seasons of Zoe's life, she'd come to this park to converse with nature, to feel its healing powers and to ground herself.

There had only ever been one occasion when the park couldn't help her. When Zoe had lost her baby. Then, nothing made any difference, and no one could help. That feeling had never really gone away.

'Shall we go, Luna?' The dog wagged her tail. Zoe looked around one last time. Perhaps it was *just* a park? Nothing special. And memories were just that. Good or bad, they were only things that had happened in the past. She needed to look ahead to the future.

When Zoe rang the bell this time, her father answered it. Zoe threw herself into his arms.

'Dad! It's so good to see you again.'

'Ditto. I left work early as I knew you'd be here—and you'd wandered off.'

'I had to take Luna out.'

'She's a little beauty, isn't she?' He knelt to make a fuss of her. Her father had always loved dogs, but her mother hadn't. Consequently, they'd never had one.

'How's work?' she asked. Her father was a bank manager.

'It's fine, Zoe. Just fine.'

They were still standing in the hall and her father seemed reluctant to move into the kitchen.

He said, 'Ready for the big family reunion tonight? Markos and Jacinda have been working flat out so that friends can take over running the restaurant, and they can join us at the table.'

'That's good. How are they all?'

'They're fine, Zoe. I'm more interested in how you are?'

'Oh, you know, fine.'

Her father looked into her eyes. Zoe couldn't lie to him, and he plainly knew why Zoe had fled the house.

'You're *not* fine, are you?'

'Oh, Dad …' She burst into tears and he enveloped her in a bear-hug, the like of which only a father could give a daughter. Zoe felt safe and secure, and about five years old again.

'Oh my darling girl, I wish there was something I could do to take that pain away. There's no point telling you that time heals all wounds, because that's rubbish. I'm so sorry, Zoe.'

He held Zoe tightly and rubbed her back, as he had when Zoe was a child. Eventually, the tears dried up.

'Better?' he asked, gently kissing her forehead.

'I'm seeing a psychiatrist,' she said. 'But don't tell Mum, I don't think she'd understand.'

'Okay. Is he helping?'

'Yes, but it's going to be a long road.'

'Well, I'm here for you, any time, you know that, don't you?'

'Yes, Dad. I love you, *you* know that don't you?'

'Of course. Come on, let's put our brave faces on and get out there and kick butt.'

Zoe smiled at her father's attempt at being down with the kids. She loved him so much, and he loved her back. For Zoe, it was all that mattered.

*

The family meal was a typical Angelos get-together, held at the restaurant bequeathed to Markos and Jacinda by their grandmother, who had returned to Greece when their grandfather died.

Zoe was greeted with open arms by the rest of her family. The children loved the Easter eggs and the adults plied Zoe with questions about Leytonsfield.

She said, 'Well, you can find out for yourselves when you come to my birthday party.'

'Where are you having it?' asked Markos, keeping half his attention on the family, and the other half on the activity in the restaurant.

'In my cottage.'

'Is it big enough?'

'I'm sure we'll squeeze everyone in.'

'Will there be dancing?' asked Avis, whose ambition was to be a dancer on *Strictly Come Dancing*.

'Absolutely, and food and drink, and lots of people for you all to meet. The O'Connors, for example.'

Her mother said, 'We can't all stay in your cottage. Is there a hotel nearby?' Ever practical, she would want to know all the arrangements.

'Yes, Mum, there's the Leytonsfield Hotel. I'm sure you'll be comfortable there. Or I could find you a B&B.'

'The hotel sounds okay. I'm sure we could make do just for one night.'

'Let's have a toast to Zoe,' said her father, holding up his glass of wine.

'To Zoe!' they all shouted. Zoe smiled and thanked everyone. It was good to be back home.

For this was what *home* was; not a place but being with the people who loved you the most.

Chapter Twenty-Eight

'Okay, Dad,' said Tom, as he put his dog carrier on and picked up Solo. 'This is Mission Socialisation and we're going to take him to as many places on the list as possible. The more Solo's exposed to things, the better behaved he'll be.'

'Okay, lead the way, Captain.'

They left the house and started walking towards the town centre. The fine spring weather had stayed, and the sun was doing its best to spread warmth on the people of Leytonsfield. Riordan had promised Tom they would spend the whole weekend together, and Tom could choose their activities. Of course, Tom chose socialising his puppy, as that was the most important thing right now. That, and persuading Jade to change the name of *her* puppy. So far, Tom had no luck with that.

'What are we doing first?' Riordan asked.

'Shops. He needs to get used to the different smells; butchers, green-grocers, delicatessens and restaurants, and cafes. He'll probably get excited but needs to learn to chill.'

Riordan smiled at the thought of his calm, sensible son teaching a puppy to *chill*. He was so proud of Tom, taking responsibility for Solo.

'You do know, don't you, that we won't be able to take him inside the premises yet? Not until he's fully vaccinated.'

'Yes, I know, but he'll still be exposed to the smells, and he'll see a lot of people on the streets.'

'True. Where to first?'

'Let's walk down High Street, then go on over to the park.'

'Okay.'

It was pleasant to stroll around their hometown, window-shopping and people-watching. Simple pleasures that were taken for granted. Things Riordan rarely had time to enjoy with all his commitments. He had a lot of admiration for his father bringing up four children and putting in long hours at the medical centre. Riordan was still worried about Dan but had accepted that complete retirement wouldn't suit his father. Dan was taking fewer surgeries and cutting down on home visits. Zoe was doing them now.

They passed the chemist, and a florist. Another dog was coming in the opposite direction and Tom stood still and waited to see how his puppy would react. Solo merely looked at the dog, who paid him no attention whatsoever, then Solo tried to climb out of the carrier. Tom gently pushed him back.

'Is it good or bad that he didn't react to the other dog?' asked Tom.

Riordan said, 'I would say it's probably good. I think you'll be able to see how he reacts when he's had his jabs and can run around. For now you're just getting Solo used to things. You're his security and while you're holding him, he won't be concerned about very much I wouldn't imagine.'

'Okay.' Tom seemed satisfied, so they moved on.

They stopped outside The Sticky Bun, a popular café on High Street. Despite what he'd said to Tom, Riordan wondered if it would be okay if they went inside—he could have murdered a cup of tea. As they stood and pondered the question, a couple who were sitting inside at a table next to the window got up suddenly and hurried out onto the pavement.

'You were with the doctor who saved that boy's life, weren't you?' said the woman, waving a teacake.

'Umm … I'm not sure that …' Riordan was at a loss. How did these people know about the rescue? They were obviously referring to Casey. Riordan was alarmed to see the man taking a photo with his phone.

'Yes, you are, I recognise you from the picture. Where's the lady doctor?'

'What picture?'

'It was in *Leytonsfield Life*, the lady doctor was bent over the boy, saving him. You and your brother were there. Can I have a selfie?'

'No,' said Riordan, and belatedly added, 'And please don't take any photos.'

'Is that your son? Can I have a photo of the two of you together, then?'

'No, I'm sorry, we have to go. Come on, Tom.' He steered Tom away from the couple.

Tom said, 'They only wanted a photo, Dad, why didn't you let them have one?'

'Why? Because it's none of their business. They're the kind of people who slow down to gawp at accidents and hold up the emergency services.' Riordan had a feeling he might be over-reacting, but the incident had left him feeling uneasy.

'Dad? Why did they say that Zoe had saved the boy's life? It was you and Uncle Casey.'

'I don't know.' And he didn't really care. He felt unsettled by the whole thing and just wanted to forget it.

'Are you angry?'

'I'm a bit disturbed, Tom, rather than angry. I'd like to know how someone, whoever it was, managed to get a photo of it, and how it made its way into the magazine. Nobody spoke to any journalists as far as I'm aware.'

'Why are you disturbed?' Tom asked quietly.

How could Riordan explain to a child, who was one of the social media generation, that not everything should be shared with the whole world?

'Because that boy, Jimmy, nearly died. If that had been you, would you have wanted people staring at photos of you lying on the ground unconscious?'

'But you and Uncle Casey saved him. He should be grateful.'

'I'm sure he is, but I'm also sure he wouldn't want what he did to be made public knowledge.' Riordan was striding fast down High Street.

'I think it's too late, Dad,' said Tom, almost running to keep up with him. 'Slow down, please?'

'Sorry.'

Riordan thought about that day. All the people on the walk had mobile phones, and some of the older generation carried cameras as well. It could have been any of them.

'It's okay, Solo, we're okay now.' Tom spoke quietly to his puppy.

'Tom, did you notice anyone taking close-ups of the rescue?'

'No.'

'Was no one taking pictures at all?'

'I don't know, I was too busy watching you save that boy's life.'

They had reached the end of High Street and turned towards the park. Tom was looking subdued and walking with his head down. Riordan put a hand on Tom's shoulder, and he looked up. Tom smiled sweetly and Riordan's bad mood changed in an instant. This was Tom's day and he wasn't going to ruin it for him.

When they reached the duck pond, Tom seemed to have perked up a bit and was talking to Solo again, showing him the mallards and swans. They stood together watching the water, and Riordan felt his breathing slow and his pulse rate return to normal. No point getting wound up about a couple of rude people and their damned selfies. No real harm done.

'Cooee,' said a woman, hurrying towards him. 'I just wanted to say how wonderful it was of you all, saving that boy. I've been a patient of your father's for years, so it doesn't surprise me that he has such talented sons. He must be so proud of you. And the woman. She brought him back to life, didn't she? It was a miracle.'

Another woman hurried after the first and they both stood in front of Riordan and Tom, gazing with rapturous expressions on their faces. Tom was smiling at the women, clearly delighted with all the praise.

'And this is your boy, isn't it? He looks just like you. What do you think of your father?'

'I think he's a hero,' said Tom with no hesitation. 'And my Uncle Casey. They're both doctors and save people's lives all the time.'

'And the female doctor,' said the second woman. Riordan realised she was clutching a copy of *Leytonsfield Life*.

Riordan said, 'Do you mind if I take a look? I haven't seen the article yet.'

'No, of course, please help yourself.'

Riordan nearly swore when he saw the two-page spread and the number of photos. He speed-read the article, then he handed the magazine back to the woman with a nod of thanks.

'Come on, Tom, we're going home.'

'Okay.'

The day was over, spoilt because of some thoughtless person's actions.

'Byee …' called the women, but neither he nor Tom turned around.

They walked home silently, Riordan deep in thought. Tom slouched as he walked along, staring at the pavement. Even Solo seemed quieter than normal.

When they arrived home, Eloise was sitting at the kitchen table with a copy of *Leytonsfield Life* open before her. She looked up as they came in.

'Have you seen this, Riordan?'

'Just now.'

'Who in the name of all that's holy would have sent these photos in? It has to be someone in the walking group, doesn't it?'

'That's what I thought at first. But those pictures were all taken from the bridge. Look at the angle.' Riordan stood at his mother's shoulder and pointed at the photos.

'Yes, I see what you mean.'

'And the central figure in each photo isn't the boy, or Casey and I …'

'It's Zoe,' exclaimed Eloise. 'But she didn't do any CPR did she?'

'No. Casey dragged him out of the water, and I did the CPR. Zoe phoned the ambulance. She was ready, of course, to take over, but it wasn't necessary.'

Tom lifted Solo out of his carrier. The puppy stretched his back legs and pottered happily to his food bowl. Tom sat at the kitchen table, opposite his grandmother and father and looked at the newspaper upside down.

Riordan said, 'Tom, did you see anyone on the bridge?'

'Not really. I was watching the action and trying to keep people from crowding around like you asked. When the ambulance came people were watching.'

'From the bridge?' Riordan frowned, wishing he had paid more attention to the onlookers.

Tom nodded.

'Who, Tom? Did you recognise anyone?'

'Just people. There was a man.' Tom stopped as if he was bored with the conversation and got up to find Solo.

'What man, Tom? This is important.'

'Aren't you pleased that your photo's in the paper?' Tom asked.

'No, I'm not. It's an invasion of privacy and whoever took those photos, sold them to a newspaper. They had no right to do that.'

Eloise said, 'They should have asked permission first, Tom. It's a bit like stealing. Taking something that isn't yours.'

Tom sighed and shook his head. 'But what about Instagram and Facebook. People put pictures there all the time.'

Riordan sat down and gestured for Tom to do the same.

'One of the biggest problems with social media is that it is no respecter of privacy.' He didn't mention all the other things about it he hated, as this wasn't the time. He needed to make Tom understand. 'Doctors have a duty of care to their patients. When they come to us, they expect complete confidentiality, and that we will never discuss their condition or concerns with anyone else without their permission.'

'But that boy wasn't your patient, Dad.'

'As soon as we stepped in to help him, he became our patient. He was in our care and that means we must do certain things. Whether we treat people in the hospital, surgery, or outside on the bank of a canal, if we are helping that patient in any way, we are responsible for their welfare. Do you understand?'

Tom nodded, but still looked doubtful. 'I liked it when the women in the park treated you like a superhero.'

'I'm not a superhero, Tom. I'm just a doctor.'

Eloise got up and filled the kettle, then set about putting mugs out and a plate of biscuits. Riordan was parched and Tom was still looking sheepish. This was their weekend together, and it hadn't got off to a good start.

Tom said, 'I'm proud of you, Dad, and Uncle Casey. You save people's lives every day, but nobody ever says thank you or well done. I wish everyone knew what you'd done for Jimmy. He would have died, if you hadn't been there.'

Riordan swallowed. It felt as if he had a rock in his throat. His eyes watered and Riordan rubbed them with the heels of his palms. Sometimes things Tom said caught him unawares.

Eloise said, 'That's a lovely thing to say, Tom, we're all proud of your father and Uncle Casey for what they did.' She poured the tea, making Tom's milky, and put the mugs on the table with the plate of biscuits.

Riordan wasn't good at taking compliments and changed the subject. 'That man on the bridge? What did he look like?'

'He was tall, with curly hair. He waved at me.'

'Did you wave back?' asked Eloise.

'Yes. Was that wrong?'

Riordan said, 'No, Tom, you haven't done anything wrong.'

As he sipped his tea, Riordan pondered. He only knew one man who fitted that description. Toby Dean.

Chapter Twenty-Nine

Riordan and Tom waited for the train from Manchester to arrive carrying their special guest for Easter weekend. It was Saturday and the warm weather had enticed visitors to Leytonsfield. The train looked packed when it drew into the station.

'I bet I spot her first,' said Tom.

'I bet I do.'

'What do you bet me?' Tom loved a challenge, and Riordan was happy to oblige.

'If you win, I'll let you stay up an hour later tonight.'

'Wicked!'

'But if I win, you go to bed an hour earlier.'

'Aww ...' Tom's face was a picture of indecision. 'Oh, okay then.'

Riordan smiled at the focused concentration with which Tom watched the doors open and the passengers spill out.

Riordan knew that Martha always travelled in the carriage nearest to the front and was usually one of the last out allowing everyone else to leave first. Sure enough, there she was, right at the front. Tom hadn't spotted her, so Riordan said nothing. He wanted Tom to win—he was going to let him stay up anyway. Tom loved Martha, and Riordan knew that his son missed having a mother figure in his life.

'There she is!' shouted Tom.

'Well done.'

'I won,' Tom said to Martha as she approached.

'What did you win, my love?' Martha enveloped Tom in a hug and stroked his hair.

'I saw you first, so Dad's letting me stay up.'

'In your honour, of course,' Riordan said, opening his arms for a hug. He held Martha tightly. 'I'll get your bag.'

'I'm perfectly capable of pulling a suitcase on wheels, but on this occasion, I'll let you play the gentleman so I can walk with this handsome young man.' Martha and Tom walked ahead with their arms around each other's waists.

'Am I handsome?' asked Tom, grinning.

'Of course you are, you take after your father.'

'Flatterer,' Riordan called.

As the three of them strolled to the car, Tom talked ten to the dozen about Solo and the rescue, and how his dad and uncle were heroes. Martha looked over her shoulder at Riordan.

'I can see I've got a lot to catch up on with you lot. I've been away too long, obviously.'

Tom said, 'This time you're staying for a long time though, aren't you, Aunt Martha?'

'I'll stay until you get sick of me and throw me out.'

'Great! Then you'll be staying forever.'

Riordan said nothing. Tom had echoed Riordan's innermost feelings. There was nothing he would have loved more than to have his closest friend nearby. Especially now, with a relationship with Zoe on the horizon. He needed Martha's support and good sense more than ever.

*

Riordan realised the only way to get Martha on her own was by going to the pub for a few drinks.

The evening meal was Martha's chance to catch up with Riordan's parents and she regaled them with stories of foreign lands, playing down the horrors she must have seen, because Tom was listening intently.

Martha had finally said, 'So, you lot have had exciting times. I've heard about rescued puppies and children plucked from the brink.'

Dan said, amused, 'Martha, you don't need to go abroad for excitement and drama. You get plenty of that in Leytonsfield.'

'So I see. And Zoe is your new locum, is that right?'

'And Dad's girlfriend,' said Tom.

Martha looked at Riordan. 'Girlfriend? Splendid. You must introduce me.'

Riordan thought he detected a guarded tone in Martha's voice. Martha was the one who suggested dating again, but perhaps she was remembering how unfriendly Sally had been.

He said, 'She's not really my girlfriend.'

Tom said, 'You spent Valentine's Day with her, Dad.'

Riordan told Martha, 'We took the kids to the cinema, so the rest of them could have time with their significant others.'

'And you took her to Rocco's, Dad.'

'Tom, why don't you concentrate on eating your lasagna and leave the gossiping to the adults?' said Riordan, taking a drink of water. This conversation was getting out of hand. He wanted to talk to Martha about Zoe when they were alone.

'Sorry it's only lasagna,' said Eloise. 'We're having a proper Sunday roast tomorrow. You'll meet Zoe then, she's spending the day with us.'

'We're going to hide the eggs in the garden so Jade can find them. I'll just pretend to look but let her have most of them.' Tom said, forking some lasagna in his mouth.

Martha said, 'That's kind of you, Tom. You're quite the young man now. So grown up.'

'Yes,' said Eloise. 'They grow up so fast.'

'You'll soon have another baby in the family though, won't you? With Casey and Lexi's new arrival?'

'Yes, she's due in July. Casey is so excited,' said Eloise.

'I bet.'

Riordan studied Martha's expression. She smiled and said all the right words, but Riordan couldn't help wondering if Martha ever felt the urge to be a mother. She'd make a good one with her kindness and endless patience. And Martha was so good with kids. Tom adored her.

Martha caught his eye and Riordan smiled, saying, 'It's good to have you here.'

'And it's good to be here, Riordan. And this lasagna, Eloise, is delicious.'

*

'How are you? Really, I mean. I know you'll say you're fine; I know you too well, Riordan, but I want the truth. How are you really?'

They were sitting in a corner of the Dog and Partridge. Riordan had his back to the pub. It was early and relatively quiet. He studied Martha's face.

'D'you know, I was just about to ask you the very same question. I was thinking at dinner that you keep your feelings well hidden. You always have, Martha. So, tell me how *you* really are first.'

He picked up his half of bitter and Martha did the same. She loved her beer and never drank any other alcohol, to Riordan's knowledge.

'I'm the same as I always am, Riordan. Nothing has changed.'

She did look the same, it was true. She wore chinos, brown lace-up shoes and a man's shirt with the sleeves rolled up to the elbows. Her hair was cut in a short style that suited the salt and pepper colour—although there seemed to be more salt than pepper since last time.

'Okay, if you say so.'

'Tell me what's bothering *you*—something definitely is.'

He took another pull on his beer.

'Someone sent photos of Casey and I doing CPR on Jimmy, the boy who fell in the canal, to a journalist. They ended up in a double page spread in *Leytonsfield Life*.'

'And you have no idea who it was?'

'I have my suspicions but no proof.'

Martha was quiet for a while, mulling it over. 'Have you asked them about it? Given them the chance to explain?' Martha would always give someone the benefit of the doubt.

'No. He's not someone I want to speak to if I'm honest.'

'Intriguing. Do I know him?'

'Yes.' Riordan glanced at Martha's face. She would never ask him outright, but he needed her common sense advice. 'It's Toby Dean.'

Martha's eyes widened in astonishment. 'I'm amazed. Why would he do such a thing?'

'Because Zoe likes him, and he likes her. Too much. He was the vet that treated Luna and spent all night at Rosemary Cottage when Luna had her puppies. I think they've been on a date or two.'

'So, when Tom said Zoe was your girlfriend…?'

'It was a bit of an exaggeration. We have… well, spent time together, quality time, but only the once.' Riordan

glanced up to see Martha's reaction to his coyness. She probably preferred him to come straight out with it and say they
had sex.

'I see,' she said. Martha sipped her beer and looked
thoughtful. 'Why would Toby take photos of something that
is clearly none of his business and sell them?'

'I've no idea. Except...'

'Except?'

'Toby Dean was infatuated with Sally. I think he's becoming infatuated with Zoe. Perhaps he's stalking her.'

'What does Zoe say about it all?'

'I haven't had the chance to speak to her.'

'Perhaps you should. Does Zoe know about Sally?'

Riordan sighed and stared into space. 'Not everything, but
enough. She knows why I loathe the vet.' Sometimes Riordan
couldn't bear to say his name, his hatred was so strong.

'After all this time?' Martha's voice was gentle with no
condemnation.

'I'm afraid so. I'm not proud of the way I feel, but there it
is.'

'You could try phoning the paper and asking who sent the
photos in. They might not tell you, of course, but considering
you were in the photos they might be more inclined to coop-
erate. And if not, you could always threaten to take them to
court.'

'Good thinking, I'll do that.' Riordan drank some beer.
Why hadn't he thought of that? Too busy feeling hard done
by.

'And what about the boy's parents? I'm sure they must have an opinion. If it was my child being photographed in such a situation, I'd be furious.'

'As would I.' Riordan was feeling better already. He knew Martha would think of the most logical solution.

'Of course, the family might welcome the publicity. People love their three minutes of fame. It's a different generation, Riordan. Everything is photographed and uploaded to some site or another. People think they have the right to know the ins and outs of a duck's arse.'

Riordan grinned. He had always been amused by Martha's tendency to resort to vulgarity. The first time she had done it, he'd laughed so loudly that everyone had turned around and stared at them. He was used to it now, but it still made him smile.

'What are your plans for the long-term, Martha?'

'In what way?'

'How long are you planning to work for *Médecin Sans Frontières*?'

'For as long as I can. I have no plans to stop anytime soon, if that's what you mean. I love the work. I couldn't imagine working in the NHS with all the frustrations you have to put up with. No offence.'

'None taken. I suppose I'm thinking of the future. When you retire, what will you do with yourself?'

'Because I've never had kids, you mean?'

'Well, yes. Kids and a spouse. I know plenty of people never have children and are completely happy, but since Sally died, Tom has been the reason I get up in the morning. He means the world to me.'

Martha asked, 'Does he get on with Zoe?'

Riordan smiled. 'He gets on really well with her. They talk together about all kinds of subjects. They're great friends.'

Martha downed the rest of her beer. 'I can't wait to meet her. My round, same again?'

'Yes, thanks.'

Riordan wondered how to broach the subject of Joe Moreton. Martha knew everything about Riordan's sessions with Joe; he had never kept any aspect of his life from Martha. But talking about Zoe's treatment would be breaking a confidence. Zoe had promised to tell Riordan when she was ready, and he should respect that.

'There you are,' said Martha, placing half a bitter in front of him.

'Thanks. Cheers.'

'Cheers.' They clinked their glasses together and Martha sat back with a sigh. 'Did I never mention to you that I can't have children of my own? I've got endometriosis, I'm afraid.'

Riordan nearly choked on his beer. 'No, you never did. Oh my God, Martha, I'm so sorry. And here I am wittering on about kids. You must think I'm so insensitive.'

'I don't think anything of the kind. I've known you a long time, Riordan, and I know that you are a sensitive man. If I didn't tell you, how could you know? I thought I had, that's all. Now you understand why kids are not in the equation for me.'

'But there's adoption?'

'Do you know, I meet orphans on a daily basis when I'm in the Yemen, Somalia and places like that. If I dwelt on the thought of adoption, I could fill the Albert Hall with kids. No, it's better that I focus my energies on what I do best, and that's being a doctor.'

'And a wonderful aunt to Tom, and loads of other kids, I should imagine.'

'Well, yes, there is that,' she said. 'But as far as any spouse is concerned, I've got someone who is the closest I'll ever get to that.'

'Oh? Who?'

'His name is Peter, and we work together. He's a widower with three grown-up children, and we're good for each other.'

Riordan hid a sigh of relief. 'That's wonderful! I'm so glad you've got someone. I don't have to think of you on your own now. When are we going to meet him?'

'Well, I'll have to ask him. We don't have much luck with coordinating our time off, but the next time we manage it, I'll bring him to Leytonsfield.'

'Good, I can't wait to meet him.'

They sat in silence for a while, Riordan thinking how sad it was that Martha would never have her own children, but thankful someone in Martha's life shared her work—which was her passion.

'I'm so glad you're here,' he said quietly.

She smiled and her eyes sparkled. 'So you said before. So am I, Riordan, so am I.'

*

Zoe couldn't decide on what to wear to the O'Connor's for Sunday lunch. The famous and oh-so-perfect Martha would be there, and Zoe didn't want to show up dressed formally and discovering everyone else casual or, even worse, walking in looking like a bag lady and being introduced to a very glamorous Martha who Riordan was secretly in love with. Zoe was feeling a bit insecure, which wasn't like her—usually she was happy in her own skin and didn't feel the need to compete with anyone. But Martha had been talked about in such glowing terms by both Riordan and Tom.

Okay, then she would just be herself and Martha would have to like it or lump it. Zoe suspected she was being childish and needed to snap out of it. Besides, Martha would go back overseas eventually and be out of the picture.

Zoe chose smart casual in the end. A pair of black trousers, black ankle boots, and a white T-shirt with a long pale-blue cardigan. With a silver pendant and silver drop earrings, and minimal make-up, she was ready.

She put the harness on Luna. Luna would be reunited with two offspring and it would be interesting to see how they all reacted to each other. Zoe put the bag of Easter eggs for Tom and Jade on the back seat and drove the short distance to the O'Connor's.

When Zoe arrived, she followed the noise of laughter and excited children's voices around the side of the house to the garden to where they were all watching Jade hunt for the hidden eggs. Tom was helping her.

No one noticed Zoe at first, and then Eloise came out of the kitchen.

'Zoe! How lovely, you've just arrived at the right time. Jade is on the hunt! Come and meet Martha.'

A woman came forward at the sound of her name and put her hand out to Zoe. She had a warm, wide smile and twinkling blue eyes, a firm handshake, and a slightly gruff voice.

'Zoe, I'm so pleased to meet you. You've certainly made an impression on the O'Connors; I've been hearing all about you and your rescued dog. Is this her? Hello, girl.' Martha knelt and made a fuss of Luna, who stood on her hind legs and put her front paws on Martha's thighs. She'd never done that to anyone else and Zoe was astonished and pleased. If Luna liked Martha, then she must be okay.

'Hi, Martha, I've been hearing all about you too.'

Martha straightened up and smiled. 'Well, maybe we should go somewhere together for a drink or two, and we can compare notes.'

'I think that's a great idea,' Zoe said. *Why on earth had she been worried about meeting this lovely lady?*

'What's a great idea?' asked Riordan. He put his arm around Zoe's shoulders and kissed her on the cheek.

'Martha and I are going to have a drink together and talk about you,' said Zoe.

'God help me,' he said, then turned as Jade squealed with delight. Luna and the pups were together in the middle of the lawn. There was plenty of sniffing going on and all three tails were wagging so hard, they were just a blur.

'Oh, how lovely, a family reunion,' said Martha. 'Dogs are so wonderful, aren't they? What a touching scene.'

Zoe glanced at Riordan watching her. He bent and kissed Zoe gently on the lips. 'Talking of family reunions, how did yours go?'

'It went well. Jo is pregnant again, due in August. We had the usual family meal in the restaurant. Everyone is fine.'

'And how did you feel coming back to Leytonsfield? Happy to come back, or did you want to stay in Manchester?'

'Well, I was happy to come back, of course. After all, I've got a lot to come back for now, haven't I?'

Chapter Thirty

Zoe was determined that her birthday party was going to be a roaring success. All the Angelos and O'Connors would be mingling in the cottage, and the combination of Greek and Irish influences meant that some serious partying was in store.

She had booked caterers who would provide a mixture of Greek and English food. Lots of sausage rolls and smoked salmon for those who weren't keen on trying something different. Her favourite Greek food would be included, of course; Souvlakia Arnisia, (lamb kebab), Keftethakia (meatballs), and Spanakotyropita (spinach pie with feta cheese). There would be plenty of salads and fruit, as well as desserts such as Baklava and Pavlova. Something for everyone.

Usually, thinking about her favourite food made Zoe's mouth water, but for the last few days she had been feeling slightly queasy and wondered if she was coming down with something. Zoe had seen so many patients in surgery, and home visits, all with symptoms of a form of gastritis, it wouldn't be at all a surprise to have picked something up. Luckily, they recovered quickly, so Zoe should be alright for the party the following day.

Dan had been very understanding and allowed Zoe to have Friday off. As everyone else was at work, Martha offered to come and help, and Zoe was delighted. She had grown fond of Martha in the short time they'd known each other. Zoe secretly called her Earth Mother. Martha had a kind word for everyone she met, and people were drawn like moths to a flame. Martha always knew exactly what to say in every situation, and Zoe understood why Riordan loved her so much.

They hadn't managed to get away to the pub together, so Zoe was determined to use the time alone with Martha to find out more about Sally, and what Riordan was like as a student. Zoe's guess was the same—only younger; studious, serious and still shy.

Martha was busy pushing the furniture to the edges of the living room and putting throws on the sofa and armchairs for protection. Zoe had a small stepladder against the wall and was trying to hang a banner that said, "Let's Celebrate!". As Zoe stretched to fix the top corner into the wall, she suddenly felt dizzy and swayed on the ladder. She grabbed hold of the top of it and held on tightly. Straight away, Martha was beside her, helping Zoe down the steps and to the sofa.

'Sit down, my love, and put your head between your knees. Do you want a glass of water?'

'Yes, please,' Zoe muttered, and closed her eyes. She felt Luna's wet nose pushing into her hands. She raised her head slightly and gazed into Luna's dark brown eyes. 'It's okay, don't worry.' Luna wagged her tail.

'There you are,' said Martha, handing over a glass with cold water.

Zoe took a sip, the coolness of the water refreshing.

'Zoe, how are you feeling now?'

'Better. Thanks, Martha. I think I've caught something from a patient, I've been feeling a bit groggy for days. I shouldn't have gone up the ladder.'

'Don't worry, I'll finish the banner.'

'I'll do it, when I've rested.'

'No, you won't. You stay on *terra firma*, we don't want any broken bones. What other symptoms do you have?'

'Well, I've gone right off coffee—and I'm a dedicated espresso drinker.'

'Do you feel tired? Nauseous?'

'Yes, a bit. I've had cramping pains in my stomach. So, it's either gastric or menorrhagic, wouldn't you say?' Zoe smiled and waited for Martha to smile too and agree. But Martha didn't. She was looking at Zoe, deep in thought.

'What is it, Martha? You're starting to worry me with that look.'

'When did you last have a period?'

'What? Well, I had a bit of one a couple of weeks ago, but nothing like I normally have. I just put it down to stress. Life's been quite eventful since I came to Leytonsfield. And to think I came here for a quiet life.' She laughed and expected Martha to join in. Again, Martha's expression was serious.

'There is a third possible reason for your symptoms, Zoe. Dizzy, nauseous, tired, gone off coffee…?'

As Martha listed the classic symptoms of pregnancy, Zoe felt cold all over, as if someone was pouring iced water down her back.

'No … no, absolutely not, it's impossible, I can't be pregnant. We used protection. Riordan was so careful.'

'It's not one hundred percent proof, no matter how careful you are. It's just a thought, Zoe, that's all. And of course, there's a very quick and easy way to find out. Buy a kit from the chemist. Do you want me to nip out and get one?'

'No!' Zoe didn't mean to shout, but the idea of being pregnant was scaring her senseless. *It can't be true.* 'Sorry, but I really cannot get pregnant.'

'Would it be so bad?' Martha asked in a gentle voice. 'Forgive me for asking, but you and Riordan seem close, and you love Tom, don't you?'

'It's not about Riordan and Tom. It's *me*, I cannot risk having a baby—I just can't. I can't explain it, but take it from me, it's the worst thing that could happen.'

Martha was quiet, watching her. 'Can you keep tea down? It's the best thing to drink in a situation like this. I'll put the kettle on. If you want to talk, I'm here and I'm a good listener. If not, that's okay, we'll stick banners on the wall instead.'

With that Martha strolled out of the living room and Zoe listened for the sound of the kettle being filled, and mugs and teaspoons being made ready.

Zoe was shaking. She closed her eyes and took a deep breath to calm her nerves. *This couldn't be happening.* But Martha was right. The symptoms didn't add up to a stomach bug. Zoe knew the difference—she was a doctor, for good-ness' sake. And the spotting period was also indicative of pregnancy. Zoe had been through this before, she should have guessed.

Oh God, no! Please, no.

When Martha came back carrying a tray with the mugs, sugar and milk, Zoe was almost near to tears.

'Milk and sugar?'

'No, just black please.'

Martha put a mug in front of her and sat down.

'Zoe, sometimes it's good to talk about it. Maybe I can help.'

There was only one way to say it, so Zoe blurted it out.

'I lost a baby. His heart stopped beating at thirty-two weeks. His name was Samuel. It broke me, Martha. It was eighteen months ago, and I still feel the pain of having my heart ripped out—and my mother thinks I should be over it, and I know I never will, and the thought of going through it again is more than I can bear—and I can't, just *bloody can't*, be pregnant.'

Zoe started crying, heaving sobs that made her want to throw up. She felt Martha's arm around her. Zoe put her face into Martha's shoulder and cried as if she was a tiny child.

Martha held Zoe and rocked her, murmuring quietly until the sobs subsided.

'I'm so sorry,' Zoe finally managed to say. 'You didn't sign up for me blubbing all over you.'

'Don't be ridiculous.' Martha's voice was kind but held a hint of anger. 'Be anything you want, my love, but don't ever say you're sorry for mourning the loss of your child. You have nothing to be sorry for.'

They were silent for a while. Zoe wondered if she was destined to break down in front of strangers every time she had to tell them about Samuel—although the O'Connors were no longer strangers. Dan was very dear to her, as was Eloise. In the short time Zoe had known them they had shown Zoe nothing but kindness and understanding. And Martha, who Zoe was sure held feelings for Riordan that would never be expressed, was being the best kind of friend.

'Do you know why his heart stopped?' Martha asked.

'No, I refused a post mortem, which is the only way they could have had a definitive diagnosis. I couldn't bear my little boy being …'

'It's okay, you don't have to explain. I would have felt the same in your shoes.'

'I'm seeing a psychiatrist, the same one that Riordan saw when Sally died.'

'Oh yes, Joe Moreton. I've heard good things of him. Is he helping at all?'

'Yes, but he agrees that I will never get over the loss of Samuel. That isn't what I should be aiming for. Funny ... he mentioned me having another child.'

'But you're not ready?' Martha drained her cup. Zoe hadn't touched hers.

'Martha, I'll never be ready. The fear of it happening again is overwhelming.'

'Even though the chances are almost nil?'

'But are they?' Zoe reached for her tea and took a swallow, the strong tannin taste causing Zoe to gag. Another sign.

'There is nothing to say that, this time, you won't have a healthy baby.' Martha said gently. 'If you want to tell me more about it, I'm happy to listen.'

Zoe sipped her tea, then shuddered, putting the mug back on the table.

She said, 'I'll never forget the moment I found out. I'd gone for my routine appointment. I knew something was wrong when the midwife had to get a second opinion, but even then, I wasn't concerned. I thought she may have been inexperienced, or the machine was faulty, but then ... then they called in the obstetrician and I had to have a scan. I think I knew then, but even so, something in my brain refused to accept it and I was making jokes and trying to make light of it. I should have realised, but it wasn't until the doctor said, "I'm sorry, but your baby has died," that I had no choice but to accept it. It was like being punched. I was in despair. I'll never forget that feeling. Never. I just wanted someone to make it better.'

Martha had her arms around Zoe again and was listening intently. 'What about the father?'

'He was on duty, so I couldn't ring him. I rang my Dad. He came straight away, and I broke down. He took me home and cared for me like he used to do when I was a child. Tucked me up in bed. The next day, we went back to the hospital. Me and Andy. Andy stayed for ten minutes, then said he had to get back to work. He was a police officer. He never wanted Samuel in the first place. The hardest part was knowing I was giving birth to a dead baby. I wanted to mourn, and I had to stay on the maternity ward with all the other mothers and wait to give birth like everyone else ... although Samuel was gone.'

'That must have been awful,' said Martha.

'It was. But the worst part was three days after giving birth ... talking to the undertaker about what coffin I wanted, and to the vicar about his funeral. I didn't want a *coffin*, I just wanted my baby to be alive and well.' Zoe brushed the tears away and swallowed, trying to fight the grief swamping her yet again.

She went on, 'In the hospital, the nurses had a room for me to be with him. Take pictures and hold him. I wanted to stay in that room forever, just me and Samuel, and not have to face the world, family, friends, strangers, all wanting to know what happened. One minute I was about to give birth, the next ...'

Zoe put her head in her hands and fought to stop the tears flowing, but they came anyway, coursing down her cheeks and falling onto Luna's fur who'd laid her head on Zoe's lap. Martha said nothing, holding Zoe while she cried and cried.

Eventually, as always, the tears ended again, and Zoe looked up to see what devastation had been wrought by her endless heartache. She found both Martha and Luna gazing at her with concern and love. It almost made her break out in tears again.

'When will I be able to think about all this without crying, Martha?'

'I don't know the answer to that, my love, but when you can, you'll have turned a corner and you'll be able to move ahead. Until that time, you cry as much as you need to.'

Chapter Thirty-One

Martha offered to finish decorating the living room while Zoe made a quick meal to keep them going. She whipped up a Bolognese sauce and cooked some pasta. There was ice-cream for dessert.

She wandered into the living room to tell Martha that it was nearly ready and gasped when she saw the transformation. There were three banners saying; "Let's Celebrate!", "Happy Birthday", and "Party Time!". Balloons saying "Happy Birthday" filled with helium were suspended in mid-air with strings dangling. The kids would love playing with those. The floor in the centre of the room had been cleared and even Luna wore colourful ribbons wrapped around her collar.

'Wow! Who bought all this?'

'Riordan mostly, and I bought some of it.'

Zoe felt ashamed that all she had contributed was one banner. And it was *her* party. Trust the O'Connors to come to the rescue.

'I just came in to see if you wanted wine with the meal.'

'Oh no, water will do just fine.' Martha climbed down from the ladder and followed Zoe into the kitchen. 'Can I wash my hands in the sink?'

'Of course.'

When they were both seated, Zoe realised she felt hungry for the first time in a couple of days. Maybe she wasn't pregnant at all and had gone through all that anguish for nothing.

'This is lovely,' said Martha, expertly winding spaghetti around her fork.

'Thanks. Not as good as Eloise's but still edible.'

'Something I've learned the hard way is to never compare yourself to anyone else. There will always be someone who does something better than you, but equally plenty who wouldn't know where to start. I've always taken that to heart. Just be the best version of yourself, that's all you can do.'

'You've known Riordan a long time, I believe?'

Martha nodded. 'Since medical school. Both of us were nerds, shy, introverted. We played chess together while the rest of the students went out and got stinking drunk.'

Zoe smiled. 'I got pretty drunk in medical school too, if I remember. So, I'm curious about Sally. From what Riordan says, she was an extrovert and loved dangerous sports. What was the attraction?'

Martha stopped eating and stared into space. 'To be honest, Zoe, I've no idea. I never understood it. Sally was the outdoor type; you know, rosy cheeks, fit and strong—well, you have to be quite strong to be a successful physiotherapist—she spent hours in the gym, ran marathons, swam, lifted weights.'

'Stop, you're making me feel inadequate.' Zoe laughed, and remembered what Martha had just said about not comparing yourself to others.

'Truly, Zoe? Would you really want to be someone like her?'

'No, not at all. Good luck to the people who are, but you don't need to put yourself through all that to be fit and healthy. My little group of patients who are doing line dancing and walking regularly are a good example. They have all lost weight, are happier and getting out and about meeting people.'

'Well, there you are then, that's a real success story. Riordan was telling me how much he enjoys the line dancing.'

'Why don't you join us, if you're going to be around for a while? I'd love you to be there and so would Riordan.'

'Thanks, Zoe. Yes, I will join in. Why not?'

'Excellent. How about some ice-cream?'

'Just a small one.'

While Zoe served vanilla ice-cream with chocolate fudge sauce, she thought further about Sally.

'Martha, I know I probably shouldn't be asking these questions, but Sally intrigues me. What did Riordan see in her?'

'I don't know, but I don't think he was using his head. He fell madly in love. Besotted, in my opinion. She was his first love and Riordan became a bit obsessed. I tried to warn him to take his time and not do anything foolish, but he didn't listen. All I could do was wait in the wings and pick up the pieces when it all went pear-shaped. I never dreamt though that she'd die. It was a tragedy, she was so young.'

Zoe was silent while she ate her ice-cream.

'You're very fond of Riordan, aren't you?'

'He's a very close friend. He's my only tie with university days. I'm not the kind of person to make friends easily, I'm too self-sufficient. I prefer my own company to others, but the O'Connors have always treated me like family. They are very special people.'

'What about your own family?'

'I don't have any now. I'm an only child of only children. Both my parents are dead.'

'I'm sorry.'

'It's probably for the best. Doing the job I do means I don't come back to England for months at a time. I'm free to go wherever I need to without worrying about the folks back home. Which is why I value Riordan's friendship. I care about him very much, Zoe, but if you're asking if I've ever had romantic feelings for him, the answer is no. I love him like the brother I never had.'

Zoe nodded. Martha was astute in wondering if that was really what Zoe was asking.

'Would you like coffee?'

'No, thank you. I think I'd better go now, I've promised Tom I'd play chess with him. Riordan is on a late shift. But, Zoe, please get a pregnancy kit and make absolutely sure, will you?'

'Yes, I promise. And thanks for all your help today. It'll be good tomorrow, I'm looking forward to seeing the two families relaxed and enjoying themselves.'

'One more thing. Tell Riordan what you've told me— about Samuel. He needs to know.'

'Okay, I will.'

Zoe had already promised that after all.

*

Zoe had tried to keep busy after Martha left, to avoid thinking of whether or not she was pregnant. After tidying the kitchen and living room, she fed Luna and let her out in the garden. Then Zoe sat on the sofa and gazed at the living room, hoping the party was a success. She yawned. She was just thinking of a soak in a hot bubble bath before bed when the doorbell chimed.

Luna immediately started barking and ran to the front door.

'Okay, Luna, let's see who it is.' Her money was on Riordan, calling in on his way home from the hospital. Zoe flung the door open with a cheery greeting on her lips.

'Hi! Oh … it's you.'

Toby said, 'I didn't expect to be welcomed with open arms, but …' He bent down to fuss Luna, who was wagging her tail as if he was a long-lost lover. 'Well at least Luna's pleased to see me. Hey, girl?'

'Sorry, Toby, I wasn't expecting you, that's all.'

'I've brought you a present. It is your birthday, isn't it?'

'Yes, tomorrow. Come in.'

'Thanks.'

'Would you like a coffee?'

'Only if you're having one.'

'I'm not, but I'll make you one.' Zoe busied herself making a cappuccino while Toby wandered into the living room.

'Wow! Someone's having herself a party.'

Zoe wondered if this meant she had to invite Toby. He'd be upset at not being invited, but Riordan would be livid when he found out. Zoe was caught between a rock and a hard place. She finished the coffee with chocolate sprinkles and took it into the living room.

'Yes, my family are all descending on Leytonsfield tomorrow morning, but they're staying in the hotel. There are too many of them for me to put them all up.'

'Thanks,' he said as he took the coffee. 'Sounds like you're in for a good time.' He took something out of his jacket pocket. 'Here's your present. It's not much, but I thought of you when I saw it.'

He handed her a small carrier bag which had the name of Leytonsfield's most expensive jeweller on the side. When

Zoe peeped inside, there was a silver box. She glanced up at Toby, watching her with a smile. He still hadn't drunk any of the coffee.

'I hope this didn't cost you a lot of money.' She took the box out of the bag.

'You're worth it,' he said, and Zoe shivered. To think she had once found this man intensely attractive. All Zoe felt now was uneasy in his company.

The box contained a silver pendant on a silver chain. 'Oh, it's beautiful, Toby, but you really shouldn't have spent your money on me.'

'Here, let me put it on you.' He put the coffee on a table then took the chain off Zoe. Toby's fingers brushed the skin on Zoe's neck as he lifted her hair out of the way, before fastening the chain. She shivered again, this time feeling it from her neck to her toes. Zoe tried to move away, but Toby kept his hands on her shoulders for a second longer than needed, before letting go.

Zoe fingered the pendant nervously. 'It's lovely, but you really shouldn't.'

'I'll be the judge of that. So, am I invited to the party?'

'Yes, of course.' *Why did she say that?* Zoe couldn't think up an excuse quickly enough.

'Great, do you need any help setting things up?'

'Oh no, thanks. The caterers will be here in the morning. The party starts about three for the kids, then will go on into the wee small hours. My family's like that.' She hoped Toby would take the hint about it being just a family get-together.

'I'll leave you in peace and see you tomorrow then.'

'Okay. Thanks again for the present.'

'You're welcome.' Then Toby added meaningfully, 'I meant what I said. I'm not giving up, Zoe. Good night.'

When he'd gone, Zoe locked the door and made sure the safety chain was secured. Then she sat on the sofa and cuddled Luna until her heart rate returned to normal.

Chapter Thirty-Two

Martha and the caterers, a local company called "Out to Lunch", turned up at the cottage at the same time, so Zoe and Martha helped carry the platters and plates from the back of the van through to the kitchen. The aroma of the delicious food made Zoe's stomach rumble. She had only eaten toast for breakfast to avoid the risk of feeling nauseous before the party had even started.

'Here,' said Martha, pushing a brown paper bag into Zoe's hands. 'I didn't think you'd have time to get one for yourself.'

Zoe sighed. She didn't need to look inside to know it was a pregnancy kit. Martha was the sensible one. Zoe didn't imagine Martha had ever been in denial about anything in her life. 'Thanks, I'll do it later.'

Martha gave her a look and nodded.

Zoe went upstairs and stuffed the bag into the drawer of the bedside table. She wasn't going to even *think* about it until the party was over. She was feeling fine now and it could all have been a false alarm. Zoe was determined to enjoy today. It wasn't often that all the people she cared about most in the world were under one roof.

With that thought, Zoe heard a car door slam. Looking out the bedroom window, she saw her parents alighting from their Volvo. Then behind them, Markos and his people-carrier arrived. Zoe hurried down the stairs to meet and greet.

After everyone had taken a good look round the cottage, the O'Connors arrived *en masse*, shortly followed by Bilal and his wife, then Louise, Imelda and Clara.

The next half an hour was taken up with introductions and pouring drinks. Someone put some music on, and the children were all out in the garden playing with the dogs. As usual, people gravitated towards others they thought they would have something in common with. Eloise was doing her best to chat to her mother who, surprisingly, was responding, while her father and Dan were talking about golf. Zoe looked around for Riordan and saw him at the other end of the room with Martha. Time to check on the caterers.

'Hi, Lainey, the food smells wonderful.'

'Thanks. Just let me know when you want us to serve.'

'Oh, I was going to let people help themselves, like a buffet.'

Lainey looked sceptical. 'There's a lot of you and a tiny kitchen. How about letting us take the food around?'

'Okay, you know what you're doing. I'll leave it to you.'

'Great. By the way, I love your dogs. I've got a dog too; a big daft thing. I love him to bits.'

Zoe didn't notice Toby arrive until he put one arm around her shoulders and the other around Lainey.

'Well, Lainey Jordan, as I live and breathe, and the good Dr Angelos.'

Zoe smelt alcohol on Toby's breath and wondered if he was drunk.

'You won't be breathing for very much longer if you don't get off me, you big lummox,' said Lainey. She was laughing, but Zoe sensed that Lainey wasn't comfortable.

'Ah,' said Toby, putting both hands over his heart. 'How many times can my poor heart be broken like this?'

'You're a daft sod,' said Lainey. She turned back to Zoe. 'I'll go and sort out the food. In about half an hour?'

'Perfect,' said Zoe.

Toby stared at Zoe's breasts, then his gaze slid to her face. 'You're not wearing the pendant. I'm gutted.'

'I, um... I didn't want it to get lost. It's lovely though, thank you.' Zoe hoped that Toby wasn't going to make a big thing of it, but he simply shrugged. Then Zoe noticed Melissa standing uncertainly behind him.

'Hi Melissa, what can I get you to drink?'

'Red wine would be great.'

'Toby?'

'Beer please, gorgeous. I'm just going outside to talk to the dogs. At least *they* like me.'

She poured wine for Melissa and handed it to her. Zoe felt a bit sorry for Melissa; she didn't know anyone at the party and Toby had just walked off and left her alone.

'Would you like me to introduce you to everyone?'

'Oh no, it's okay, I'll probably not remember their names anyway.'

'How are you liking Leytonsfield?'

'It's a bit quiet for my tastes, I'm used to London, but I'm sure it'll grow on me.'

'And your daughter?'

'Oh, she's in London with her father. I go back home every weekend that I'm not working. I'm on a late tomorrow, otherwise I would have gone home. I'm hoping my husband and daughter will join me soon. It gets a bit lonely on my own. Toby's been great.'

'Yes, I bet he has.'

Toby came back and put his arm around Melissa. 'Have you missed me, darling?'

Then they kissed. Zoe slunk away and retreated to the bathroom. *What the heck was going on with those two*? Melissa was married, openly admitted it, but was getting down and dirty with Toby Dean. Zoe wondered if TAO still existed and the two of them were part of the club. The whole thing was slightly sordid, especially in light of what Riordan had told Zoe.

The party had been in full swing for at least an hour and Zoe hadn't had the chance to speak to Riordan. After touching up her make-up, Zoe went in search of him and found him out in the garden with the children.

'Hi,' she said walking up to them.

'Hello. I didn't want to interrupt, or I would have said hello before now. Loving that dress, by the way.'

Zoe was wearing her favourite little black dress, because she needed a confidence boost—and knew she looked good in it. She had worn it when they went to Rocco's, but Riordan had apparently forgotten. Zoe put her arm around Riordan's waist. He hugged her and kissed the top of her head.

She said, 'You can interrupt any time you like. It's good to see you again. It seems ages since we … you know.' Being in Riordan's arms reminded her of the pregnancy test in her bedroom. She couldn't ignore it forever.

Her mother's voice echoed around the garden. 'Zoe! They're serving the food.'

'Thanks, coming,' Zoe called back, then told Riordan, 'She's got a voice like a foghorn; she would make a great town crier.'

Riordan laughed. 'Food, then.'

*

The caterers had done a wonderful job. Riordan took full advantage of the plates being passed around by taking two of everything. He noticed that Zoe hardly ate a thing. She seemed distracted and Riordan wondered what was wrong.

He said, 'This food's amazing, Zoe, aren't you eating?'

'I've had something thanks, and yes, the caterers have done a great job.'

'Are you enjoying your party?'

'Yes, Riordan, I am. Please excuse me, I'll just be a minute.' Zoe slipped away through the crowd of people and made her way upstairs.

Suddenly Riordan lost his appetite. He caught sight of Toby Dean leaning against a doorjamb and drinking what looked like a whiskey. He had noticed him earlier and had done his best to avoid him, but as everyone had congregated in the same place to eat, Riordan was now confronted by him. Toby noticed Riordan watching him and raised his glass in a mock toast, then knocked the contents back in one go. By the way Toby weaved about when he turned to go into the kitchen, it was clear that he was drunk.

Why had Zoe invited him to the party?

Riordan wandered around the living room, admiring the banners and looking for someone he could talk to. He hated parties and had hoped he and Zoe could be together as a couple, so people would know that they were an item. But Riordan never seemed to get a chance to speak to Zoe. Apart from the brief time in the garden, he never got her alone.

He spotted Martha in a corner. She looked as if she was enjoying the food and seemed perfectly happy on her own. Riordan needed Martha's good sense and comforting presence, so he joined her.

'Hello, Riordan, splendid party, isn't it?'

'If you like parties.'

'Oh dear, that doesn't sound good. What's the matter?'

'You're going to think I'm being childish, but I can't get to talk to Zoe, and I thought that we were ... well, together. And she's invited Toby Dean.'

'Yes, I noticed that. He's brought someone called Melissa, but he's treating her very badly, practically ignoring the poor girl.'

'The man's an idiot. In fact, a drunken idiot.'

'That's the very worst kind of idiot,' Martha said, wiping her fingers on a paper napkin.

Riordan chuckled. 'You're laughing at me and you have every right to. I'm feeling sorry for myself instead of going to find Zoe and asking what the problem is. Right?'

'If you want my advice, I'd let her enjoy the party, then ask Zoe later tonight when you two are alone.'

'Why? What do you know that I don't?'

'I'm merely suggesting that serious conversations aren't suitable for parties. Have fun, dance, eat, drink and be merry. Then later you can talk.'

'Okay, oh wise one, I'll take your advice. I'll just nip to the bathroom, then when we've all finished eating, I want a dance, okay?'

'Good, I can get in some practice before the line dancing class. Zoe's persuaded me to join in.'

'Excellent. Don't go away.'

'I wouldn't dream of it,' said Martha, swapping her empty plate for a serving of Pavlova.

Riordan climbed the stairs, hoping there wouldn't be a queue for the bathroom. He remembered student parties, many years ago, when couples locked themselves in the bathroom to do drugs or have sex, or both, forcing the more boring people like himself to pee in the garden. Not that this was that type of party, of course.

Riordan was just wondering what Zoe was like as a student, when he heard crying coming from the bathroom. He walked quietly up to the closed door and listened. The sound stopped. Maybe he'd imagined it. He knocked tentatively on the door and tried the handle, but it was locked.

The door opened and Zoe came out with red eyes and tried to squeeze past him.

'Zoe? What is it?'

'Nothing. I just need a minute, please Riordan.'

'Why are you crying?' He tried to put his arms around her, but she evaded his embrace and hurried to her bedroom.

'I'll talk to you later, okay? I'll tell you everything. Please go back downstairs, I just need some time to myself now.'

'But Zoe…' She turned and went into her bedroom leaving Riordan standing on his own staring at the closed door. He had no choice but to do as she asked.

After he had used the bathroom, Riordan hovered for a while outside Zoe's bedroom, but there was no sound; her crying had stopped.

He walked down the stairs feeling puzzled and rejected. Why wouldn't Zoe confide in him? She kept shutting him out.

He wanted so much to be part of her life, but she obviously didn't feel the same about him.

When he reached the kitchen, he looked through the open door to the garden and saw Toby Dean talking to Tom. A feeling of white-hot rage came over him, making his hands clench into fists and his jaw ache. All the frustration he had been feeling watching that nasty piece of work strutting around as if he owned the place, blinded him to common sense and he strode out of the kitchen towards his nemesis.

Chapter Thirty-Three

Before he had even reached them, Riordan shouted, 'I want a word with you.'

Toby turned and, swaying on the spot, said, 'I was just talking to your son. Fine boy. Loves dogs. Always a good sign of character.'

'Get away from my son.'

'Dad…?' Tom looked anxious.

'Over there, where we can talk privately.' Riordan pointed to a weeping willow tree in the corner of the garden.

'What's the matter, O'Connor? You're frightening the boy.'

Riordan put his hand on Tom's shoulder and spoke reassuringly. 'It's okay Tom, you stay here with the dogs and the other kids. I just want a quick word with Toby.'

'Are you angry?' Tom hated confrontation and his face was pale with concern.

'No, I'm fine. Sorry if I frightened you. Do what I say, there's a good boy, it won't take long.'

'Okay.' With a last lingering look at Toby, Tom turned away.

'Right, let's go,' Riordan said to Toby.

'And what if I don't want to?' The man was obviously drunk but not so much that he didn't know what he was doing or saying.

'Then I'll tell everyone what kind of a cheating, odious scumbag you are.'

'Brave words, O'Connor.'

Riordan strode off before he took a swing at him and stood under the weeping willow tree, where he couldn't be seen by the other people in the garden; especially the children. This discussion was likely to get heated. He tried to calm down, but his breathing was erratic, and his hands were clenched so tightly they ached.

Eventually, deliberately taking his time, Toby ambled over to the weeping willow tree. He took a packet of cigarettes from his jacket pocket and offered one to Riordan. 'Smoke?'

'I don't.'

'No, of course you don't. Mr perfect.' Toby laughed and lit a cigarette then took a long draw and blew the smoke out slowly.

Riordan suppressed the urge to cough; he had always hated the smell of cigarettes.

'I want to know the truth. You owe me that at least.'

Toby frowned and gazed up at the sky. 'Truth about what?'

'You know damn well what.' Riordan didn't know how he was going to keep his temper in front of this arrogant imbecile.

'Do I?' He stood swaying slightly and pretending to contemplate the question. 'No, I'm afraid you need to be more explicit. I really have no idea what you're talking about.'

'Did you have an affair with my wife?' Riordan spoke through gritted teeth and resisted the urge to smash his fist into Toby Dean's smirking face.

'Ah, so we get to it at last. It's taken … what? Seven years for you to ask that question. Seven long years when you've been eaten up with the thought of Sally and me together. What took you so long?'

Riordan said nothing. He didn't owe this man anything. Certainly not an explanation. 'Just answer the question.'

'Yes, Sally and I were an item. I loved her and she loved me. Life with you was intolerable to her. She said that being with me was the only thing that kept her sane.'

'How long?' Riordan could hardly get the words out. All he could see was a veil of red over his vision and he was shaking with a hatred so powerful he knew he was in danger of losing control altogether.

'How long was what?' Toby Dean's voice was controlled and calm. He was playing with him and enjoying every minute of it.

'How long were you together?'

Toby again frowned and stroked his chin as if he was thinking deeply. 'Now let me see. We met at Uni, so... oh, I would say from then on.'

'You're lying.' Riordan was reeling from the implications. If what he had said was true, they were having an affair before Riordan had even met Sally, then all through their marriage. It can't be true. Dean was just trying to wind him up.

'Am I?'

'Sally would never have married me if she was seeing you.'

Toby stared at him and smiled slowly. 'I remember the night she told me about your proposal. You even went down on one knee. What a loser you are...'

'You bastard!' Riordan took a step towards Toby, then felt hands holding him back.

Casey and Zoe's brother Caleb held him fast. 'Let me go!'

Casey said, 'The kids are just over there, Riordan. Tom's worried about you. For his sake and Zoe's, this isn't the time or place.'

'Let me go.' He spoke calmly and Casey and Caleb let go of him but stayed where they were, one on either side, in case they needed to restrain him again.

Toby was watching the scene with amusement. He held an empty glass in one hand and a burning cigarette in the other.

Riordan took deep breaths and tried to empty his mind of the vision of Toby Dean and Sally together.

'Let me ask *you* a question, O'Connor. I mean, it's only fair. Why should you have all the fun.'

Riordan said nothing. Casey and Caleb were still standing close to him, ready to grab him again.

Toby took a long drag on his cigarette. 'Why did you let Sally die?'

'What?' Riordan was shocked. He hadn't expected that.

'That's sick,' said Casey. 'I think you should leave.'

'Not until I've had an answer to my question.'

Casey said, 'You don't have to answer that, Bro, the little shit's just trying to be provocative. Ignore him.'

'No, it's okay. I'll answer. She was brain dead as well you know. Yes, she could have been kept alive on a respirator, but she would have hated that. I let her go because I loved her. It wasn't the easy option; it was the hardest thing I've ever had to do in my life. But I loved my wife and I knew it was the right thing to do.'

'It is possible, isn't it, that coma patients can wake up weeks, sometimes months after an accident? Sally could have recovered. You never gave her the chance.'

Riordan shook his head. 'She was brain dead. That means incompatible with life. I know you're only a vet but even you must understand what that means.'

Toby stepped forward, angry suddenly. Riordan stood his ground feeling stronger now that he had managed to rattle Toby's cage.

'You patronising …' Toby stopped and then smiled. 'You love playing the big doctor, don't you? Sally used to hate that about you. Saving lives, getting your name in the paper. You love it.'

Riordan had never had his name in the papers until the canal rescue. He'd written articles for medical journals, but all consultants do that. Research was an important part of his job.

They stood facing each other, neither speaking.

Casey said, 'Come on, let's go and find the kids. Forget him.'

'Just one more question,' Riordan said.

'I need another drink.'

'It was you, wasn't it? You took the photos from the bridge and sold them to the paper. And tried to make out it was Zoe who had saved the boy.'

'Zoe… ah yes, the lovely Dr Angelos. Let me tell you something, O'Connor. You ruined Sally's life but you're not going to ruin Zoe's. I won't let you.'

'How in hell do you think I ruined my Sally's life? We were married. We had a child.'

'She never wanted children. Everything changed for Sally when you got her pregnant. You thought you had her then, didn't you? You'd clipped her wings and kept her grounded. But you were wrong.'

Riordan was ready with a caustic response until he realised that someone else was listening to the conversation. Zoe stood to the left of them, half-hidden by the branches of the weeping willow. She'd been crying and her make-up had run.

Toby started to walk towards her, but she put her hand up to stop him. He slowed down but kept walking towards Zoe.

'Toby, can you leave please.' Zoe's voice shook and Riordan moved to stand next to her, glaring at Toby.

'Zoe, come on, let's go and have a dance or some food.' Toby reached out his hand as if to touch Zoe, but she turned away, and Riordan put his arm around her. Casey and Caleb walked over to Toby Dean.

Casey said, 'You heard the lady—do one.'

Toby didn't move so Casey and Caleb escorted him back to the house.

Riordan stood with his arm around Zoe's shoulders, waiting for her to look at him. When she did, he said softly, 'I think it's time we had that talk, don't you?'

Chapter Thirty-Four

Zoe wanted the ground to open and swallow her. She needed time to let the fact that she was pregnant sink in. Time to plan what to say to Riordan. But suddenly Zoe didn't have that luxury. Riordan was standing right there and gazing at her.

The clouds had gathered, and it had turned dark. Dusk was settling in.

'I don't understand what's going on here, Zoe.'

'Let's go inside and I'll tell you everything.'

They walked back to the house. Riordan turned and smiled at Tom as he passed the children. Tom smiled back and returned to the game the children were playing. They all seemed to be getting on well. It was a pity the adults couldn't take a leaf out of the kids' book.

They didn't speak to anyone when they arrived back at the house but went straight to Zoe's bedroom.

Riordan stood in the middle of the room and waited for Zoe to speak. She didn't know how to start, so sat on the bed and said nothing. Then Riordan noticed the pregnancy kit that she had left on the bedside table.

Slowly, Riordan walked over to it and picked up the plastic stick. He glanced at it, then put it back.

'You're pregnant,' he said in a flat voice.

'Yes,' she said quietly.

'Is it his?' Riordan wouldn't meet her eye. At first Zoe didn't understand the question, then realised. Toby Dean.

'No! Good God, no! You think I've slept with Toby? After everything you've told me about him. Really? How could you think that of me?' Zoe could feel the fear giving way to anger, but she had no right to be angry with Riordan. They'd used protection but no contraception was one hundred percent safe.

He said, 'Well, what am I supposed to think? Why were you crying?'

'It was a shock. We'd been so careful.'

'So, *we* are pregnant, you and me?' The smile on Riordan's face was like a stab to Zoe's heart. She hadn't expected him to be pleased. And now she was going to have to disappoint him.

'Riordan …' Zoe was still lost for words. How could she tell him?

'That's wonderful news, Zoe. I know we haven't known each other long, but—'

'Riordan, wait ...'

'It'll be okay. I know it's been a shock, and it is for me too, but a baby, it's a positive thing, isn't it?'

Riordan looked so happy. Stunned, but happy, nonetheless. Zoe was just about to bring all that crashing down to earth. Riordan would hate her—the whole of the O'Connor family would hate her. Why did this have to happen?

'Riordan, I *can't* have this baby.'

There, she'd said it. Riordan stared at Zoe and the look in his eyes made Zoe hate herself even more.

'Why? Just talk to me, Zoe, please. Tell me why it would be so bad. Casey and Lexi had one night together, and then didn't see each other for four years. But now they're a family with another baby on the way. It worked for them.'

Zoe got up and started pacing around the bedroom. She was suddenly filled with nerves and tried to remember what Joe Moreton said to do when the feelings became overwhelming. Feelings of grief, rage, sorrow—how could she even contemplate the risk of losing another baby?

Riordan was looking determined.

'Riordan, you don't understand. It isn't *you*.'

'Oh, please spare me the "it isn't you, it's me" speech. Are you saying you don't have any feelings for me? Don't you feel anything at all? That night we spent together was, well for me anyway, it was amazing. Are you saying you didn't feel anything, that it was just sex?'

'No! That's not what I'm saying. I do have feelings for you, honestly. More than you'll ever know.'

'Then why? Is the idea of having my child so repugnant?' Riordan's words were full of pain.

'It's not because it's *your* child. I just can't risk going through it again. I can't lose another baby.'

Zoe stood and watched the emotions playing across Riordan's face. He usually kept his feelings hidden with rigid self-control. Now his guard was down, and Zoe saw shock mingling with pity. He was speechless for several seconds, gazing at her.

'Another? Zoe … you lost a baby? I didn't know. I'm so desperately sorry. Is that why you're seeing Joe?'

She nodded and quickly Riordan enveloped her in a hug. She clung on to Riordan and was determined not to cry but could feel the familiar lump in her throat and stinging eyes. Riordan picked her up and laid Zoe gently on the bed. He removed her shoes, and then his own, and lay next to her. He put his arm around Zoe, the two of them huddled together in the gathering darkness. It had started to rain.

He said, 'Tell me.'

So she did. Zoe told him everything, sparing no detail. Riordan listened and said nothing, occasionally squeezing Zoe's arm or kissing the top of her head. Zoe laid it all before him and hoped Riordan would understand why the memory of Samuel was too fresh to contemplate going through another pregnancy.

Muffled sounds of the party floated up the stairs. Occasionally someone turned the music up and there were shrieks of laughter. They heard the opening bars of "Zorba the

Greek". That would be Zoe's father; he always wanted to dance when he'd had too much to drink.

It was peaceful lying in the dark next to Riordan with the soft sound of rain against the windows.

Zoe didn't want to talk anymore but knew that they had to. She needed Riordan to understand.

'How long ago did you lose Samuel?'

'It'll be two years in June. June the twenty-first, to be exact. I remember Lexi telling me how she met Casey at a Summer Solstice ball, and how *she* has always loved that date ever since.'

'Yes, I've heard the story.'

'Well, it's the date I gave birth to my dead son.'

They fell silent again and Riordan hugged Zoe closer. She breathed in the smell of him. A mixture of his cologne, and healthy male. Zoe relished the feeling of being listened to, combined with being held in strong, caring arms.

'What did you do afterwards?' Riordan's voice was calm in the darkness. Zoe couldn't see his expression or read any body language, so she closed her eyes.

'Me and Andy had stopped seeing each other before the birth. He never wanted a child. He didn't seem to feel anything for the baby. The fact that Samuel was his son too didn't seem to matter to him. I told him where Samuel's grave was, but I don't think he's ever visited it. I haven't seen him since.'

'You stayed with your parents?'

'For a while, but I think I got on my mother's nerves moping around the house all day. She works from home, you see.'

Riordan sighed. 'What did you do?'

'I went to stay with my grandmother in Greece. A tiny village where she grew up and everyone knows your business. It got around the village that I had lost a child, and it seemed that all the villagers came to my grandmother's house to mourn with us. They brought food and wine and stayed for hours. Then they came back again the following day. So different to this country, where I lost friends because they didn't know how to act around me. The villagers were genuinely sad for me.'

'Tell me about the village.'

'It was a picture-postcard place. Built on a hillside, whitewashed buildings with blue doors, and a deep sparkling sea and white sandy beaches.'

'Sounds idyllic. Did it help, being there?'

'Oh yes, I loved my grandmother with a passion. She was my role model. I loved her so much that when she died, six months after I lost Samuel, I thought I'd never get over it.'

Riordan hugged Zoe harder. Zoe was willing herself not to start crying again. She'd had enough of tears.

'I do understand, Zoe, and I'm not going to try talking you round. You have my support with whatever decision you make. But please, don't shut me out. Let me help you, okay?'

'Okay, I promise. But now I really think we should go downstairs and join in the fun.'

'Do we have to?'

Zoe wished they could stay just as they were; Riordan holding her in the darkness, talking about things that mattered. But it was her party and she had been absent for too long.

'Yes, I think we do.'

Chapter Thirty-Five

Zoe went in to work on Monday to be greeted by Imelda, who had a head cold.

'Don't come too near,' Imelda said from behind the reception desk. Her nose was red, eyes streaming.

'Shouldn't you be in bed with a hot lemon and honey?' asked Zoe, telling herself to double up on the use of hand gel.

'Oh, that's a luxury I can't afford. Far too much to do,' Imelda said, bustling about busily.

'We can cope,' said Mandy, one of the receptionists.

'Yes, and we don't want your bloody germs,' muttered Clara, the other.

'The girls are right,' said Zoe. 'Go home, if you don't feel well.'

Imelda ignored this, so Zoe went to her office and fired up the computer. It looked as if surgery would be busy that morning.

Zoe had no sooner got settled, when the phone rang. It was reception.

'Yes, Clara, what's up?'

'I've just had a call from Mrs Bannister. She's concerned about one of her neighbours who's a patient of ours. Jack Dempsey? She's called an ambulance.'

'Yes, Jack's one of mine. Are Bilal and Louis here yet?'

'Yes, they're both in. Do you want me to allocate some of your patients to them?'

'I'll have a word with them first.'

The other two doctors were willing to take on a few extras, and Zoe left.

When Zoe arrived at Jack Dempsey's house, Mrs Bannister was peering through the letterbox and calling Mr Dempsey's name.

'Oh, thank goodness you're here, Doctor. I'm sure something's happened to him. I've phoned an ambulance—he might have had another heart attack or fallen down the stairs.'

'Thanks. You did the right thing.' Zoe peered through the window but couldn't see anything through the net curtains. Then she looked through the letterbox too.

'Is there a way to get around the back?'

'You'll have to go through the alley, but the gate's locked. Jack probably has a key, but that's no good here is it?' Mrs

Bannister was looking worried and wringing her hands. 'Oh dear, I should have phoned the police or the fire brigade.'

'I'll ask next door.'

The neighbour had a key and opened the gate. She stayed outside gossiping with Mrs Bannister while Zoe went round to the back, but Mr Dempsey was security conscious and his backyard gate had a padlock on it. It seemed there was no way into the house.

Zoe tried ringing the bell again, but there was no answer.

An Ambulance Service motorcycle came tearing down the street and stopped.

'Oh, how exciting!' said the neighbour. 'It's like that programme off the telly.'

'Is this Jack Dempsey's place?' the rider asked as he climbed off the bike.

'Yes, I'm Dr Angelos. We can't get in, I'm afraid. The place is too secure.'

'No worries. I'm Jay O'Connor, by the way. Are you *the* Dr Zoe Angelos that my big brother keeps banging on about?'

'If your big brother is Riordan O'Connor, then yes.'

Jay put his hand out and Zoe shook it. He said, 'Pleased to meet you, now let's get inside this house, shall we?'

Jay went around the back, and Zoe and the neighbours followed. Jay climbed over the wall and looked up at the top storey. 'There's a window open. I'm going to see if I can reach it.'

'Be careful. Shouldn't we call the fire brigade?' Zoe asked. She didn't want to be treating Jay as well as Mr Dempsey.

'Nah, we'll be in faster than you can say Spider-Man.'

Jay scrambled up to the roof of the extension over the kitchen, then managed to reach a window that Zoe thought was the back bedroom. Jay disappeared inside, so Zoe returned to the front door to be let in.

'He's here, downstairs,' said Jay. They both hurried through the house. Mr Dempsey was in the back room and still in his pyjamas, lying in a doorway. He was unmoving, but conscious.

'Jack? I'm Jay, and you know Dr Angelos.'

'Aye. I'm not going to hospital, you can't make me. Or a home. I'm staying here.'

Jay was listening to Mr Dempsey's chest and taking vital signs, such as pulse and respiratory rate. He took his temperature and blood pressure. Then he asked about any pain, in case Mr Dempsey had twisted something or broken a hip. But the old man insisted he was fine.

'What happened, Mr Dempsey?' asked Zoe.

'I fell, that's all, then I couldn't get up again. There's nowt wrong with me. I just need someone to help me up.'

'Did you lose consciousness at all, Mr Dempsey?' Zoe asked.

'No, I just tripped, could happen to anyone.'

'How long have you been on the floor, mate?' Jay asked.

'Not long.'

'All night?'

'Not *all* night, no.'

Jay turned to Zoe. 'His vital signs are okay. Don't think there's any bones broken, and his heart rate is fine. Not tachycardic.'

'You'll be due your meds won't you?' Zoe watched Mr Dempsey's face for any signs of pain or discomfort, but he just looked embarrassed at being found in this situation.

'Aye. They're in the kitchen.'

'Right, come on then, let's have you up.' Jay pulled him up into a sitting position. 'Just stay there for a while in case you feel dizzy.'

'What?'

Jay repeated it and Mr Dempsey waved his hands impatiently. Between them, Jay and Zoe got Mr Dempsey to his feet and they shuffled him to the living room and into an armchair.

'Fancy a cuppa?' said Jay.

'Aye, go on then.'

'I'll get your meds while I'm there.'

While Jay was gone, Zoe knew she would have to convince Mr Dempsey to accept help. Once an elderly patient started having falls, further ones soon followed.

'Mr Dempsey?'

'Call me Jack, I don't mind.'

'Okay, Jack. You're going to have to allow some professional assistance. We want to keep you at home for as long as we can, but you need to meet us half way. I'll organise for a carer to come in once a day, okay?'

'I don't want people poking their nose in.'

'They won't, Jack, I promise. They won't do anything you don't want them to. Otherwise, you may not be able to stay here. I know it's what you want.'

'Aye, all right then. I'll try it, but if I don't like them, I'll not let them in.'

'Okay, we'll give it a try.'

Jay came back with the tea and a glass of water to take the medication. Zoe watched as Jack held on to the mug. No shaking or tremors. That was a good sign. He was in quite good physical condition considering his heart disease. Underweight, but if Zoe could persuade him to accept meals-on-wheels too, that could be rectified.

Jay said firmly, 'D'you know, Jack, I should be ringing an ambulance now to take you to hospital, just so you can be checked over.' Jay stood in the middle of the room and Zoe was struck by the strong family resemblance. He was definitely an O'Connor.

'There's no need, you've just done all that. Don't make such a fuss.'

'What do you think, Doc?'

Zoe glanced at Jack. 'I'm just concerned about your mobility, Jack.'

'What?'

'Whether you can get around the house easily.'

'Of course I can. I told you, I just tripped.'

Jay said, 'Let me hold your mug and we'll see how easily you can get up from the chair on your own.' Jay took his mug and stood watching carefully as Jack stood quite easily.

'Bravo,' said Jay. 'Now walk across the room and come back.'

Jack was grumbling, but he walked and turned without going dizzy and returned to his chair.

'Can I finish me tea now? It'll be cold with all this silly business.'

'Of course you can, and you seem okay to me.' Jay handed the mug back. 'Right then, I'll be off. Nice to meet you, Jack, and you, Dr Angelos.'

'Likewise,' said Zoe, and Jay winked.

'Aye, thanks lad.'

'No problem. You stay upright now, Jack. I'll see myself out.'

When he'd gone, Zoe took Jack's pulse again, just to reassure herself.

'That seems fine,' she said. 'Is there anything I can do for you before I leave?'

'No, you get off and go and help genuine sick people. There's nowt wrong with me a bit of peace wouldn't cure.'

'Right, I'll leave you in peace then. Take care of yourself, Jack, and think about having an alarm in case of emergencies. Okay?'

'I'll think about it.'

'And don't forget, I'm arranging for someone to come in. Okay?'

'Aye, alright.'

Zoe left, knowing that she'd done everything possible.

Chapter Thirty-Six

Riordan and Casey were having a quick lunch in the hospital dining room. Riordan had no appetite whatsoever and was picking at a salad. Casey had the shepherd's pie and was wolfing it down too fast, as usual.

'So,' said Casey, between mouthfuls. 'What did you want to talk about?'

'Zoe. You've been through it with Helen and I need advice; I'm floundering and have no idea what to do.'

'Zoe's pregnant?'

'Yes, but she doesn't want to go ahead with the pregnancy.'

Casey stopped eating and stared. 'Why ever not?'

'She lost a baby at thirty-two weeks and is still suffering the grief. I don't know what I can do to help but demanding that Zoe go through with this pregnancy isn't the way forward.'

Casey was silent, and Riordan tried to eat more of his lunch. He needed his strength to face a large outpatient clinic that afternoon.

'She's thinking of getting rid of it?'

Riordan winced at the question. 'Zoe's frightened of having to go through it again. She had to give birth, knowing the child was already dead. This way, I suppose, she's in charge.'

'And what about afterwards? Helen regretted the termination and it sent her over the edge.'

Riordan nodded and pushed his plate away. He drank some water, thinking all the while that it was his child they were talking about, not some anonymous blob of cells.

'It's Zoe's decision, Casey. All I can do is be there for her.'

'But it's your baby too. I remember how I felt when I discovered that Helen had aborted our child. I didn't even know she was pregnant. It was one of the worst days of my life. I felt so helpless.'

'This is different,' Riordan said. 'Zoe has been totally honest with me. She told me exactly what had happened, down to the last detail. It was so sad listening to her relive it all over again.'

'So what happens now? With the two of you, I mean. Can you still have a relationship? How are you going to feel afterwards, knowing that she didn't want your baby? My advice would be to cut and run. End it while you still can. This will only end in heartache.'

Riordan was silent. He'd wanted his brother's advice, but maybe Casey wasn't the right person to ask after all. Helen and Zoe were different people, and they were in a completely different situation.

'Riordan? Did you hear what I said?'

'Yes, I heard you. I'm afraid it's a bit late for that. I love Zoe and I'll be there to support whatever decision she makes.'

*

When the doorbell rang, Zoe knew it would be Riordan. He'd been so kind and supportive, which made what she was about to do doubly hard. But it had to be done. Zoe had no other choice.

Luna was barking and wagging her tail.

Riordan stood on the doorstep with an enormous bouquet of flowers.

'I thought you might need cheering up,' he said, walking into the cottage.

'Thanks. These are really beautiful and *will* cheer me up, I know. I'll just put them in water.'

Riordan followed Zoe into the kitchen.

He said, 'How have you been? Jay told me he saw you today.'

'Yes, so that's the whole family I've met now, I think.'

'He was very impressed with your doctoring skills. And Jack Dempsey has agreed to carers coming in to look after him. Result.'

Zoe took a large Italian crystal vase and put the flowers in it. She was hopeless at flower arranging but messed about with them to avoid having to turn around and look Riordan in the eye.

'Do you want a coffee?'

'No thanks.'

Riordan was right behind her and Zoe was tempted to hug him and find solace in his arms. She could just forget the speech that she'd prepared, and take Riordan upstairs to make slow, sensual love. But that was the coward's way out and would only postpone the inevitable.

'There,' she said. 'I'll put them in the living room.'

Riordan followed and sat on the sofa as Zoe placed them in the front window.

'We have to talk about it, Zoe.'

'I know.'

'I just want you to know that I understand. But I *have* to ask whether you've really thought this through.'

Zoe felt a surge of anger at Riordan's calm tone. If he only knew the anguish she'd gone through since taking the pregnancy test.

'Riordan, I need to say something to you.'

He sighed. 'Go on.'

'I can't have this baby. I can't risk going through it again. I know the statistics, and that I'd get more help this time, but

I'm not ready. I don't think I'll ever be ready … which is why I can't see you anymore.'

'What? But why? Zoe, I don't want this to end. I've said I'll support you whatever you decide, and I will, I promise. You mean so much to me. I can't lose you too.'

The pain in Riordan's eyes almost made Zoe back down, but she knew that Riordan would only end up despising her after the termination.

'Riordan, it'll never work. This has come between us, and it would always be there. It's better that we stop this thing now before we get in too deep.'

'I'm already in too deep. I love you and want you in my life. And I'll put up with not having any more children, if that's the only way I can have that. Please don't end it, Zoe.'

'I'm so sorry, but I don't think we can get past this.'

'Have you seen Joe? Asked him about it?'

'No, not yet. But whatever Joe thinks, I'm not going to change my mind. I'm sorry, but that's my decision. I never meant this to happen. But it has and …well, I think it's best all round if we keep away from each other.'

Zoe couldn't look at him, or she'd never be able to let Riordan walk out of her life.

'Will you stay in Leytonsfield?'

'I don't know, I can't think that far ahead.'

Riordan stood up. 'Okay, I'll go, but you know that you can contact me any time if you change your mind, or if you need any help. Anything. Whatever happens, I'll always be here for you.' Riordan was quiet for a moment. 'Would you do me a favour?'

'If I can.'

'When you've … well, when it's over, will you let me know? A text will do. I just need to know.'

Zoe nodded, still too distraught to look Riordan in the eyes. She was going to lose control, if he didn't leave.

After a while Zoe heard the door close quietly. Luna came over and laid her head on Zoe's knees. Zoe didn't cry this time, she just felt numb. As she stroked the dog, Zoe told herself sending Riordan away had been the right thing to do.

So why did it feel as if someone had ripped her heart out and stamped on it?

*

Riordan arrived home to a quiet house. Martha was sitting on the sofa, watching the news. She turned the TV off when he came in.

He asked, 'Where is everyone?'

'Your parents have nipped down to the pub for a swift half, Tom's asleep.'

'Right.' He collapsed next to her.

'And you, my dear friend, look as if you have been put through the wringer.'

Riordan closed his eyes. 'Zoe doesn't want to see me anymore. She said we can't get past this. I wanted to convince her otherwise but couldn't think of anything to say.'

'Because she's right?'

'No, because I love her, but I don't know *how* to convince her.'

'Do you want me to speak to her?'

'No, thanks anyway.'

They were silent for a while, and then Martha got up and left the room. She came back with a bottle of brandy and two glasses.

'What a good idea,' said Riordan. 'I'm so glad you're here.'

'Well, you better make the most of me, because I won't be here forever. In fact, I'm thinking it's time I went back.'

'Where to, the Yemen?'

'Yes, Peter sent me a text and asked if we can meet up before the fun begins again.'

'What's he like?'

'He's older than me, has three grown-up children, all doing something important in the NHS, and is a widower. He never wants to get married again but likes the thought of having someone in his life. And that someone is me, apparently.'

'And how do you feel about him? The same, obviously. Well, hopefully.'

Martha laughed. 'We're both realistic enough not to make plans. Life is so transient.'

'Especially doing the job that you two do.'

'Exactly. But, suffice it to say that we stop each other from getting too lonely so far away from home. We're good for each other.'

'That's marvellous. I'm so pleased.' Riordan put his glass down and hugged Martha. Then, as he didn't want to let go, they sat with their arms around each other until Martha pulled away.

She said, 'I hate to leave you at a time like this, and if there was anything I could do, I'd stay.'

'I know you would. This is something I need to sort out myself. I got us into this, and it's up to me to find a way out.'

'If Zoe did have a termination, would you be able to have a relationship with her afterwards— if she agreed to see you?'

Riordan sighed. He seemed to be doing a lot of that lately. 'I love her, Martha, and I don't want to be without her.'

'I'll take that as a yes, then.'

Chapter Thirty-Seven

Riordan tried to do as Zoe asked and stay away from her. Every time he looked at the calendar to check appointments—dates for patients to have operations and a million other things—all he could see was the twenty-first of June, summer solstice, the date that Zoe gave birth to Samuel. It would be gruelling for Zoe and Riordan wished he could be with her to offer love and support.

He went along to the line dancing class. The numbers had dropped with Lexi getting too big, and Shelley and some others deciding to skip the class and go straight to the pub on Wednesday evenings. Shelly and Andrew were getting closer and, Josie told him, had been seen holding hands on a number of occasions. Good luck to them, Riordan thought.

Zoe didn't look at him all evening. There was a definite lack of energy and enthusiasm in the community hall that night. Nobody smiled, and even Mavis and Millie had little to say for themselves. Riordan decided he wouldn't go to any more.

He threw himself into work, staying later each day, so he could be kept busy. Riordan took Tom to the cinema on several occasions but had no recollection of any of the films they'd seen. Riordan's mind was on one thing and he couldn't shake it free. He desperately wanted to see a text from Zoe. It would be the only thing that stopped the turmoil in his soul.

If it was done and over with, he'd *have* to move on, there'd be no choice. Until then, Riordan was on tenterhooks waiting. He didn't know which was worse; waiting for the text, knowing that Zoe hadn't yet had the termination and there was a chance for a change of mind, or being told that she'd done it, and it was over.

By the time summer solstice was upon them, and Casey and Lexi had made plans to have a romantic dinner at Rocco's, Riordan couldn't just sit around doing nothing any longer.

*

Zoe went through the next couple of weeks on automatic pilot. She listened to the patients, filled in forms for blood tests, referrals to specialists, had staff meetings on a Monday morning, and enquired of Imelda how her bunions were—and was she over that nasty cold? Zoe felt as if she was watching herself move through the days, going through the motions and doing what was supposed to be done, while the real Zoe Angelos was suffering the hell of indecision.

At first, the choice had seemed clear. She couldn't go through another pregnancy, so there was only one thing to do. Now, as Zoe studied the calendar every day, she was aware of the milestones slipping past. Going ahead with the pregnancy, she would have had the first scan at six weeks, and be entitled to more appointments and scans, and under the care of a consultant, not just midwives. Zoe would be protected and monitored very closely, having lost a baby once.

They would do everything in their power to stop that happening again.

Because Zoe wasn't going to keep the baby, she didn't need all that. Only to make an appointment at the clinic and within a short period of time it would all be over.

*

When Zoe arrived at the children's section of the cemetery, carrying the flowers, she was trembling. Samuel's last resting place was in a beautiful spot. Ancient trees stood guard around an area that was immaculately kept. The afternoon sun threw shadows on grass that was like a soft green blanket, and the graves were tidy and bright with flowers and toys.

Zoe gazed at the shooting star inscription on the black granite with the words, *"Held for a moment, loved for a lifetime."* Someone else had left fresh flowers on the grave. They were brightly coloured; carnations, daisies and freesia. They should have lifted Zoe's mood, but instead brought Zoe to her knees with guilt.

She knew who had brought them and looked round the cemetery. Riordan was standing near a copse of trees and watching. When Zoe lifted her hand in acknowledgement, he came across to the graveside.

'Riordan. Thanks for the flowers and coming all this way. They're lovely.' Zoe laid her bouquet next to his. Zoe's was a more classic selection; white roses and purple freesia. How strange that they should both have chosen freesia. They had always been Zoe's favourite flowers.

'I didn't want you to go through this alone,' he said.

'Thanks. It's kind of you.'

'Where are your family?'

'I told them not to come. I needed to be alone today, just myself and Samuel.'

'Oh, sorry, you don't want me here. I'll go. I was just worried about you, that's all.'

Riordan made to leave, and Zoe put a hand on his arm. 'Please don't go. Now that you're here, I'm glad. It's such a beautiful day. I just want to sit in the sun for a while. Will you sit with me?'

'Of course.'

There was a bench nearby, close enough to still see the grave and the flowers. Riordan sat next to Zoe but didn't put an arm around her. They sat in silence. There was no awkwardness, no need to fill the silence with idle talk. Zoe breathed deeply trying to imprint the scene on her memory. Whenever she thought of her baby boy, Zoe would think of this place in the summer sunshine and how peaceful it was.

She longed to put her head on Riordan's shoulder and breathe in the scent of him. She wanted Riordan to kiss and hold her. She wanted … Oh God, she wanted him *so much* the yearning was almost unbearable.

Riordan must have felt her mood. 'Are you okay, Zoe? Is there anything I can do?'

'Talk to me, tell me how everyone is.' She wanted to hear his voice—and might not have another chance.

'Well, Tom is fine, but he misses you. Solo is growing at an alarming rate, as Princess Leia is.'

She managed a smile. 'Tom's managed to persuade Jade to change her puppy's name then?'

'He has. Jade loves the idea of her puppy being a princess. Tom and Jade watched the first Star Wars movie and she gave in and agreed.'

'Clever boy.'

'Chip off the old block.'

They were again silent for a minute or two.

'Oh, and Martha is going back to the Yemen in a week or so. She has a boyfriend, did she tell you?'

'No! How wonderful. I'm happy for her. Everyone needs someone in their life. I hope Martha calls in to say goodbye before she leaves.'

'I'll tell her.'

'Thanks.'

It seemed they had run out of conversation and had said nothing of any importance either. Nothing that would change things. Zoe was at a loss. If Riordan had been angry with her, she could have dealt with it. But he was still being so supportive, kind and loving; it was a constant reminder of what she was losing. Zoe had lost too much already and didn't think she could lose much more and stay sane.

He asked, 'Have you seen Joe recently?'

She sighed and felt tears coming. 'No. I suppose I should, but every time I see him it's like rubbing salt in the wound. I'm there because I lost my baby, but I want to move on with my life and I can't do it with constant reminders.'

'There'll come a time when you'll know you're strong enough to live your own life again. That's what happened to me. Then you won't need Joe anymore.'

'Maybe I've reached that point already.'

'Maybe you have. Just be sure, Zoe, before you do anything.'

Was Riordan talking about her appointments with Joe Moreton, or was he making an oblique reference to the termination? Zoe had to know.

'Riordan? What is it you want from me?'

'I don't want anything *from* you, I just want you in my life. I love you, Zoe, more than I've ever loved before. And I want to share my life with you. No conditions or demands. I'll accept whatever you're willing to give.'

She said in a dull voice, 'You deserve more than that, much more. You're a wonderful father who should have a big family. Tom needs brothers and sisters. If we tried to make a go of it, both of us would be constantly reminded of everything I'm preventing you from having. The life you should be living with kids around you—I couldn't live with myself.'

He said, 'And what about you? One day, you may want to be a mother again. I know you'll never forget Samuel, and that's right and proper. But you would make a wonderful mother. I've seen you with Tom and Jade; they adore you. Don't close the door on the chance of happiness. I understand how you're feeling, but you may not feel this way forever.'

'Oh, Riordan ...' Zoe put her hands over her face, and Riordan put an arm around Zoe and hugged her close.

'I love you, Zoe, and whatever the future holds for both of us, I want us to face it together.'

He held Zoe, stroking her hair, and she clung to him, feeling Riordan's strength and warmth. She wanted to stay like this—with the man she loved and the baby she lost, forever, locked in an embrace that bound them together.

The sound of sobbing disturbed the moment. A woman was kneeling at a headstone, one hand tracing the engraving and the other clutching a tissue. A man was standing next to her, wiping his face, his head down.

'Oh dear,' said Zoe. 'I think we should leave them to their grief.'

'Agreed,' said Riordan.

They stood up and, with one final glance at Samuel's grave, Zoe started walking away. Riordan followed and caught up. When they got to the gates of the cemetery, they stood gazing at each other. Zoe didn't want to say goodbye, but knew she had to.

'Thanks for today, Riordan. It meant a lot to me.'

'You're welcome. I hope I helped, at least a bit.'

'You helped a lot, more than you'll ever know.' She wanted to tell Riordan that she loved him and always would, but that wouldn't be fair.

Zoe couldn't ever be the person Riordan deserved.

He said sadly, 'Right, I'll be off then.'

'Yes, thanks again.'

'Don't forget about the text,' he said uncertainly.

'I won't, I promise.'

He nodded, and Zoe watched him striding away, his head down and hands in his pockets.

'Goodbye my love,' she whispered.

Chapter Thirty-Eight

Zoe could feel time running out, moving past in a blur. No sooner had she arrived at the medical centre, then the day was over, and Zoe was back in the cottage, alone. Weekends were the hardest. Apart from taking Luna for a walk and going window-shopping in the town centre, she just sat around watching movies and wondering what Riordan was doing.

On one foray into Leytonsfield shopping centre, Zoe saw Toby and Melissa walking along with their arms around each other. Melissa had smiled at Zoe as they passed, but Toby merely inclined his head as if Zoe wasn't worth bothering with anymore. Perhaps the fact that she was pregnant with Riordan's baby had cooled his ardour. Thank goodness.

Zoe needed to make the call and book into the clinic. Terminations were safely performed up to the twentieth week, but the longer she left it, the harder it would be to make that call.

The strange thing was that Zoe was automatically doing everything as if she was going to have the baby. Not drinking alcohol, and being inexplicably drawn to Mothercare, and spending ages looking in the windows at prams, high-chairs and other baby paraphernalia.

When Zoe had been pregnant with Samuel, she had brought so much stuff in readiness for his arrival the small flat was crammed. Only a blue blanket was ever used. Samuel was wrapped in this after the midwife had cleaned him up—the same blanket he was buried in. The rest went to Oxfam, the staff delighted with Zoe's donation until they realised she had lost a baby. They said all the right words of commiseration. Zoe had been desperate to leave and get home to the empty flat.

*

In the cottage, knowing she was setting herself up for heartache, Zoe went upstairs and brought down the box of treasures. She opened the box and took out the photo of her holding Samuel. Zoe waited for the familiar overwhelming grief to come, but looking at the photo this time, Zoe found she could smile. Her eyes were gritty, and there was a lump in her throat, but Zoe felt calm. She picked up the hand and foot prints and traced their contours with a finger. Again, she felt immeasurably sad, but in control.

The doorbell made Zoe jump and she stood to answer it, with Luna dancing about at her feet. Zoe made no effort to hide the treasures.

Martha was standing on the doorstep, holding a Tupperware dish.

'I come bearing gifts,' she said, her kind face breaking into a wide smile. 'Eloise has been baking again. This time she was making fairy cakes with the kids, and they wanted you to have some of theirs.'

'Lovely! Come in, Martha. Would you like tea?'

'Oh, yes please.'

'Go through to the living room.'

She went into the kitchen to make the tea and could hear Martha talking to Luna. Zoe arranged some cakes on a plate, then, when the tea was made, carried everything through on a tray.

Martha was holding the photo of Samuel. Zoe put the tray down and offered Martha a cake.

'Thanks. This, of course, is Samuel. What a lovely photo.'

'Yes, the midwife who took it was kind. She couldn't have done enough for me.'

'Midwives tend to be like that. At least from my experience of working with them.'

Zoe sat on the sofa next to Martha and waited until the tea brewed.

'So, you're going back overseas, and Riordan tells me you have someone waiting for you there?'

'Yes, Peter. You'd like him. Next time we're back home I might drag him to Leytonsfield to see if he can stand up to meeting all the O'Connors. He's made of strong stuff, fortunately.'

'I'd like to meet him too,' said Zoe quietly.

'Of course, I was including you.'

'I'm not an O'Connor, and don't deserve to be.'

Martha sipped her tea, searching Zoe's face. Zoe said nothing.

'You are too hard on yourself, my dear. Riordan loves you and isn't about to let you go easily.'

'He deserves better than me.'

'What utter rubbish.' Zoe was startled, but Martha was smiling. 'I'm not a naturally romantic person, but I do believe in love. And, in my humble opinion, the opposite of love isn't hate as a lot of people think, but fear. You, my dear girl, have lived in fear for too long. It's time you gave love a chance. Now, that's all I'm prepared to say. How about pouring that tea before it gets too strong?'

*

Riordan hadn't heard from Zoe since the day in the cemetery. Martha had left and Riordan missed her dreadfully, but at least Martha promised to return in the New Year with Peter in tow.

It was now the middle of July and still there had been no text from Zoe. The suspense was killing him, and Riordan was living on his nerves. He couldn't settle to anything and dozens of times during the day his finger hovered over Zoe's phone number. He nearly rang her to beg her to put him out of his misery.

Casey was also living on his nerves—Lexi was due to give birth at any time. Between the two brothers, they were driving everybody around them nuts.

Riordan went into work early, thinking of immersing himself in other people's problems as a way of forgetting his own. There was a huge pile of correspondence that his secretary had opened, date stamped and sorted into different categories. Deciding to glance through the letters later, Riordan attacked the pile of investigation results and was soon examining ECG results, echocardiograms, angiograms and the like. One paper was ear-marked as having come to the wrong place, with a post-it note asking if it should be sent on to Maternity.

Riordan picked it up. It was an ultrasound scan of a pregnancy taken at between ten and thirteen weeks. Riordan felt a shiver in the pit of his stomach looking at the perfect, tiny human form. There was no point torturing himself looking at someone else's baby, so he tossed it on the growing pile of things for his secretary to deal with. Then, he picked it up again and read the name in case she was one of his heart patients.

Zoe Angelos.

He stared at the name in disbelief. Zoe had sent him a picture of their child. The first-ever picture that would be taken. A picture that told him the baby was alive and well.

Riordan stood up and paced around the office. He stared out of the window at the uneven roofs of the hospital buildings. Building work was taking place all the time, expanding departments, adding new ones. Change going on continually.

Riordan sat down again and picked up the scan, reading the name once more in case he had been hallucinating and seeing Zoe's name had just been wishful thinking. But no, it clearly said, Patient: Zoe Angelos. Address: Rosemary Cottage, Leytonsfield. Age: thirty-two. It was his Zoe.

Zoe had sent Riordan this. She was telling him … what? *That she was keeping the baby.* Did this mean Zoe wanted him as well? Maybe. But then again, maybe not.

Riordan desperately needed to talk to Zoe, but had a long, arduous day ahead of him that couldn't be avoided or postponed.

Chapter Thirty-Nine

Zoe jumped every time she heard a noise outside. Her ears were straining for the sound of the doorbell. Luna was keeping a close eye on her. She was in her bed but, watching intently every time Zoe moved.

Riordan would have received the scan by now. She had put a first-class stamp on it. In fact, put two on to make sure he got it as soon as possible. Maybe it had gone to another doctor, or department. Perhaps Riordan hadn't understood the significance and didn't read her name. Maybe … but she could sit there second-guessing all she liked. If Riordan didn't get in contact soon, she'd ring him and tell him in person.

Tea, that was the answer. Zoe was still right off coffee but seemed to have acquired a taste for tea worthy of any northerner. Yorkshire tea was her favourite, and she could do with a cup now.

Zoe made it as far as the kitchen door before the doorbell rang. Once, a sharp ring. Was that Riordan's ring? Only one way to find out.

She opened the door and Riordan was standing on the doorstep with an enormous bouquet of flowers. Even bigger than the last one he had given her. He didn't speak, just gazed at Zoe as if he'd never seen her before.

Zoe stood back and he came in.

'Hi,' she said.

'Hi.'

'Are those for me?' She gestured at the flowers and he handed them over without a word. 'They're lovely.'

'I got the scan.' Riordan's voice was croaky as if he had a cold or was fighting tears.

'Good, that's our baby,' she said simply.

These were the magic words to break the spell. Riordan picked Zoe up, flowers and all, and carried her into the living room. He sat on the sofa with Zoe and the flowers on his knee. He kissed her. A long, lingering, wonderful kiss that Zoe felt all the way down to her toes. Then the kiss ended and they both came up for air.

'I just need to know one thing,' he said breathlessly.

'Anything,' she whispered.

'You're having the baby, and that's wonderful. But am I part of your plans?'

'Of course. I couldn't have made the right decision without you. I couldn't imagine my life now without you in it. I love you, Riordan, so much it would scare me if I hadn't made a promise to myself to stop living in fear.'

'Ah,' he said, as if a penny had dropped. 'So, what—or perhaps I should ask who—brought you to that conclusion?'

'A wise woman who told me to give love a chance, and the realisation that I have never been loved the way you love me. You are the best thing that has happened to me, ever.'

Riordan said with a catch in his voice 'I feel the same way. I love you, Zoe, more than I could ever say.'

They kissed, tenderly.

'I'm so glad you get on well with Martha. She's a gem.'

'Yes, me too,' said Zoe. 'When I thought about the life she leads, in war zones, and people risking death and being maimed for life by land mines and yet, through all that, Martha has someone she cares about enough to go back, again and again ... well, it's humbling and puts my fears into perspective.'

'She's a remarkable woman, and so are you.'

'Me? I've done nothing special.'

'I disagree. You're facing your fear and beating it.'

'I can only face my fear if you're by my side. I love you, Riordan, and need you.'

'I'm not going anywhere, Zoe. I'll be by your side every minute.'

Riordan kissed her again, gently, with so much tenderness and love that Zoe thought she was going to melt.

She said, 'I'm sorry I put you through the torment of thinking I was going to have a termination. I wasn't in my right mind. I just panicked and tried to run away. But no more, I'll face my demons head-on from now onwards.'

'It was understandable that you reacted like that.'

'Have you told Tom?'

'Not yet. He'll be thrilled. He's always wanted a brother or sister.'

Zoe wriggled on his lap. 'I'd better put these flowers in water before we kill them between us.'

He walked into the kitchen with her and watched as Zoe stuck the flowers into a vase.

'Flower arranging isn't your forte is it? And you a member of the WI as well.'

She put her arms around him, and Riordan hugged Zoe to his chest. She could feel his heart beating strong and sure, making her feel safe and cherished at the same time.

'Let's go to bed,' she said.

'I thought you'd never ask.'

'Race you!'

She ran up the stairs with Riordan following closely behind. Zoe flung herself on the bed and he followed. Then he undressed her slowly and kissed every inch of exposed skin until she was panting and wet, desperate to feel him inside her.

He started to unbutton his shirt and she said, 'Let me', then copied him by stroking and kissing his chest and stomach. He groaned but didn't move, letting Zoe do whatever she wanted.

Soon they were both naked and Zoe straddled him, staring down at his face. Riordan's eyes were open, and Zoe saw love swimming in the grey. He smiled.

'I love you, Zoe.'

'Not as much as I love you.'

'I'd better prove it to you then.'

He entered her and Zoe cried out feeling his hard length filling her, completing her, making Zoe whole again. Riordan held her hips and watched as Zoe orgasmed, her head thrown back with a loud cry. It was a triumphant sound as Zoe rode the waves of ecstasy, and Riordan's climax followed swiftly.

Zoe rolled off him and they both started laughing as they heard Luna barking outside the bedroom door.

'Oops …' said Zoe

'Poor Luna,' Riordan said. He got off the bed and went to open the door to let her in. Luna jumped up onto the bed, wagging her tail. As she stroked the dog, Zoe's gaze was firmly fixed on Riordan. She remembered the first time she had set eyes on Riordan when he was serving tea and wearing the sexy gladiator costume. Zoe had thought Riordan was gorgeous with long legs, slender hips and a firm upper body—a purely physical attraction. Now, as she took in the sight of Riordan naked, she marvelled that he loved her as much as Zoe loved him. She would never stop loving Riordan, never stop wanting him.

'What are you thinking about, Zoe? You have a dreamy look on your face.'

'I was just thinking how lucky I am to have you.'

'I'm the lucky one.'

'Are we going to argue about this?'

Riordan crawled into bed next to her. 'Only if we can make up afterwards.'

'Good, then let's make up.'

Luna jumped up on the bed to join in the fun.

As Riordan kissed Zoe, his mobile rang. He ignored it, and then there was the ping of a text message. He sighed, scrambled off the bed again and plucked the phone out of his jeans pocket. As he read the message, Riordan broke into a huge grin.

'What?' asked Zoe.

'That was Casey. Lexi has just gone into labour.'

Epilogue

It was Christmas Day in the Maternity Unit of Leytonsfield General hospital, and Zoe lounged back on the hard hospital pillows and listened to the festive sounds filling the Maternity Ward. Christmas carols could be heard, bursts of laughter, the sound of newborn babies crying, someone hurrying past the door, and the phone ringing incessantly.

Riordan sat beside Zoe in an armchair, cradling their new baby. Abigail Dorinda Eloise O'Connor had been born twelve hours earlier after a long, painful birth. Zoe had been induced in the morning and labour started in the late afternoon. She had been given gas and air, and had waited desperately, listening for the sound of her baby's first cry. When it came, Zoe had burst into noisy tears and clung to Riordan. He, too, was crying and they held each other in exhausted relief.

When they had put the baby on Zoe for skin-to-skin time, and Zoe had felt the warmth of the tiny body and the softness of her skin, she thought her heart would explode with love and relief. It was finally over. All the fear and doubt had gone, and Zoe was a mother at last.

They had been put in a private room and it was filled with O'Connors. They'd all come to see the baby. Casey held Lucy, his second daughter, while Lexi and Jade cooed over Abigail. Tom had told them that next time they had to have a boy, because he was outnumbered by all these girls. Dan and Eloise declared Abigail perfect with tears in their eyes. Josie had popped in on her lunch break, and Jay would drop by later on his way home from his shift.

Martha sent a text congratulating them and saying she was looking forward to seeing them all again in the New Year and meeting the new O'Connor babies.

They had texts, messages on Facebook, and the room was full of flowers and pink balloons.

Zoe couldn't help comparing it to the day she had given birth to Samuel. There'd been no celebration then, just silence and solitude as she spent a few precious hours with her baby.

Eventually, later that evening when their visitors had all gone home to wet the baby's head—as they described it—Zoe breathed a sigh of relief. They would have to do it all again the following day when *her* family descended. The Angelos family had graciously agreed to come on Boxing Day, letting the O'Connors see the baby first. Zoe was looking forward to meeting the new edition. Maya had been born in August and Caleb and Jo were anxious to show her off.

The three of them were alone at last. Riordan sat on the bed with his arm around Zoe's shoulders as she cradled Abigail. Zoe couldn't stop looking at her daughter and stroking the skin of her cheeks.

'She's beautiful,' murmured Riordan.

'Perfect,' Zoe said.

'Happy?'

'Completely. How about you? You looked shattered, Riordan.'

He kissed Zoe on the forehead. 'I'm a consultant, remember? I'm used to being shattered.'

'Well, you should go home soon and get a good night's sleep.'

'I'll dream of you and our daughter.'

'I love you, Riordan, so much.'

'I love you more.'

'No you don't.'

'Do.'

Then they both burst out laughing until tears rolled down their cheeks. And baby Abigail slept peacefully on, safe in her mother's arms.

THE END

ABOUT THE AUTHOR

Jax was born in Manchester where she now lives, after having lived and worked in Australia. Jax attempted various jobs before deciding on a career as a medical secretary.

She has been writing for fun all her life, but now takes it seriously, concentrating on creating sexy alpha heroes and the strong, empowered women who fall in love with them.

If you enjoyed "Healing Hearts", you may enjoy reading Book One in the series, "Worth Waiting For", which is Casey and Lexi's story.

Please also consider writing a review on Amazon, it doesn't have to be long, a sentence or two would do. The author would greatly appreciate it. Thanks.

Printed in Great Britain
by Amazon